ELVIE CANN

Coming Back Stronger

First edition

This book was professionally typeset on Reedsy.
Find out more at reedsy.com

To anyone that understands the hollow feeling that Carly mentions, this is for you.
I see you. You are coming back stronger.

Content warning:
Marital Abuse
Trauma PTSD/Anxiety/Mental Health
Open Door Spice Scenes
(Please skip those chapters, mom)

Acknowledgments

This book has been a work in progress for so long because it was a story so important to me. I never imagined that I would achieve "The End" and publish it, but here we are. It turned out better than I originally imagined and whole lot spicier than I thought it would be. Carly's story is purely fictional, however a lot of her mental health issues and emotions are ones that I could feed from my own experiences. Seriously, my therapist got fired during my healing process, so I needed something to lean into, so you get a book filled with sarcastic humor, sexy moments, and one of the sweetest book boyfriends.

While I have built such a sense of strong independence while writing it, there are a huge handful of people in my life that have been cheering me on and holding me up. First, of course, is my family. My daughters will always be my reason. I love you, divas! Thank you to my mom for being my fan club President. Also, my brother (you are only allowed to read this page) and my sister-in-law, plus her family, are the best cheerleaders!

When my loneliness hit the hardest, I unfortunately did not have a hot neighbor move in, but I did find my soulmates. On a whim I decided to go on a solo trip and met my best friends, which we have become the Smut Hut. Thank you to these girls for never judging and always supporting.

To my Brunch Girls, our friendship has gotten me through some dark days for 20+ years. You are my rocks! And J, thank you for being my Amber... everyone needs a best friend like you.

My writers group, Writer's Obscurity - I still think there may be some magic involved in bringing the seven of us together. There is no doubt that I would not be about to hit publish without your support. Having our little community to learn from each other and work through the hardships has been crucial for me.

Lastly, thank you to all that are about to read my first novel. This is a labor of love and it may not be perfect but it's special. I hope you love it as much as I do!

-Elvie

Chapter 1

Ten years. One entire decade has gone by for me, and I have been stuck in the same spot. Ten years ago, I fell in love in a whirlwind and thought I had it all. We would go out to fancy dinners, take spontaneous trips, and could not get enough of one another. At some point that slowly stopped, and he began to want to stay home more. We could not afford the vacations suddenly, though I knew that was not true, I was convinced that it was. On the weekends we had things planned, suddenly we would have to stay home for one reason or another. Before I could take in what was happening, we were reclusive in our home, and this was before we had even gotten engaged. Then there was marriage and babies then the global pandemic. There seemed to be no turning point until I finally broke.

* * *

I met Jake in the Winter, shortly after my 30th birthday. My boyfriend of two years and I had recently broken up simply because we wanted different things. I wanted to get married and have kids, but he had a teenager and was not interested in starting the parenting time line all over again. After dragging it along as long as we could, we amicably went our separate ways. I was ready to go out and have some fun. My best friend, Amber, was about to get married, which lead me to be on a complete health kick to prepare to be her maid of honor.

Jake came into my life while I was working as an on-site auditor for an accounting firm. His office was in the same building as my company's client. On the way down at the end of the work day, Jake and I were on the same elevator going to the lobby. It stopped at a floor to pick up a sweet looking older woman. As she stepped in the elevator, she put earbud-headphones in and pressed a button on her phone. That resulted in her phone to play an audiobook during a very strange scene in a thriller audiobook. She did not realize her error, even turning up the volume louder assuming it was only in her ears. The elevator became a full crime scene in the making with the descriptions. The elevator opened to the lobby and she just walked out towards the sidewalk, none the wiser. Jake and I doubled over laughing together which led to us going out for drinks after. It was so natural.

I was in love immediately. We liked the same music and laughed all the time. He made me feel seen and special like I had never experienced in a relationship before. In past relationships, I felt like I had always been chasing the guy, begging him to want me. Jake seemed instantly devoted to me. He brought me flowers. He came up with fun dates.

At five months, we were living together.

My life was content in my city apartment and I did not need much for just me, but now there was an us. Jake made me feel like his house was warm and cozy every time I was there. He started to ask my opinion on paint colors for the living room so that I felt connected to it. Sure enough, as soon as my lease was up for renewal, he suggested I move into the house instead of signing again. I had been staying there so many nights already, it made sense. I was head over heels in love with this man and his son, Stevie, from his first marriage, who I had begun to form a strong relationship with. So, I agreed.

The first month was like a never-ending slumber party. On nights we had Stevie, it was movie nights, pizza parties, building forts in the living room, etc. When he was not there, we would go out to new restaurants or order in and eat in front of the fireplace. We would have an early dinner just so we could spend extra time in the bedroom making love all night long. Our hunger for one another was unsurpassed. I was so attracted to him and so in love with our life. The rose-colored glasses were so thick that I missed the early signs that things were not going to stay like this. I brushed off the concerns that my family and friends expressed or that I had in my own fleeting thoughts. This was my happily ever after, or so Jake told me to believe.

* * *

Six months of perfection. Nine and a half years of anything but. Those years were filled with emotional and mental damage that I came out on the other end with. I was not clueless the entire time, but I was in too deep to escape. That is something about a toxic relationship, you take one step towards leaving, then get pulled two steps back. Jake made sure I was dependent on him.

By the time we got married, we ended up quietly eloping in August. The only people we invited were our immediate families, my best friend, and a few of Jake's friends. Amber had only met Jake a handful of times in the first two years. After we married, Amber and I barely saw one another until my oldest was born.

Once the rings were on, the verbal abuse became more frequent. Looking back, it did not start after we got married but it was less targeted and less aggressive before. Jake convinced me to quit the job that I loved to take a part-time job closer to home. He said I was spending too much time at work. I refused to stop working completely, which is what he really wanted. He wanted me to be solely dependent on him financially, which I was because the little bit I was making went to the household food and goods I shopped for, I barely had enough left over to buy myself a coffee at the cafe. He began telling me what to cook and making a scene if I made something that he did not like. It was no longer take-out in front of the fireplace, but rather greasy food in front of the television watching his shows. I have never been a naturally thin girl, I have always had to work to stay at a healthy weight, and with this lifestyle, I gained weight and lost a lot of self-confidence.

About two years after getting married, we had our oldest daughter, Millicent "Millie" Grace on a summery day in June. She came into this world as perfect as could be and I was at once in love. Becoming a mom to this little girl felt like the most natural thing I had ever done. She was, and still is, my tiny best friend. After she was born, I was so tired from trying to learn to be a new mom, I did not see I was the only one doing the work. This little girl that needed me and I started to feel a shift in my realization of the situation. I began to question things and push back to Jake, but every time he turned it around. By the end of the conversation, I felt guilty and/or crazy. Between horrible postpartum anxiety and his constant gaslighting, he would belittle me into feeling like I was not good enough or strong enough. My internal light was so dim that it felt like it may go out completely, leaving me numb and alone in mental darkness.

Shortly after Millie's second birthday, we were pregnant again, about six and a half years after we originally met. Three days before Easter, my second tiny best friend, Remi Lynn, was born. Since I had experience having a newborn, Remi seemed like a much easier baby than Millie. Also, I did not have as many of the postpartum issues I had experienced with Millie.

Jake helped even less this time, going as far as to brag about not having to change diapers because he had me do it every time. Remi gave me a new sense of drive that I had been missing. I began fighting back against Jake more. On a locked document on my phone, I would journal conversations we had so that I could organize my thoughts clearer. I saw what was happening and while I was sick of it, I was still very stuck.

By the time Remi was born, I had only been working extremely part-time and mostly only during tax season. I took the entire summer off to be home with the girls and Jake's son during his school break. I had no source of solid income and was unsure of where to generate any savings. I did not have a support system really, because I was too embarrassed to tell anyone what my life was really like. This continued for a while with no changes. I just went through the motions of day-to-day life. Raising my little girls, who brought me so much happiness. Watching them learning new things and hitting milestones was my reason to keep going. I was not attracted to my husband any longer, but he was too wrapped up in himself to realize that. As long as I performed my "wifely duties" for him, he did not see anything wrong with our relationship, even though we barely even spoke to each other. He would come home from work, eat dinner, and sit in front of the television. Maybe he would play with the girls a little bit and let them sit with him. He was an awful husband and wanted none of the responsibility of parenting, but wanted to be the fun parent. Of course they did; he was not the one forcing them to take baths or making them blow their noses when they are sick, he was the one that cuddled and tickled their feet.

When the pandemic plagued the world, Jake, like so many others, transitioned to working from home. Instead of going to school at the local elementary school, Millie started her educational career virtually, with me having to home school her through it all. Plus, I still had to handle taking care of the entire household. The pressure of having Jake in the house "critiquing" my teaching skills all day and making me feel like I was at fault for the baby crying because I coddled her (in his words), all led to the beginning of my plan.

The next two years were devoted to a get-out plan. I started doing independent consulting work where I was paid per meeting, not in one lump check. It was good money for the time spent on it and all virtual, but it was only a few clients a week at first. As I started picking up more clients, I would schedule them back-to-back. This way Jake was unaware that I was taking two separate meetings and subsequently was not surprised by only one check being deposited into the joint account, while I had a secret bank account in just my name. At the grocery store, I would get cash back at the register then throw the receipt in the garbage outside of the store. Everything had significantly increased in price throughout the pandemic and Jake had not been grocery shopping in many years to really have a comparison.

Deciding when to make the move and leave was a decision that was tough to make, until he made it crystal clear. I had just turned 40 and Jake had bought me socks for my birthday, yes just socks with dogs on them. I had always talked about wanting to do a big, fancy trip for my 40th birthday, but he blamed the pandemic and not feeling comfortable traveling. At that point, the kids had all been back to in-person school for going on their second year, including Remi starting school. People were traveling regularly again, and masks were not even needed on airplanes any longer. Jake did not see why I was upset and told me I was ungrateful for not being thankful for my gift.

Later that night after the kids were asleep, I went to bed early but was just lying awake thinking about things. Jake came in and told me he was sorry that we could not go on a trip this year, but hopefully we can plan something next year. He then said he had another birthday present for me as he grabbed my breast like a stress ball and grabbed my hand to put it on his erection. I told him no, that I was tired and just wanted to go to sleep. He did not listen to a word I said and just kept forcing my hand. I kept saying no but it did not matter as he was convinced that his wife wanted to perform her duties for him on her birthday. At this point, I just did what I needed to do to have it just end quickly, then I turned over and I cried myself to sleep. This was not the first time that had happened, but it sure as hell was the last time.

* * *

That is how I ended up here, keys in hand for a cottage just for me and my girls. It is a little outdated and dusty, but it is ours. I have gotten this far, but where to go next is unknown and a little scary. I am free to be me again for the first time in a decade, but I keep asking myself, who even am I anymore?

Chapter 2

E ven after more than half a year of living here, it still feels like a layer of dust is thick on everything. We are the first tenants to live here for some time. Every free minute I have, I am scrubbing and organizing. My hands are raw. It feels symbolic in so many ways for my own self. I have spent this time focusing on keeping us financially stable and making the transition to a two-household family as easy as possible for Millie and Remi. I just want them to feel comfortable and loved, I will worry about myself once they are a little bit older.

We have a nice little routine down. I am still consulting, so I can make my own hours around the girls and their busy schedules. My workflow is consistent. The girls visit Jake every Wednesday night for dinner and then they stay for two nights every other weekend. This has allowed me flexibility to pick up more hours and try to get ahead instead of just staying current. There are so many unexpected expenses that keep popping up that it feels like I only get ahead to be pushed back to struggling. If I put aside an extra $1,000, then suddenly the car needs a $1,500 repair.

Overall, the bills are taken care of each month between my work, plus the measly alimony and child support that I receive from Jake. He got a mean, aggressive lawyer and used the girls as pawns to threaten to take more custody if I asked for more than what they offered. I could not afford an attorney at that same level, so I had to surrender to his intimidation. He does not want them more than every other weekend; he just needs them enough to take photos for Facebook to maintain the facade that he is an involved dad to people online, but he knows how to play with my emotions and he continues to at every opportunity. I do not think he will ever stop trying to twist my emotions to control me. One minute he will act like we are friends, then the next he will use that against me to make me feel insignificant, sometimes to get something he wants or sometimes I think it is just a game to build himself up to feel like he has control.

The divorce finalized two months ago, but we followed this custody schedule from the very beginning. Somehow, I am still not used to the quietness without the girls being home. I feel like I just go through the motions while they are gone. I never go out. What few friends I have left, are all out doing couple things with their husbands and their couple friends. Even when I was a couple, I never had that life, and it is one thing I envied when I saw those outings on social media. All I have are my daughters. Amber is long-married with a miracle baby on the way, and we still talk often but making plans with her is tough and usually scheduled well in advance. We went to brunch the last time the girls were with their father, and it was nice to catch up in person, but it felt so far removed from the days when we would party until sunrise.

I crave having friends that I can go out with on a whim for a drink on Saturday night while the girls are with Jake. I spend most kid-free nights alone with a glass of wine watching Hallmark movies. I also have done nothing to put myself out there to meet friends. It is tough to even know where to even begin to meet new friends in your forties.

The girls are with Jake this weekend, so I am just filling the time. The summer is coming to an end in New England; the sun is shining with a slight crisp in the air. It is comfortable to spend some time outside. I remember noticing that the stairs and front porch are all muddy from the summer activities and recent rain, so I gather up what I need to give them a good scrub and head out to fill my day with another task.

I only have one mop, which I really do not want to use outdoors. Instead, I grab a scrub brush with the handle. I start on the first stair while kneeling on the walkway in front of it. I am trying to scrub the time away until I get to the point where I can pick the girls up tomorrow. As I scrub more, the more I obsess over the stagnant state of where I am. I just keep scrubbing harder and harder trying to force myself to think about something else, something positive, but it is hard to find the good. We are all okay and the girls are happy, but I am just existing. I can laugh and enjoy our activities, but it does not fully reach my core. Those moments are what keeps me going and functioning, but there is still a feeling of cement encasing my internal organs. My lungs feel exhausted from taking so many deep breaths, my heart is still hurting from all it has gone through, and my brain is overwhelmed and overthinking in a constant loop. I scrub harder. I am breaking into a sweat and my arm hurts as I am still cleaning the same bottom stair. If I stop, it feels like I might explode, or finally let go and my tears will flood the whole house. So, I scrub.

I feel like I have been scrubbing for hours, even though it was probably only a few minutes, but I am hollow and cannot force myself to stop. I am battling between my body stuck in this motion and my head telling me to move my hands off the brush, when from behind me I hear, "Carly! What the actual fuck are you doing?"

I jump up, spilling the bucket of soapy water next to me all over my pants in the process. I look over to find Amber standing there looking at me like she has no clue what I am going to do next. Truthfully, I do not know what my body and mind are about to do. I stand frozen, still startled, then the adrenaline wears off.

"The stairs are muddy and... and... I," my voice breaks, and I am not prepared for what happens next.

The tears just start falling hard. I do not think they will ever stop. I am crying for every ounce of loneliness I felt leading up to the point when I left Jake and the fact that I still feel lonely but in a new way. I am crying about the promises that I believed in and the hopes I had for my life. I am crying because I feel like I am not strong enough or brave enough. I am crying because I am crying.

Amber puts an arm around my shoulders and leads me into the house. Once inside the door, I lean against the wall and slide down to the floor, putting my head between my legs to try to regulate my breath. The tears just keep coming and coming.

* * *

When I wake up the sun has set, and I am lying on the couch in the living room. My face feels swollen, my mouth is dry, and my body is weak.

"Here, drink this first," Amber says as she pushes a huge glass of water my way, "then we are heading into the kitchen to eat something. I ordered your favorite stuffed shells from Pacino's."

I shake my head a couple times trying to clear my thoughts and gather my bearings. I pick up the water and down half the glass before I even try to speak.

"You're still here? What time is it?" I ask. I look at the clock on my desk, it says 9:04 PM. I slept for around 5 hours. I am not in the same outfit as before; Amber changed me out of my wet clothes and into comfy pajamas.

"Of course, I am still here," Amber says, in a way that sounds as though she is surprised I was even questioning it, "I was not going to leave you alone."

I start to choke up a little. I do not want to start crying again. I take a bunch of deep breaths and I manage to hold back the tears from restarting, but it is clear that this is only temporary.

"No more crying until you hydrate more and get food in your stomach. Come on, let's go to the kitchen," Amber stands up with a little extra effort. I did not realize how big her baby bump had gotten, I just saw her a couple weeks ago, but she has really popped. She still has a little less than two months to go before her baby boy arrives and she has been really stressed about making sure everything is ready. Her baby shower is scheduled for the weekend after next, which her mother-in-law has taken over completely.

As we walked into the little eat-in kitchen, my thoughts were starting to come together, and my head was processing details again. Once the smell of the garlic and sauce hit my nose, my stomach rumbles with anticipation. I had breakfast, but I had forgotten to have lunch. Amber opens the oven door to reveal a pan of stuffed shells that were staying warm.

"How did you end up here? I am so confused and disoriented still," I ask her as she grabs two plates out of the first cupboard she opens, like she is familiar with the kitchen. I don't know how she can always do that, making everything seem natural with her movements and actions. I swear everything I do looks clunky and is never easy.

"Paul's sister lives one street over and I had to drop off baby pictures of myself for the shower. Lord only knows what she's planning with those. She will probably use one of those weird programs that merges two photos together to predict what the baby will look like, but the photo always looks creepy," Paul is her husband and a complete anomaly in his family with his easy-going personality. Amber laughs in a way that she reserves for Paul's family. It is a fake laugh that resembles when a Southern woman says bless your heart, "I was on my way home when I saw you out front, so I was going to stop in and say hi. As I walked up from the driveway, you looked like you were tearing apart the stairs one layer at a time with a scrub brush. Don't take this the wrong way, but you looked manic. In nearly thirty years of knowing each other, I have never seen you lose control, so I knew something was wrong. Do you want to tell me what is going on?"

"Oh jeez," I am so embarrassed, "you have wasted your entire evening on my meltdown. I was overthinking things. I am totally fine, everything is fine. I don't want you to have me to worry about on top of getting ready for the baby and dealing with your in-laws. I am so sorry I put this on your plate too, I am just overtired. I don't sleep well when the girls are at Jake's house."

"Bullshit, Carly!" Amber says in a tone much harsher than her normal melodic voice. I sit back in my chair, startled.

"What?" I have no clue what to even say to her.

"I called you out on your bullshit, Carly," Amber starts back up, "we both know that this was not just you being 'overtired.' This was you snapping and now we are going to sit here, eat this delicious Italian food, and you are going to tell me what the hell is going on, even if it takes all night."

She puts a plate of stuffed shells in front of me and grabs a bottle of red wine. She pulls two wine glasses off the rack on the wall. I give her a look to question what her next move is going to be over that big baby belly. She pours the wine in one glass and grabs sparkling water from the fridge which she pours into the other. I laugh a little.

"What? Just because I am pregnant doesn't mean I can't be fancy. I miss wine and I am telling myself this is a bubbly wine not boring water," she says as she picks up both glasses and walks over to the table. She actually smells my glass, like a huge whiff of my glass, before she sits it in front of me.

"That was weird, you know right?" I laugh again as I take a bite of the pasta and a sip of the wine. It is a euphoric combination. I start to feel centered once more, and I am processing my thoughts better.

Amber just shrugs and dives into her plate.

"Okay, we have food and drinks, now spill," she demands.

I sigh, take another bite, and give in. I am too emotionally drained to keep pushing it all down and I am at a point where I know something has to give. I feel so disconnected from the world and the weight of trying to wade through it all alone has maxed me out. The problem is that I have never spoken about it out loud and I am lost just trying to find words that describe my internal roller coaster.

"I'll do my best to talk about it, but I do not know if it is going make sense," and with that I tell her everything I have been feeling. I tell her about the emptiness inside of me. I tell her about how for the first time in my life I do not know how to meet friends- I cannot even fathom the idea of dating. I lay out everything that has been bottled up. She asks me questions here and there but mostly just listens. When I finish telling her everything, I am certain that I lost her. Even if I have, I take that silence to take a deep breath and I realize that suddenly I feel like I can breathe better. The tension of holding everything so tightly inside has given way just a little and for a moment I am okay. Nearly at the same moment, it hits me that I just told her my deep secret, and I feel a panic attack building up in me. I begin formulating excuses of insanity. She speaks before I can fully design the excuse of chemical fumes from the cleaning supplies.

"Wow, that is a lot you've been holding in. I knew that you had a lot to heal from, but I had no idea that it was weighing you down so much. Since you left Jake, you have seemed free and happy, but I never stopped to think about that being just freer and happier in comparison to life with him, not necessarily in the full spectrum," she says slowly.

I can tell she was still processing but she is quick to think, as always, and continues, "First, we are getting you in with my therapist. If you don't want to see the same one that I do, we will get someone else in her office. I helped her kid get an interview at my Alma mater, so she owes me."

I open my mouth to argue, "Don't argue," she knows me all too well, "You are talking to someone. A therapist who is experienced in domestic abuse."

"Jake never hit me. He was controlling, yes, but never violent," I say quickly.

"What he did to you was abusive. You had to plan to escape him, and he still looms over you," Amber says carefully, like she is afraid if she pushes too hard, I will clam back up and stop talking. That is fair, this is the most vulnerable that I have been in years. It feels wrong talking about my own needs.

After she lets that sink in for a beat, she keeps going, "Carly, stop making excuses for him. You are the victim here. You deserve to find your happiness."

I do not attempt to make excuses. I realize that it might be true. I need to start fighting for myself. I need to start to heal. It is time to get angry and to do better not only for me, but also for my girls.

I am ready for the next chapter.

Chapter 3

꧁꧂

I sit next to a little tabletop fountain listening to the water flowing, it is peaceful, but also makes me feel like I need to pee. I look around trying to find the nearest restroom for when I need it. Now, I realize that I have not drank much water during the day, so I hope my voice does not get scratchy. I am looking around the room to see if there is a water fountain when I hear, "Carly Kennedy?"

My heart jumps out of my body, startled. I look at where the voice is coming from to find a woman with long blondish-brown hair and a soft face. She is dressed in linen pants with a simple shirt and long cardigan over it. I do not know what I had expected a therapist to look like, but I suppose it was not as approachable as the woman in front of me.

"Carly?" She repeats.

"Yes, I'm sorry, that's me," Jumping up trying to get myself together and not seem so disheveled. I take the hand that she put out for me to shake.

"I am Dr. Nicole Rose. It's a pleasure to meet you finally! Amber has always spoken so highly of you. I guess I am not supposed to say that, but it is just amazing to see such a long-standing friendship like

16

yours," she begins, "Please follow me and we will get settled into my office."

She leads me down a hallway into a small office. It is much more friendly than what I was expecting. I had assumed that it would look like all the movies where therapists have stark, minimalist offices with a chaise lounge type couch to lie on. There is a couch, but it does not make me think about laying down and there are several chairs of varying comforts, from an oversize fluffy chair that looks like I could sink into with a good book to a desk chair with a stiff back.

"Sit wherever you feel comfortable, Carly," Dr. Rose gestures to the options.

Like most things in my life, I am overthinking the seating arrangements. I know I used to be impulsive, but after years of walking on eggshells and constantly fearing that I was doing something wrong, I cannot make an easy decision without thinking about if I might upset someone else by doing so. A simple decision, such as a chair, could feel like a landmine with Jake. If you picked the wrong one, there would be an explosion. I end up picking an armchair that seems like an in-between of the reading chair and desk chair, a safe compromise within my intrusive thoughts.

"Thank you for coming, Carly. I know this can be intimidating and feel strange when you first begin therapy," Dr. Rose begins, "I do not want you to feel forced into answering any questions and silence is okay. Feel free to think to yourself or out loud. I may ask some follow-up questions, but it is your choice to consent to answering."

Consent. My choice to consent. I went so long without having my consent cared about that this feels like a joke. I accidentally chuckle out loud a little bit, but Dr. Rose does not seem taken aback by this.

She just says gently, "I can see that triggered something and that did not feel like a truly humored laugh, can you tell me where your mind went just now?"

I pause for a long time, so long that I think Dr. Rose might start talking again. She does not.

"I was thinking about how easily you assigned consent to me, and that I believe you," I pause again to question how ready I really am to dive into this therapy session. I decided that I was long overdue to get my life back, and if it starts here by being open, I was going to try. My kids deserve to have the best version of their mom, and I deserve to be happy, "I do not even remember the person I was the last time I felt in control of my own decisions, it seems so long ago."

"Tell me about the last time you felt that control."

"It was definitely before Jake came into my life," I thought back to those days, "I was living and working in the city. I would go out to dinner with friends or just stay in and order take out. No one ever made me feel guilty or stupid for doing what I wanted. I took really good care of myself. I know it's hard to imagine now but I used to be very fit and cared about my appearance."

"I think you look great, give yourself a little grace. Being a mom is not an easy job and, again, I probably shouldn't mention my conversations with Amber," Dr. Rose says with a small grin that tells me that she knows Amber will not mind, "but on more than one occasion she has named you as a mom she wants to be like with her little one. Let's try to make this a space that you can build yourself back up, not bring yourself down. It's okay to have those feelings sometimes, we all do, but it is important that we work on those feelings as we move forward, not get stuck in the mud with them."

"Okay," Is really all that I can manage because I feel a lump in my throat like I am about to cry again. I did not know Amber saw me in that light as a mother, she is always so poised, and I am not at all. I also desperately feel like I want to reach the point where I can appreciate myself again, but that feels so far away. I can barely imagine marginally tolerating myself, much less loving who I am.

"You mentioned Jake, can I assume that is your ex-husband?"

"Yes, sorry I should have mentioned that!" I say, embarrassed that I am talking about people in my life like Dr. Rose will magically know who's who.

"No apologies are necessary. I want you to feel comfortable talking organically and finish full thoughts. If I need more clarification, I will ask, but I am pretty good at figuring out where everyone fits in," Dr. Rose says, again in that tone that makes me feel like there is no judgment from her, "Tell me, how did you and Jake meet originally? What was it like in the very beginning?"

I tell her all about how charming and kind he was then. I keep talking as the story turns into being about controlling behaviors. I talk about when both the girls were born, for a moment, I thought everything would be okay, as brief as that was. I go on and on, not even getting into my head about the fact that I am saying this all to a perfect stranger.

Finally, I mention Amber stopping by my house and finding me melting down while scrubbing the stair a little over a week ago. Looking back at that day, I struggle to not be hard on myself. I still cannot believe that I cracked like that. Parts of it are still spotty to me.

I finish with, "Amber insisted that I need therapy to help with the trauma from the abuse. I hear and see what she is saying, but I still have a hard time seeing what I have gone through as abuse."

"Why is that?" Dr. Rose asks.

"Because he never hit me or left bruises on me," I start. I take a deep breath and continue, "it feels more like I was stuck in an unhappy marriage, and I did not have the strength to leave. He was controlling, but that does not feel like abuse."

"Do you know the basic definition of abuse?" Dr. Rose asks me. I kind of just shrug and wait for her to say more.

"Abuse is manipulating someone in a way for one's own benefit.

Yes, abuse can be causing one physical pain, but it is also causing one mental turmoil," She provides and then pauses to let me digest this. I feel a throbbing pressure in my chest when she says that, remembering the emotional pain of living with Jake. As if she can read my thoughts, she continues, "How often did Jake turn a conversation around so that you felt at fault or inferior about what you wanted or knew? That is gaslighting, which is a form of mental and verbal abuse. How many times did Jake not let you have money for something or say that you could not afford it even though you knew it was not true? That is financial abuse. Those are just some examples, but you do not have to fully accept it because I said so. These are things we will continue discussing and unpacking. We will go at your pace."

I cannot think of how to respond to that. Her words start to crack through my guard, just a little, just enough to start to make me wonder if it is true. The lingering fear of how Jake would react to those accusations are pushing against my acceptance. I hear my own thoughts trying to work out how that fear proves the point, but I am just not there yet. All I can manage to say is, "Okay."

Dr. Rose shifts towards the computer on the desk. I had not even noticed it, but she types a few things, "I am just creating a file for you so we can track certain things. We want to be able to celebrate milestones, big or small. Also, we want to be able to see if some things are not working so we can alter the plan, as needed. This will all make much more sense over the next few sessions as we establish a routine and treatment plan.

The purpose of today essentially is to get to know one another. If you decide that you would like to continue with our sessions, which is completely your decision, we will continue our conversations and dive into certain hurdles that you face."

"I definitely want to continue," I say, maybe a little too quickly, so I slow down for the next part, "It feels nice to not bottle it up and to have a safe space to just talk. I constantly feel like a burden on my family and friends if I tell them about how badly I am struggling. I am ready to feel like myself again."

"I am glad to hear that, Carly. I want you to know that you are not alone, a lot of people, especially moms, try to hide the negative and do not allow themselves a chance to feel out loud," Dr. Rose says, "Alright, I like to give homework. Feel free to groan, most of my clients do, but guess what? I am a mom, as well, to three teenage children, so groans and moans about homework do not faze me."

I laugh a little at her candidness. I do make a face at the thought of having homework, but I am listening and willing to do what is needed. I figure she will want me to write out a list of people I might talk about, or I should read a motivational quote every day. I did not expect what she actually assigned as homework.

* * *

"Join a club?!" I practically scream into the phone with Amber after my appointment with Dr. Rose. I called her as soon as I got in the car, "what is this? Fucking high school?"

"Carly, settle down and think about what she told you to do. She really told you that you had to join a club?" Amber sounds kind of amused by this homework assignment.

"I mean she did not say exactly join a club, it was one of her suggestions though," I reply.

"Okay, what was the actual homework then?"

I groan and tell her, "Dr. Rose asked me to push my comfort zone and do at least one thing social, without the girls, before our next appointment. She gave suggestions like join a book club or some other club, find a local group with similar interests, or just reach out to someone I haven't talked to in a while and make plans."

"Well, that sounds reasonable. Isn't that what you have been wanting to do?" Amber asks.

"Yes, but I pictured doing that after therapy cured me," I am just being a big baby now and whining. I do not want to admit that I have no clue where to even start and it scares me to try.

"Carly, I have been in therapy since I was 8. It's not a magic cure. It's a tool to help you live consciously and help you direct the shit train that is life in a direction that hopefully will make it not crash into another shit train that causes an explosion of double the shit. We are trying to figure out how to keep the shit on board and not lose it."

"The places your brain goes amazes me," I say laughing at her imagery.

"I'm pretty sure it is because I am an only child and had a lot of pretend friends," she says, "But let's not dive into why I am in therapy, let us get back to you. So, she wants you to get out in the world. I like it, now let's figure out what you can do."

"Is there a waking up too early and drinking coffee in the quietness club? I'd be great at that!" I suggest satirically. I hear typing.

"The Early Bird Café Club meets at different coffee shops nearby. You don't have the girls this weekend and they are meeting this Saturday at that shop on Main with the cats on the front sign," she quickly replies.

"What?! How did you even find that information?"

"The Meetup app. Haven't you heard of it? I have used it a few times for things like networking and stuff," she tells me.

"I see, well even if I had any desire to go to this thing, I can't. Your baby shower is on Saturday, and I promised your mom I would come early to try to play buffer to your mother-in-law, remember?" I remind her.

"We do not have to be at the venue until one at the very earliest and this is at seven-thirty in the morning. Next excuse please," she counters.

I do not have one readily available. A Saturday morning coffee chat actually sounds nice; it is the not-knowing-anyone-else-there part that freaks me out. I used to be so outgoing and could make friends anywhere. I would go have dinner in a restaurant alone when no one was free and usually end up meeting people to chat with. I miss that part of my personality and if a latte with strangers helps take me back there then I guess it is not so crazy.

"Okay I will go," I tell her as I pull into my driveway.

"Really? Yay! I was prepared for at least two more excuses," she says and then in a softer tone she adds, "I'm proud of you, Carly. It takes a lot of strength to put yourself back out in the world after being hidden away for so long. You will not regret this!"

I hope she is right.

Chapter 4

Saturday morning rolls around faster than I can talk myself out of it. It is not really early for me. I have never been one to sleep in, I like being productive earlier in the day. I calculate the amount of time that it will take me to get there and leave 10 minutes earlier than that. I hate being late, or even just on time.

As I am putting my purse in the car on the passenger side, I look over to the house on the left of mine. It is a beautiful old farmhouse, but it is very unkempt and, from what I can tell, completely abandoned. The house looks massive, but I could not be sure through all the shrubs and unruly tree branches. I have never seen anyone there before.

Until today. A truck is pulling up in front of the house with a trailer behind it carrying a lawnmower and other landscaping tools as I am getting into the car. Maybe the city has finally decided to take care of the yard. It is such an eyesore. I cannot help but do a double take when the driver steps out. The guy who stands next to the truck is tall and handsome, throwing me for a loop, since I have not looked at anyone that way since the divorce. Attraction feels like a disabled function since the damage of my marriage.

I shake my head a little and remind myself to stop ogling this stranger who is probably a city employee working overtime on the weekend. My smart watch lights up with the calendar reminder about the coffee thing and I see the time. It is very early, much too early for yard work. I have met most of the neighbors and I knew that Barb across the street would be the first to complain about a lawn mower making noise before a reasonable hour.

I laugh at that thought since she is one of the neighbors who often calls the city about the property to complain. Not that I blame her, it is overgrown and there are some trees that have about as much life in them as the house does.

It is strange how lonely a house can look. In a way, I feel connected to that farmhouse. It was strongly built but now sits neglected and forgotten. It is stuck in the same spot and cannot help itself. I can see how the house, at least the exterior, could be beautiful again and be a home to a happy family, it just needs work. I am glad it is getting at least a little help on the outside.

As I am staring at the house, the handsome man, in his jeans and flannel button up shirt, turns on the lawn mower and starts driving it off the trailer. Right on cue, Barb's front door swings open and she hurries across the street in her robe and curlers in her hair.

I quickly get into my car and buckle up. I know Barb will call me over if Mr. Hot Landscaper argues with her and I do not want to be late.

As I back out, I can hear, "What is with all this racket so early in the morning?"

* * *

I pull into the parking lot of Kat's Café, appropriately decorated with cats on the sign, and look at the clock. I am about 5 minutes early for the meetup. I take a deep breath and question what the hell I am doing here. I would much rather be comfortable at home in my pajamas with coffee in my favorite mug while listening to Barb yell at Mr. Hot Landscaper. I don't know what has gotten into me, but the fact that I have a name for him like I am on Grey's Anatomy is a little alarming.

I shake off the thought, slightly embarrassed, but it is kind of nice feeling flirty thoughts again.

"Okay, it is time to do this," Big breath. I made it this far and cannot back out now.

As I walk up to the coffee house, I have to force my feet to keep going forward. My heart rate is unusually high, and my mouth feels dry. I feel like I might pass out as I realize that I have no idea how to locate the group.

'I can't give up now," is what I keep saying in my head, pulling open the glass door and stepping into the café. I'm in.

I look around the tables in the small front area, but my vision feels blurry, and my mind feels foggy. I had never experienced social anxiety before my marriage and during it we never did anything or went anywhere to trigger me, but the trauma response seems to be real, at this moment, in the wake of having to meet new people.

Then something clicks. I have two amazing daughters that look up to me and I preach being brave to them, so now it is my turn. Several deep breaths in and out before I keep going. My palms are still clammy and gross, but my vision clears, and my heart rate has started to go down. What would I tell the girls to encourage them? Stand up straight, hold your head high, and open yourself up to a new adventure because you never know where it can lead you.

I get in line to order some coffee, since that feels like the natural thing to do. This gives me an opportunity to look around the café without standing out. As the older couple in front of me bickers about which flavor of scone to share, I look over to the back wall at a large table. That is when I spot it— a little chalkboard easel with "Early

Bird Café Club" drawn on it with top tier artistic skill. I already like whoever wrote the sign.

The couple lands on a cranberry-orange scone, pays their bill, and scoots to the side to wait for their drinks. I give the barista my order- a regular coffee with a blueberry muffin. I just could not resist a muffin with the crumbles on top but feel self-conscious, wondering if I am going to be the only one eating. I crane my neck towards the table and see a couple other people with baked goods. My lungs exhale the panicked breath I was holding.

I take the plate and the coffee, which I had asked for in a to-go cup. I love coffee in a mug, but when I was ordering I had a scenario ridiculously play out in my head that I might spill it if I start shaking, or I would trip as I got over there, scorching all my new acquaintances before I can even introduce myself. I know I am being ridiculous, but at least I am functioning, and the panic has mostly subsided.

As I approach the little sign at the table, a couple of people look up as it becomes clear that I am coming to join them. A woman who I am guessing is around my age, maybe slightly older, with wild, brown curly hair and she has a boho style that I could only dream of pulling off, looks directly at me and smiles.

"Hi! Carly, right?" She jumps up from her seat to greet me. I do not mask my surprise because she continues, "I recognized you from your little picture on the app. I am Marti, I am the founder of this group. I am so happy you came! We are so excited to get to know you. I am so glad you are here—"

She is speaking faster than I can process through my nerves. When she finally pauses, I manage a weak, "Hi. Yes, that's me."

"Oh my gosh, Marti, stop being so fucking creepy. You are already scaring her. Can you act a little normal for a minute and try to trick people into thinking you are sane?" chides the guy on her right. I can tell he is just kidding around, well mostly. I think.

Marti throws him an over-dramatized look of angst and then breaks into laughter, "You're right, Miles. Sorry, Carly, I am happy to have you here with us. Please sit down, I promise I will behave and chill out."

I laugh and pick the seat across the table from Marti, "I am glad to be here. I have driven by this place a bunch but have never been inside."

"Same for most of us, that is why we picked it this week. It is cute here, maybe three dozen too many cats, but cute still," the woman sitting next to me says, "I'm Lana."

"Hi," I like her immediately. I look around the table. Six people, besides me, are sitting there with a few extra empty chairs.

"Carly, let me introduce you to everyone," Marti says, and she starts pointing at people, "This is Lana and over there is Talah. Then our lonely and only straight guy, Dylan. And on this side is Jayna. This is Miles, and of course, I am Marti. Everyone, say hi to Carly."

Everyone gives a little hi and/or waves. I start to feel the nerves lessen more. No one at the table is intimidating or giving off bad vibes. They all seem familiar with one another. I just hope that maybe they could make space for me in their circle, but I refuse to get my hopes up too high. It has been a long time since I found somewhere I belong as more than a supporting character, including my own life.

"There are a few other regulars in the group that are either not here yet or unable to come this week. Plus, of course, we get occasional new people joining us from the app," Marti explains, "We are really informal around here. If you can make it, great! If not, we are not going to hold it against you. I generally am what the app calls the host, but occasionally I am not free and someone else hosts. Honestly, the only thing we do as the host is bring the sign and get here a little early to grab a big table. We have a meetup every Saturday morning. We pick a different café each month."

"Wow, every Saturday?" I read that in the group description but hearing it out loud sounds like a huge commitment.

"Don't worry, none of us are here every single week, but it is nice to know that every week there is something we can do to get out of the house and have adult conversations," Lana says from next to me. She chuckles and continues, "Sorry, I'm a single mom and sometimes I forget how to adult. I am usually here every other Saturday when the kids are with my ex unless I have a Friday night date that goes really well."

"Which means she is here every other Saturday without fail," Talah says from the other side of Lana. With that comment, Lana swats at Talah and rolls her eyes. The table breaks out in a fit of pure belly laughing and I cannot help but join in.

"They poke fun, but they are not wrong," Lana smirks at the rest of the table, "My tales of 'single mom out in the dating world' are a fan-favorite around this table. I seem to be a magnet for the weirdos on every dating app."

"Don't you have greater odds of finding someone? And yeah, you do find some doozies," Dylan asks. I look at Lana, because I do not know what he means by that.

"Common misconception there, my friend. Just because I am bisexual does not mean I have so many more choices." They are super comfortable as a group and not at all phased by a new person with them, "If anything, it just means I have more less-than-quality people to weed through to find just one to go on a date with."

"Hey! What did I miss?" Another person rushes up to the table and sits down on the other side of Jayna. When she looks my way, she says, "Ooo, new person! Are you totally new or have I just missed you before?"

Marti replies, "We were just talking about Lana's dating messes, and this is Carly, she is brand new today. Carly, this is Paula."

"Hi, Carly, it is nice to meet you," Paula says to me then she looks over to Lana, "Please tell me you went on another date with the guy that asked if he could pour a beer in your shoe and drink it so that it tasted like your feet. I mean he wasn't all red flags; he did pay for the beer!"

I nearly spit out my latte.

"Please tell me I heard that correctly," I need to know more.

"Oh, you did," Lana shakes her head, "and there will be no second dates for that guy. Carly, tell us more about you."

"I'm really not all that interesting," I start, "I am an accountant by trade, but not the 'do my taxes' kind but rather consulting and helping companies with audits. I am a single mom of two little girls. Um, I don't know what else—um—"

"That's cool," Dylan picks up where I trail off, "I am a solo girl dad. I have two as well. They're 13 and 15. How old are yours?"

"Millie is 7 and Remi is 4," I tell him, picking at the sleeve on my coffee cup. Talking about myself makes me want to slink under the table. What if the conversation turns to them asking me about my marriage- a total mood killer- or my relationship status – nonexistent.

"Those are great ages! The teenage girl years are turning my hair so gray. I swear I was not this salt and pepper when they were little," Dylan pushes a hand through his, as stated, gray mixed into a dark brown that gives him a more sophisticated look that some guys are just blessed with. He is an attractive man, not really my type but I couldn't tell you what my type is anymore. I can feel my thoughts diverting to Mr. Hot Landscaper, until luckily the conversation restarts.

"I remember when my oldest daughter was about 15. She just turned 24," Paula starts and then adds, "She was a terror. They say that terrible twos are hard, but no one warns you about the terrible teens. She would be laughing one moment and crying the next. Luckily my other two are boys. They were mischievous but much easier to raise. Now they are all in their 20s and starting adult lives, I can confirm that my daughter is much more pleasant now, we are very close."

"Good to know that there is a chance of survival!" I joke. The table laughs. I feel silly about how much I like knowing that I was able to make this group think that I am funny, even if only for a split second.

"So, you're a single mom too," Lana says, and I brace myself for the questions, "Are you dating? Any funny dating app stories that can help take the pressure off me?"

There it is, sort of. I take a deep breath and prepare myself to answer in a way that does not sound off-putting, "Honestly, it's all still really fresh. I have only been separated for 8 months, divorced for two. I just haven't even thought about getting out there again. I don't even know if I would know where to start," It really was not too hard to say that, and no one gave me any judgmental or pitiful looks, "And seriously the shoe beer story is not selling the idea of dating!"

The whole table roars with laughter again.

Marti leans across the table and puts a hand on mine, "You have to go at your own pace, no rush, but when you are ready, we are here to vent to. Many of us have been divorced and are all just trying to figure it out. Then others are figuring out other things in life. Sometimes we just need to laugh it off to not pull our hair out and let it take over. Our group is not for everyone and that's okay, but I have a feeling you'll fit in just fine."

I let that sink in as I just nod along with her. I smile back at her because it is nice to hear that I am welcome somewhere after feeling so isolated. Inside though, I am trying to not cry with relief and release.

While I am thinking this over, the conversation turns over to Miles telling the group about something cute his twin toddlers did recently. The rest of the time at the table is just that, conversation about life.

As we get ready to leave, Lana says to me, "I'm on the same schedule you are with weekends with the kids. I hope to see you again in two weeks, I would kill to have a mom friend on the same parenting cycle.

Coffee meetups are great, but this mama needs to go out for drinks sometimes!"

We chat as we walk to the parking lot, and I am smiling at the thought of being able to see myself going out like I used to. I feel like a kid in school. I want to call Amber and tell her that I made new friends today. I am proud of myself.

Chapter 5

I pull in my driveway around 10:30 AM. I had to run errands after the meetup, including grabbing my dress for the baby shower from the dry cleaners.

The truck is still in front of the house next door. The front yard looks much cleaner and there is a pile of branches and leaves at the curb. It is nice to see that progress is happening.

I can hear the lawn mower somewhere on the property. It is a large plot of land that goes far back, so Mr. Hot Landscaper could be anywhere back there. A glance at my watch tells me that I do not have time to wonder any longer. I have to get ready and head over to the venue to help set up.

I shrug and smile again at the abandoned house getting a makeover and head inside for my own makeover.

By the time I head back to my car to drive to the baby shower, the truck is gone. The yard looks a lot more presentable, but there is still a lot of work that the poor old house needs. I have always dreamed of owning an old farmhouse like that. I can imagine myself taking on projects, using YouTube to learn how to DIY it. For now, that was just on my mental vision board while we got on our feet, but it is nice to feel like I am dreaming about a future again.

* * *

As I pull up to the venue, I see Amber sitting on a bench at the front entrance. There are employees and other people going in and out of the doors, so I know she is not locked out, but she seems checked out. It looks like she is trying to meditate away violent thoughts.

"I'll take it your mother-in-law has arrived?" I say as I walk up to her.

"She is currently mushing different things into baby diapers so that the guests can guess what it is," Amber sucks in her breath through her teeth. I have rarely seen her mad but her mother-in-law, Sheri, has a talent for bringing her to that point, "And what was the number one game I said I did not want to do?"

"Oh no, Guess-The-Belly game?" I guess, referencing the shower game where the guests cut a piece of ribbon to the size that they think the baby bump is all the way around. Sheri is notorious for corny games. Amber's wedding shower was proof of that with the toilet paper wedding gown contest. Amber hates being touched, especially while she is pregnant.

"Let me handle Sheri," I reach into my bag and pull out a pile of papers, "I printed these out last night in anticipation. A few on paper, harmless games, Baby Gift Bingo and cutesy stuff like that. Give me a minute. I will be right back."

In the banquet room, I scan the area. I cringe at the blown-up canvas on an easel in front. There are baby pictures of Amber on the left and Paul on the right, with arrows from both pointing to a mockup of a strange, distorted AI-generated picture of a baby that looks about 4 months old with a full set of teeth. There is a table of game supplies, baby diapers loaded with God-knows-what in them. Sheri appears to have finished that task and now is torturing the event planner. I head over to her.

"Hi, Sheri, it's nice to see you," I say politely.

"Carla, I'm glad you are here, there is still so much to do!" Sheri says with a wrong name again, as she always does despite having known me for almost 20 years.

"It's Carly," I correct gently knowing that I need to keep the peace here. I look across the room and see Amber's mom setting up place cards with a plastered-on smile like my own, "I have one more load to grab from my car, but I did want to drop these off. I know you have things planned but I printed off some backup games just in case we needed them."

"Carly, yes, so sorry," she apologizes half-heartedly. This is a step up since for the first decade she would reintroduce herself each time like she had never seen me in her life, "That is very thoughtful. I think I have the games covered but if you want to place them at the game table, we can have them on standby in case we need to fill time."

"Sounds great, I will do that, and I will be right back in," I turn to leave.

"And if you see Amber on your way through the lobby, send her back in here, she went to the bathroom quite some time ago!"

I nod and head over to the game table. As luck would have it, I get to the table as I hear Sheri yelling something at the event planner and they shuffle into the kitchen entrance. I look all around and lock eyes with Patti, Amber's mom, who is like a second mom to me. I put a finger to my lips to motion to stay quiet. Other than Patti, no one else is around, so I put the papers on the opposite side of the table and scoot down to the ribbon. I have a big purse today, which is working to my advantage right now. With a quick sweep of my arm, the spools of ribbon fall into my bag without a sound. I take the pen that is closest to me from the table and drop it on the floor. Oops!

As I bend down to pick it up, I lift the tablecloth to look underneath. Sure enough, there are four more spools of extra ribbon with other supplies hidden away. I quickly stuff those into my bag as well and stand up to return the pen to its place.

I brush down my dress and look around again. I can still hear Sheri in the kitchen yelling about pickle juice seeping onto the cheese on the charcuterie boards. An amused Patti waves at me to get out while I can.

As I walk back outside, I look over at Amber still meditating on her bench. I peek out one spool of baby blue ribbon and say ominously, "The deed is done."

I can hear her laughing as I walk over to my car. I open the trunk and empty the contraband into a gym bag, then zipper it up and grab the wrapped gift I left there.

With my slightly less full bag and the gift, I walk back up to the venue and Amber stands up, links her arm in mine as we walk into the wildfire.

* * *

The rest of the shower is relatively low drama. When Sheri goes to get the spools of ribbon, Patti and I manage to convince her that we never saw ribbon there, so she must have left it at home. We play one of my games instead, which ends up being a hit. The baby diaper game is as disgusting as expected, especially after the one she had avocado in turns brown and looks like what should go into a diaper. Luckily no one threw up, but it was touch and go for a minute. Plus, I stole the answer key and gave it to the table of our high school friends to make the game go faster. Paul comes by towards the end with a beautiful bouquet for Amber and my heart is full for my best friends.

As the shower is winding down and we are cleaning up, they realize that some of the gifts are too large to fit into the sedans that Patti, Paul, and Sheri drive. There is too much to fit into Amber's smaller SUV. I have a larger SUV with a third row I can flip down, so I volunteer to bring gifts over to their house. We manage to pack everything into mine, Amber, and Paul's cars, so there is no need for Sheri or Patti to follow us, much to Sheri's protest. I am pretty sure she wants to come to their house immediately to set up the nursery the way she has envisioned it. Luckily, Paul steps in and insists the mommy-to-be needs to get some rest.

As we get to their house, Amber, Paul, and I all pull into the driveway. Amber throws her keys to Paul and says, "Just pile it in the garage for now, thanks and love you, babe!"

As I pass by him, I throw my keys towards him and mimic Amber, "Thanks and love you, babe!"

He just laughs and shakes his head. He is such a kind spirit; it is amazing that he is so different and independent from his mother. For a long time before I met Jake, it had been just Amber, Paul, and me. Amber and I went to different colleges, but she visited me often at my school since my roommate flunked out after one semester and they never gave me a new one. I had an extra bed and there were some dive bars that did not ID around the campus.

One weekend she came to visit me and as she arrived, I was just finishing up working on a group project with Paul and two of our classmates. The other two left shortly after, but Paul had stuck around chatting with us. It was not love at first sight with them, rather Paul just made his way into the circle of trust that Amber and I had with one another. It was not until senior year of college that something shifted between them, and they both admitted to me that they had a crush on the other one. This was no surprise to me; I had suspected it for some time but was not sure if either of them was going to make a move.

After their individual confessions, I set into motion the opportunity for them to decide what they wanted to do next. One weekend Amber came to visit me. I had a nice sized one-bedroom apartment off-campus with a fancy futon, which means it was made out of fake wood instead of metal, for her to crash on. This was our normal routine, except this time right after he arrived, I volunteered to go pick up the pizza. We had planned a wine and movie night but needed to carb-up first. I made sure to take my time getting the food and when I returned, they were both sitting on the couch deep in conversation, but still with some distance between them. They both had a hand on the couch cushion in between them outstretched. I had a feeling they were close to figuring it out.

I made an excuse that the pizza place forgot something, and I had to run back. Instead, I went down to the bar near my house where a lot of students hung out. I was bound to know people there and let them have their time together, once upon a time I had no problem being outgoing. Once I got there and found a group of other accounting majors. I texted Amber (which cost me like $.60 back in those days!) to tell them I bumped into these people and had to talk to them about our senior capstone project, so get started on the night without me.

I came home a few hours later to find the two of them cuddling on the couch, fast asleep. The television was still playing reruns of Friends in the background with an empty bottle of wine on the coffee table. I put a blanket over them and headed into my bedroom to call it a night.

After that night, they were officially together and have been since. While they had their own date nights, we still had our nights together. Our friendship never wavered until I met Jake. He was uncomfortable with how close I was to Paul, even though there was never anything to warrant that, and drove a wedge between our group of three. They never liked him, and I did not listen to my friends when I should have.

I shake out of my memories and walk into the house behind Amber. She is already grabbing snacks and drinks out of the kitchen. She gestures for me to sit at the bar stool seating that separates her living room and kitchen.

"Okay, now we have that shit show over with, let's talk about you," she says as she sits down with a handful of different chips bags and a variety of dips and salsa, "How was the meetup? Did I send you into a group of old retired men meeting for coffee or college kids sharing their poetry for the next slam night?"

"Neither. I think I actually enjoyed myself. I think I will go back."

"Hmm, I guess I really am a genius," she says with a hint of smugness, "This is why everyone should just listen to my advice, I am usually right."

I laugh at her, knowing she is only half joking. I start by telling her about the meetup and how I pushed through my nerves. I tell her a little about the people I met, though I do not know very much about them yet. Every few minutes Paul's head pops through the garage door asking if something needs to come inside, or what something is. He may never recover from us trying to explain the post-delivery kit she received. He legitimately lost his footing when we told him that the squirt bottle was not for drinking from and where the ice packs were going.

As he retreats back outside, a little pale, we chat about how long we think he'll make it in the delivery room before passing out.

Chapter 6

꧁⬦꧂

The day after the baby shower should be a quiet Sunday. The girls do not need to be picked up until late afternoon.. Besides my homework to join a club, Dr. Rose also encouraged me to not feel so much pressure to fill time every second of every day.

I might as well embrace her suggestion. The club homework ended up not being all that awful. I let myself sleep in a little, which means about 8 AM for me. After I roll out of bed, I decide to take a long shower to pamper myself. I am so used to showering quickly between clients and kids. No need to rush this morning. A 10-minute facial mask to start then an everything-shower sounds just like what the doctor ordered to relax. I sit on the toilet seat and do some breathing exercises to relax while the mask does its thing.

I make it about 2 minutes before the relaxation is stressing me out. I need to do something to keep my hands busy. Learning to relax will be a work-in-progress.

For the rest of the face mask time, I reorganize my skincare products. Laying out the ones I will need after my shower and arranging all the rest in order of frequency of use. I put the last bottle of aloe vera sunburn gel in the back just as my alarm indicates that I can take the mask off. Thank god! It has hardened and feels like cement on my cheeks.

The little cottage has two full bathrooms in it. There is a bathroom that the girls and guests use, which has a regular bathtub in it. However, one of my favorite parts of this house is something I have always dreamed of – a master bathroom. It is not fancy by any means, not like the homes in the magazines or on television, but it is nice to have my own space. It is just a toilet, sink, and walk-in shower.

I turn the water on and let it get hot before walking into the stream to rinse the mask off my face. I mentally pat myself on the back for the job well done with self-care, but it is time to get on with the day. I quickly wash my hair, wash my body with my shower poof, then do a quick shave on my under-arms, like I normally do. As I finish up, I reach to turn off the water but then pause. I take a deep breath and remind myself that I am supposed to be relaxing. I turn back into the stream of hot water and let the heat fall onto my shoulders. I can feel the tension knots in my neck releasing ever so slightly under the water. As I roll my neck down and look at my legs, my eyes squint in thought to try to remember the last time I shaved my legs, which is extra scary since I wore a dress to the baby shower yesterday. I had on dark tights so no one would have noticed, but I cannot believe that the thought of shaving never crossed my mind. When did I stop caring about myself?

I sit on the small bench in the shower and take my time shaving. I use a good smelling shaving cream and take long careful strokes. I finish up the last bit and take the shower head down from the cradle above to rinse off all the leftover cream. I lathered up higher than I normally shave so I rinse it off, but the cord catches a little and turns the shower head right up the center into my sensitive parts.

I gasp as the stream hits a place ever so briefly that has not been touched in so long. I have not taken care of myself in all ways, apparently. I have not even thought about sex since long before the separation, but even before then it had never been about my pleasure. It had always been over once Jake reached climax. In the beginning I would finish myself after he turned over, but after a while I did not care enough to even do that. Since I moved out on my own, it just has not even crossed my mind. I am always so focused on everyone and everything else to consider my forgotten needs.

But now here I am with no reason to need to leave that shower quickly and my heart is racing with anticipation. I switch the shower head to a little more pressure and keep rinsing the shaving cream off my legs. I look around the empty bathroom sheepishly, like I am about to do something forbidden. My breathing hitches as I move the water farther up my thigh and it hits exactly where I need it. The water power moves up and down the length of my center and a little noise escapes, like a cross between a groan and a whimper. The sensation is almost too much to handle but it feels too good to stop. I do not want to tease myself anymore; I just want to take myself over the edge. Leaving the heavy stream on the spot, I give myself over to it. I feel the building, closer and closer. Suddenly, a surge moves through my entire body. I shudder and shake as I let the feeling race through my body. I am panting as I come down from the high, the water still on me creating little aftershocks of pleasure. I move the shower head away and start floating back down to reality.

After a minute or so, I snap back into my surroundings. I look all around again like there was someone there to catch me in the act. Why am I being so ridiculous right now? I am a single adult woman alone in her own home. I take a deep breath and have a sense of being lighter, I am relaxed in a way that I forgot existed.

I return the shower head to the cradle and its previous pressure setting. The warm water envelopes me one more time before I turn it off. As I open the shower door and reach for my towel off the rack, I catch a steamy view of myself in the mirror. I smile at the reflection. I feel sexy and feminine for the first time in a long time – I like it.

* * *

By the time I get dressed and throw my wet hair up in a messy bun, it is still only a little after nine. I put on a pot of coffee and look out the front window. The sun is shining, and it looks so calm outside. Autumn just started, so I might as well enjoy it.

As my coffee is brewing, I grab my comfy flannel shawl out of my closet. I wrap it around me and go back to the kitchen. Some peace and quietness with my coffee in the fresh air sounds heavenly now. Apparently, a little relaxation earlier that morning made me a new woman.

I pour coffee into the oversize mug that I bought many years prior at a pottery stand during a craft show at the city park. I grab the morning paper, which yes, I still have delivered every Sunday, to sit at the little table on the porch to work on the crossword puzzle. This neighborhood is so serene, especially this early. Occasionally, a person will jog by, or a couple walks by with their dog, but otherwise it is all still.

I am really leaning into how nice that silence is when I hear, "Carly! I thought I saw you out up there!"

"Oh hi, Barb," and just like that my quiet morning is done. Barb is very nice and kind-hearted, the girls adore her, but she is a chatty person. There are no short conversations with her, and she loves to fill everyone in on all the neighborhood gossip. It is not Wisteria Lane, so gossip is far between, but Barb will talk about anything from someone's new car to a neighbor leaving their trash cans at the curb too long.

"You look great today, so relaxed. I can't remember ever seeing you not go-go-go," Barb says. I smirk with a flash of memory as to why.

"I decided it was time to slow down and take some me-time. My daughters have such busy schedules between school and activities that I forget to do that," I pause to take a sip of my coffee, "and it's just lovely out today."

"Good, it is important to do that. I was a lot like you when my kids were little, except that I was a kid. I was only 18 when Bud and I got married. Our oldest was born one year later. I put everything into the house and took care of everyone else, but forgot to think about what I wanted," Barb starts. In all our conversations, she talks very little about herself and her family. Sadly, it might be because I am always on the go and do not stop long enough to let her tell me about her family.

"Do you want to sit for a cup of coffee with me? I don't think I know anything about your kids, sorry that I've never asked," I gesture to the seat across the table.

"Honey, I get it. Time flies and before you know it, you're a great-gran. A cup of coffee would be wonderful, just a dash of cream and sugar, please." she replies as I am heading inside.

I carefully set down the mug in front of her and sit back in my chair, just as her last statement clicks, "Did you just say 'great-gran'?"

"Any day now! My first-born's oldest is just about ready to pop. Plus, two of my other grandkids are expecting early next year. It's an incredible season of life that not many are blessed to see, but dang was it tough getting here. For so many years, we were so broke that I wondered how we would survive, but we did and have so much to show for it," she goes on to tell me all about her four children, 11 grandkids, and all their significant others. She is so animated talking about them all and telling me stories of all their antics. It makes a lot of sense as to why she is so good with my girls, she is well-practiced. I have noticed family members coming around, but never noticed how many really. She warns me that I will see the full spectacle on Christmas Eve when they have their party. Barb mentions that since the pandemic kept them apart for a couple years, they now make it a point to have everyone together. It is a true testament to her and Bud that all the generations want to be together, even flying in from other places to be there, "there will be cars up the whole street. I used to have some park in the driveway across the street, but I don't know if they'll be able to this year now that there has finally been work happening there."

"I saw the truck there yesterday from the city or something," I think back to Mr. Hot Landscaper.

"That wasn't a city worker, dear," Barb says, shifting back into her role as neighborhood gossip, "That young man is Phil's nephew."

Her story stops cold there, like that was supposed to make any sense to me. I take the bait and ask, "Who is Phil?"

"Was, unfortunately, died about three years ago," Barb says solemnly, "Phil McMulley's family owned this whole plot of land back when. When Bud and I bought our land and built our house decades ago, the street was much different, a true dirt path. It was just our house in addition to Phil's mom, dad, and younger sister in the big house, and Phil lived in your cottage. He never married, heck I don't remember ever even hearing of a lady coming around. We bought our lot from the McMulley's, Bud worked with Phil at a factory over on Center Street back then and they decided to start parceling parts of it off. We were the first that they had agreed to sell too. Phil's sister had gone off and married a guy out of state, there was a lot of family drama there, and I don't think she ever returned to that farm once she left. Mr. McMulley's health declined soon after and he passed away shortly after we moved in. Phil left the factory to help his mom out on the farm. They had a fair number of cows and other animals. Over the next decade they parceled the land out to the point we are at now. It became a regular old neighborhood. Phil's mom passed away at some point during that time and Phil moved into the big house."

Barb points over to the house and looks around the neighborhood. I try to imagine it without the paved streets and sidewalks, but rather farmland with cows roaming around. The girls would have loved it if that was still the case. They have been begging me for a dog since we moved in. Their dad keeps a very anti-pet household – hating puppies should have been a major red flag.

"I did not know that someone even owned the house," I say, "it has always been so dreary since we moved in."

"Henry - the nephew - did not know they owned the house either - until recently, it seems," Barb says and now Mr. Hot Landscaper has a name, "I only found out a little from him yesterday. He was really a grumpy-pants."

I laugh and say slyly, "Barb, did the grumpiness come from you yelling at him from across the street before you even reached him?"

She smirks and I can tell she is not offended, "I did come out pretty hot. It was just so early to start yard work! I was trying to let Bud sleep in, he was at the hockey game with our son Friday, and he didn't get in until late. I swear I was nice once I knew who he was and what he was doing."

"You said that Phil died years ago but Henry just found out about the house? What's the story there?" I ask.

"Remember the sister that never came back? That is Henry's mom!" she tells me like she unearthed a big secret. I already figured as much, but I let her have her moment, "I didn't get much information out of him. He did not seem like he was in a sharing mood. Just assured me that he was not doing anything illegal by being on the property and that he had just learned of the place while helping his mother with some estate planning. It sounds like he might be a lawyer."

"Really? I mean he was really making that landscaping outfit work for him," I slap a hand over my mouth as if to create a dam, so no more words flow out. I feel a blush rising; I didn't mean to tell Barb that I noticed how attractive Henry is.

"He certainly is easy on the eyes," she smiles at me, "He said his mom deeded the house over to him and told him to do whatever he wants with it, keep it, flip it, sell it. It seems like he's starting with just cleaning it up a bit. He was grumpy but respectful and he apologized for it being so early. He told me enough that I was not calling the police on him for trespassing. After he got the lawnmower off the trailer, he spent the next few hours doing things that did not make a lot of noise. But he did mention that he would be coming around a bit more now to clean up the yard and figure out what he wants to do with the old house, in case you were wondering."

"I wasn't wondering," I was. "I'm glad someone is fixing the yard up."

Why am I fixated on a perfect stranger who is being described as grumpy? I do not need negativity in my life, I am on the path to a new chapter. I decide to push Mr. Hot Landscaper Henry out of my mind. However, I do like this giddy feeling of finding someone attractive and I am very interested in more experiences like the shower that morning, maybe at some point not alone. Maybe it is time to consider going out on dates, but I feel helpless to even know where to start.

Chapter 7

I pull up to what used to be my house around 3PM. I cannot pull
into the driveway like I normally do. Next to Jake's SUV is a little
shiny black sports car that looks like it would fit in my tank of
an SUV's glove compartment.

"He got a freaking sports car?" I say to my empty car as I pull up to
the curb in front of the house and beep once to let him know I was
there. It still feels strange being there, like it is familiar in a sense but
never has been mine. In all actuality it never had been mine. Jake
bought it before we were married, and he never put me on the deed.

The front door swings open and the girls come running towards
me. I do not see Jake at the front at all before the door closes behind
the girls, which is strange because he normally watches to make sure
they get to the car. I get out of the car and meet them with a hug when
they reach me. The girls climb up in their seats both talking at the
same time about a million different things. I think I hear Encanto,
dandelions, and hot dogs in the same sentence as I help Remi with her
car seat buckle. My head is spinning trying to keep up with them, but
I love how animated they are and that they love telling me about what
excites them. They are such amazing kids.

I get into my seat and look back to check to make sure Millie has put her seat belt on. The girls are not chattering anymore but they are having an entire conversation with their eyes. Remi looks like she is about to burst from holding back something she wants to say, and Millie looks like she is shushing her sister with a look, then Remi looks confused.

"Okay, girls, what's that about?" I ask as I pull away from the curb. My house is only about ten minutes from Jake's house, "Is this about daddy's new car?"

"What new car?" Remi sounds confused.

"The black one in the driveway?"

"That's not dad's car, it's Riley's," Remi tells me.

"Remi!" Millie says sharply.

"Who is Riley?" I am thrown off by Millie's reaction, she doesn't usually get that tone with her sister.

"Daddy's friend," Remi said. I cannot think of why they are being strange about Jake having a friend over. Since we divorced, he has become social suddenly and goes out with friends that I never knew he had. The Patriots are playing today, so maybe he has one of the guys over to watch.

"Is he over to watch football with your dad? Why wouldn't you want me to know that?" I ask, still feeling in the dark. I start thinking the worst, like Jake did not come to the door because he passed out drunk.

Millie sighs dramatically and says, "Mom, Riley is a girl. And dad told us she was his friend, but they are definitely boyfriend and girlfriend. I didn't want you to know because you always look so lonely, and we don't want you to be sad."

My jaw drops as I ease to a stop at a red light. There is a lot to unpack in the information my seven-year-old is giving me. She has always been wise beyond her years and very well-spoken, but to hear her say she thinks I am lonely is like a shot in the chest. The worst part is that she is not wrong. Then there is the information that they just told me about Jake bringing someone new around our girls. I take deep breaths before I speak in hope that I might inhale something to say.

Beep, Beep

The car behind me sounds its horn and I realize the light is green. I shake it off enough to get the car moving again. I take a couple more big breaths before I speak.

"I'm sorry that mommy has made you guys feel like she's lonely. I am learning through all this and sometimes it's tough being a one-mom-show, but I have you two and I am never lonely hanging out with my little besties," I say, trying to sound upbeat.

"But mom, you need big besties too. More than just Auntie Amber," Millie says and Remi mutters an agreement.

"Well, I went out for coffee yesterday with some new friends, so I am trying" I tell them, now feeling extra proud of myself that I can honestly say that to them, "But you shouldn't worry about me, kiddo. Your job is to be a kid, let mommy handle the worrying and hard stuff."

"Okay, well that's good, I guess," Millie responds reluctantly, "And are you upset we told you about Riley?"

"No, I am not upset, I want you to feel like you can tell me anything," I respond, still trying to figure out how to talk about this when inside I want to scream, "I was just surprised. Did you like this Riley?"

"Yeah, she brought us ice cream with sprinkles in so many colors!" Remi practically shouts from the backseat. She is easily won over with sweets. Again, I work hard to not react and show my jealousy of this random woman hanging out with my kids.

"Meh," Millie sounds a lot less enthusiastic, "She was trying way too hard. And she kept asking me about things like Paw Patrol and asked me if I knew my ABC's, like I am a baby. I haven't watched Paw Patrol since I was like five. But she was not mean or anything, just very energetic. And she kept touching daddy, which was weird, like hugging him a lot. And when she thought I wasn't looking she kissed him! Super gross! That's how I know she is his girlfriend."

Tough cookie. Millie has been reading since Preschool and now in 2nd grade she is reading at minimum a 4th grade level, probably much higher. She is very easily insulted if anyone classifies her as a little kid. I look up in the rear-view mirror to find both girls staring intently up at me. I am not getting out of this conversation. Inside I am grappling between wanting to cry, being angry, and at a complete loss as to how I am supposed to handle this with grace in front of my kids. I am so mad at Jake for both bringing a new woman into their lives so soon and for letting me be blindsided with this news.

"Did you talk to daddy about how you felt?" I ask, still at a loss about how I should address this. This is not my conversation to have and somehow Jake gets to do all the fun stuff, while I tackle the emotions and hard topics.

"No, there was not any time alone with daddy. She was there all day today," I sigh a little bit of relief that Millie did not say that she had spent the night, "But I will talk to him a little about it on Wednesday night, if she is not there."

"Sounds like a good plan. And it is okay to be nice to her and even like her, your daddy will always be dad and I will always be your mom," I am starting to process better and thinking of a few things I should address, "Daddy and mommy are not married anymore, and we might have new people in our lives. If those people are special enough to get to meet you two, then it is just another person to care about you! But if either of you have feelings about each of us dating, or that person we are dating does not make you feel comfortable, our ears are open to listen to you. Do not be afraid to talk to us about it."

I park the car in our driveway and turn around so I can make eye contact with the girls to try to gauge how well this is going over. I can almost see the wheels of their brains turning.

"If daddy's girlfriend is Riley, then what's your boyfriend's name, mommy?" Remi asks. Just when I think I have a handle on this conversation, these kids keep throwing obstacles in front of me.

"I don't have a boyfriend, honey," I tell them honestly.

"You need to go on dates too, mom. Those movies you always watch say that a Christmas party is a good place. Do you know of any good Christmas parties?" Millie suggests earnestly. She means the Hallmark movies that I love. This makes me laugh and relax a tad.

"It's only October, so I have not been invited to any Christmas events yet. And don't worry about mommy's dating life, I will start dating when I feel ready. Right now, I want to keep focusing on the three of us," I respond.

"Gotcha. Well, I guess that is okay, mom. But we are okay if you do start having a boyfriend, just please don't kiss him because that is just yuck-o," Millie talks in a way that I forget how young she is sometimes, but then little things will jostle my memory and her true age shines.

"Yeah, mom! Kissing is gross and you should never do that!" Remi chimes in.

The girls never saw Jake and I kissing. We were never happy together in the years after the girls were born. We co-existed and what martial relationship we did have was behind closed doors. There was never a kiss hello or goodbye, not even a hug. They have never seen me in a loving, affectionate relationship, which makes me a little sad. I want them to have an example of a healthy relationship, but I don't even know where to start with dating and I have doubts that Jake's new relationship will be that example. Part of me feels bad for Riley, I remember the love-bombing with activities with his son. He made me feel special for having met Stevie and being let into their special times together. I wonder if Stevie ever felt like Millie did about me.

"I see. Thank you for talking openly with me, girls," I am desperate to be done with this conversation, "Let's head inside so I can get dinner started."

The topic is not brought up again that evening, nor do they really mention Riley again. Even so, the thought about dating stays on my mind. I keep churning thoughts in my mind about whether I was ready to date and what I want that to look like. Do I want a full-blown relationship? Do I just want to go out on dates? Do I want to have casual hookups?

I dated one person shortly before I met Jake for a few years but before him, I didn't really have serious relationships. I would not say I was slutty in college and into my twenties, but I definitely was not a prude. I had fun, no shame in that. That was a totally different version of me though. I have no clue where forty-something women meet decent guys now.

* * *

After dinner, I help the girls with showers and get them tucked into bed. I am relieved when Remi goes to bed easily, which is not always true. Millie will read in bed for a little bit before she falls asleep, or until I go back to her room to tell her lights out. I go into the kitchen and pour myself a glass of red wine, then sit with my computer at the kitchen table.

I open a web browser and type in a search 'Best Dating Sites for Single Moms.' The results are overwhelming. I select the first link, and it shows blog ratings for a few of the sites. I click a few other search results to compare. There are 2-3 sites that are showing up on every list.

I navigate to one of them that is supposed to let the women be in charge of who they talk to. I am greeted by happy couples of all ages, a good sign. I click the 'Sign Up' button and start filling out the questions. I get through the basic questions and then hit a roadblock.

Headline (up to 100 characters): _____ _____

What the fuck is a headline and what should mine be? I keep staring at the screen before I get up and go into Millie's room to tell her lights out. Back at my computer, I look at it again with no more clarity than before about what to write. I look at the rest of the fill-in-the-blank questions and almost shut the laptop completely.

My Bio: Where I need to write a quirky blurb about myself.

Additional Prompts: Where I get to pick three questions out of a list to torture myself with answering about me and my lifestyle.

My Interests: Just in case I miss something in the previous FOUR boxes, here I am able to check up to five activities/topics/etc. that I enjoy

I pick up my stemless wine glass and take a large sip. I hold the glass up to my forehead for a moment, as if to will the alcohol to give me what courage I need to fill out this damn questionnaire. I will not drink more than that one glass since the girls are home, so I need liquid courage by osmosis for this. I think about calling Amber, but I do not want to say out loud what I am doing.

"Okay, we got this," I say to the empty kitchen and then take another big sip. With the help of Google, I come up with generic answers that do not feel too corny or off-putting.

I make my way through all the sections without issue, until it prompts me for a photo. I feel like I have not been in front of the camera in over 10 years. I open Amber's Facebook page and find the photos from her shower. There is one that has me in it, laughing at whatever Amber's cousin was saying to me. I actually look genuinely happy, so I crop out the other people and add it. I hit the save button, and just like that I am officially on a dating site. I slam my computer shut quickly before I can do anything else on there. I tell myself that this is all silly and push it out of my mind for the rest of the night.

Chapter 8

M onday morning is hectic. Millie is not a morning person. She actually may not be human in the morning at all. She moves like a sloth around the house getting dressed and all the things she needs to be ready for the bus. We reach the door and as I about to yank it open to send her to the driveway, she yells that she forgot the book she wants to read at lunch and runs back inside.

I look like a base coach during the World Series telling her to go out the door, while she is at a completely different speed, moving slowly still. The bus flies by without even attempting to stop for my kidless driveway.

I take a few deep breaths and tell her to go sit on the couch while I get her sister ready. Looks like I am driving them both to school today.

It is easy enough to get them both to school on time, but it is just a lot easier when Millie takes the bus, plus she prefers it since her two best friends are on the bus route too. Now, she has the audacity to give me attitude because she is mad that she is not on the bus.

Remi is all ready to get out the door when I hand her a pair of shoes. She crosses her arms and rolls her eyes at me and the shoes. She proceeds to tell me she wants the blue ones not the pink sparkly ones. I am lost because I buy all her shoes, and I have not bought this kid blue shoes. We go back and forth for two excruciating minutes before she goes and gets the shoes she wants. They are mostly yellow with one stripe of blue, but she insists that since she has two pairs of shoes that are yellow, these are her blue shoes. The logic of a four-year-old.

With drop off complete at both schools, it is now coffee time. I have earned it after this morning of parenting-whiplash. As I am deciding on a pastry, I hear the barista at the other end yell, "I have a Grande Flat White for Henry."

My head pops up and I look over to see my new neighbor, of sorts, pick up his coffee and walk out the door. I can see the same truck and trailer in the parking lot that had been at the house next door on Saturday. I do not have too much time to think about it before the barista in front of me says, "Ma'am, have you decided? There is kind of like a line behind you?"

"Sorry! I'll take the blueberry scone." I pay and wait for my drink. When I look at the parking lot again, the truck is gone. It is strange that I feel disappointed that someone I have never met did not see me. It makes no sense, but something makes me want to be seen by Henry.

* * *

I make it into the house with my latte and empty pastry bag. The scone did not make it through the drive home. I swore it was going to only be one little bite in the car and then I would eat the rest while I started work- I lied. The truck is next door, but no sign of Henry anywhere. I rush inside like if he sees me, he might know how weird I had acted in Starbucks.

My computer is still on the kitchen table. I sit down to start checking my email and see what I have on the calendar today. As I open my computer, my eyes nearly bug out of my head. I have not closed the dating site, and I have 48 notifications. It takes some clicking around before I find what kind of notifications I have received. They are guys that gave me a thumbs up. That is apparently good, but they are all blurred out unless I pay for the Premium account. I start getting frustrated because I have no clue what I am doing and I want to figure it out, however I also need to get some work done.

Minimize the screen, I open my Outlook to check if there is anything pressing for any of my clients. I worked a little bit on Saturday night, so I am hopeful there is not too much on my calendar or in my emails. After confirming that it is a light day, I open the screen again.

The first profile I open is a 50-year-old guy named Rob, and he is holding a fish in every one of his photos. He is not my type, thumbs down.

Next up is 46-year-old Dan who is very attractive and is in an ENM relationship. What are all these acronyms I am supposed to know? With the help of a quick internet search, I find that "ENM" means he is in an ethically non-monogamous relationship and dates outside his marriage with his wife's knowledge and consent. That is great for Dan and Mrs. Dan, however I do not think that would be the best avenue for me as I get back out dating. Thumbs down. A notification pops up, 'You missed a potential match.' Nice to know.

The next profile is 43-year-old Pete. He is a good-looking guy with an adorable dog in his first picture. Reading through his profile, I discover he is also a single parent and seems down to earth, with no fish in any photos. His description makes him seem quirky in a dad joke way. Thumbs up. Another notification, 'You and Pete are a match. You can now start a conversation." In the chat screen, there is a little disclosure at the top reminding me that I have to start the conversation, that the men cannot. There are also a few options of prompts that I can send for both of us to answer. That seems like the best option.

'What is your ideal first date?' It seems casual enough. I smile at the computer; I sent a message and am online dating. Screw Jake and his sports car driving little girlfriend. I can get out there too.

I look around the profile for about 20 more minutes before it feels like I have overloaded my brain. I liked a bunch of profiles, thumbs-downed even more, and even sent 3 more messages. As I am closing out of the website, I notice there was a little "1" on the envelope icon. I figure out that it means I have a message; that one of the men I messaged sent me one back.

I open the inbox to see a reply from Pete with the cute dog. I feel my stomach do a couple flips with anticipation. I click it open.

'My ideal first date would be grabbing drinks at one of the restaurants downtown. Then–" I brace myself for what he might say next, "we could go for a walk through the Fall Harvest Market in the square. Have you ever been to that? They have the little wood sheds for the vendors, and a bunch of fall themed snacks and drinks. Which is better, Pumpkin Spice or Apple Cider?"

I am in shock. I am pretty sure that this guy was plucked out of one of my Hallmark movies and put on this site for me. As the shock wears off, I start to feel a little giddy. I click to look at his profile again to learn more about him. His profile says he is 5'10" — not bad next to my 5'5" — and he works as a financial planner. He is originally from Cleveland, Ohio, but now lives in the town next to mine. This all seems really good.

I click back over to the message and type my reply, "That sounds like a lot of fun! I have not been to the FH Market but have heard it is a lot of fun!"

I stop and look at my message. I am not doing well here. Clearly it sounded like "a lot of fun!" to me since I said it twice in just as many sentences. Delete. Try again.

"That sounds like a lot of fun!" Once is fine, right? "I have heard great things about the FH Market but haven't made my way over there yet. I am definitely a Pumpkin Spice lover but will never turn down a cup of hot apple cider. How about you?"

Send. I put my hands up like if I touch the computer again, I may somehow type something stupid. I start strategizing what I can ask next and fantasizing a little bit about how this might work out. I find myself getting a little excited to start dating again.

Pete seems to be actively at his computer or maybe using the mobile app – I need to download that still. About 15 minutes later, he replies that he is strictly an apple cider guy but will not hold it against me that I may order a PSL. He says things in a way that makes me smile and sometimes chuckle out loud. We talk back and forth all day long. I want to be cautious and will be incredibly nervous about actually going on a date, but it is nice to talk to someone and flirt.

* * *

For the next week, Pete and I talk every day. I get excited to see the notifications pop up on the app. I even downloaded it on my phone so that I do not miss a message.

There are a couple other guys that I message with on the app too, but none of them make me feel like Pete does and most of those conversations fizzle out. There are also a couple of weirdos. One guy asked in his first message, completely ignoring the question I had asked him, "Hey girl, what's your address? No need to talk, I am just going to rock your world." That made me gag a little.

Pete is different. He does not make me feel like he is only looking for sex and I am comfortable talking to him. We chat about our jobs, kids, and likes/dislikes. We do not get too into our ex-spouses which is fine with me. I don't really want to explain my marriage to someone

I have not met yet, even though I feel like I could.

After a week of chatting, Pete starts today with a different kind of message, "Hey! I have really loved getting to know you and would love to meet you for real. Can I take you out one night this week?"

My heart starts racing. I know that this moment was inevitable but still for some reason I am freaking out inside. I check my calendar to see when I am free and what the girls' schedules look like. They are at their dads for dinner on Wednesday, but I would have to pick them up. However, it is Jake's weekend with the kids.

I respond by telling him that I would like to meet and giving him the times when I am free. We go back and forth figuring out a real, in-person date. The butterflies in my stomach are going insane. We decided on a date downtown on Friday night. I am going on my first date in over a decade. My mind goes from giddy to panic almost immediately. I start to freak out about what to wear. I feel self-conscious about my mom-body. I worry that I will not be able to proofread my side of the conversation before sending. I try to calm my nerves but there is no use. I am going to be a basket case until I meet Pete on Friday.

Chapter 9

֍

We decided to meet at a little wine bar near the Fall Harvest Market. I wear dark jeans with a cowl neck sweater in a hunter green color that brings out the green in my eyes and brown booties. I curl my hair and put effort into my makeup. I feel pretty, and it is certainly the confidence boost I need going into tonight.

Pete and I are still talking through the app's chat feature and I do not have his real phone number. I am a little nervous about giving my number to someone that I do not know but this also makes me nervous- how am I going to find him in the busy bar. I was 10 minutes early in true Carly fashion. I close my eyes and take some deep breaths to calm my nerves. I feel very similar to how I did before the Café Club meeting a couple of weeks ago. I plan to go again the next morning, so I start thinking about them and find myself looking forward to it.

With five minutes until our designated meeting time, I check the app. There is a new message from Pete, 'I'm on my way, ETA 6:04.'

I can appreciate the head ups and let being a little late go. I truly hate being late and it annoys me to no end when others do not abide by my rule-of-thumb to always be a smidge early. This is a new chapter, a new Carly. I can roll with the punches and be cool as a cucumber, both sayings I am sure no one uses anymore.

I head into the bar to grab two stools at the bar. It is a busy night, but I luck out and a couple is leaving as I walk up. I sit on one stool and drape my jacket on the other one. My phone lights up with another message, 'Just parking. Be in shortly.' I reply to him where I am sitting at the bar, so that he can find me.

My stomach does a complete twist and flip as my heart rate starts increasing. I am most nervous about whether I can spot him in the crowd. I only have two little pictures to reference. I look towards the front doors, and I see a man walking directly towards me. I freeze in place waiting for this man to turn or stop at one of the other groups at the bar. Stuck there looking like a deer in the headlights, I hear a nasally voice say, "Carly? Hi, I'm Pete."

I stand up and find myself at eye level with the Temu version of Pete.

* * *

"He was the same height as you?! Was he at least sexy short, you know how some men can own it," Lana asks. I am back at Kat's Café with the Early Birds dishing about my first online dating experience. They are quickly invested in the story.

"Did you miss the Temu version part?" Miles says from down the table, "Have you ever gotten something off one of those shopping apps that looks like its picture?"

Half the table grimaces and nods in agreement that they did not find quality on Temu nor did I find quality in Pete.

"Unfortunately, Miles is correct. Pete used a picture of his younger brother for the app, but that came out a little later in the date…" I trail off for dramatic suspense. If I had to relive this story, I at least am going to have some fun retelling it.

"Later in the date? How long did you stay after this?" Marti asks.

"So, fun fact about Carly," I shrug as I say this, "I hate confrontation. I will avoid it at all costs, especially since my marriage. I cannot tell someone where to shove it when I am mad, and I apparently will not call someone out for catfishing me."

"We will work on that but for now, go on! What happened next?" Lana nudges me.

"Okay, so, there I was looking at the supposedly 5'10" man who really was a hair above my own 5'5" with a face that looked somewhat like the pictures, but slightly off. I will grant him that he and his brother do look very similar. The saddest part is that he is sort of cute, but in a nerdy way instead of the sexy way his brother is," I pause to remember the rest, "Anyway, he comes in and hugs me. I am so stunned that I just mumble a nice to meet you or something as I am sitting back down. I gathered myself at this point. I try to remember our great conversations and decided to not be so judgmental about the outside appearance."

"Backfired, huh?" Talah asks.

"Big time," I laugh under my breath, because I had to laugh at myself in this situation, "We ordered some wine, and it was going okay for a bit. Then we started talking about our jobs. He had mentioned that he was at a bit of a crossroads in his career."

"Ooo! I know that one! Unemployed, right?" Dylan contributes, looking proud of himself for keeping up with the spilling of the bad date tea.

"Not only was he recently fired from his job at a bank's call center, which, apparently, he had translated to financial planner in his profile, but his plan to get out of the hole is using his mom's money to invest in bitcoin and take a cut of the profit. This is the point I realized it was not the match I anticipated, and it was very unlikely it was going to turn around. But again, I don't like to be confrontational, so I did what any slightly unbalanced people-pleaser might do, I stayed all the way to the end of the night."

"Shit. And how late was that?"

"I managed to fake being tired at about 8:30, but really with the conversation we had it was not a far stretch. It is exhausting to listen to someone talk so much about themselves and never ask about me. He didn't even seem to care about what he was telling me. This is where he slipped and mentioned that it was his brother's photo. But he just kept on talking, unbothered by it."

"Did you stay at the bar the whole time?" Paula asks.

"No, after I paid our tab." A collective cringe went around the table. "Yeah... We went over to the Fall Harvest Market. You would think that this would help and give us something to do, but nope it made it worse for me. He walks like he is constantly stepping over a puddle."

"Like what?" Marti scrunches her face in confusion.

"I know that walk that she means, I haaate when guys do that," Miles says with dramatic length on the word hate, but Marti and a couple others still look perplexed. Miles rolls his eyes and gets out of his chair, "Like this."

Miles walks up and down the space in between tables, taking strides that stretch his entire leg span while stomping down hard on each step. He does not care in the least that other tables are looking at him. I burst out laughing, "Yes! That is exactly it!"

I am getting more and more comfortable. Everyone at the table's attention is on me ready for the story. I am feeling hyped up to finish my recollection of the date. It is not an insanely crazy story by any means, it is rather tame actually. However, it is nice to share and get it off my chest, it helps me feel humored by it and not so embarrassed, like I did the night before. I had been hard on myself on the drive home and felt a deep gut lonely the rest of the evening, but here, with them, I feel supported in a way that I have been missing. I love Amber and she is irreplaceable, however, she always tries to fix things. I didn't even tell her about my date because she would take that as a cue that I am ready to date, therefore she should find suitable men to set me up with on blind dates. I am not ready for that pressure. The environment with the Café Club is different; no pressure and easy to share.

"Then after chasing him around the market with my little steps for about an hour, I told him I had to be up early – not a lie - and needed to get home. That's when he insisted on walking me to my car," Now I am the one who cringes, remembering what happens next. Everyone is leaning towards me a little after seeing my face react, "When we got to my car I thanked him for a nice evening – lies but oh well – I started to turn to my car as he thought it was an appropriate time to try for a kiss, but he missed my mouth."

"I thought that only happened in movies," Gwen states. She was not there the first time I came here but she seems just as nice as the others.

"Me too, but he got my cheek. He had closed his eyes and actually did not realize that it wasn't my mouth somehow. He was standing there licking his tongue all over my cheek like a puppy, with equal amounts of drool, with no signs of stopping." The whole table makes grossed out sounds, "So, again I did what any sane grown adult would do. I said 'Okay, bye,' removed my cheek from his tongue, got in my car, and drove away quickly."

They all laugh loudly, then Lana snorts, and we all laugh even harder. We laugh until some of us are crying, and other tables start shushing us. We look at each other sheepishly and try to calm ourselves down.

"And that, folks, was my first post-divorce date. A complete shit-show and I doubt I will be doing that again anytime soon," I say still laughing, a little softer now.

"Naw! You can't give up now after just one bad experience," Jayna says, "we have all had bad date stories when getting back out there, you are just lucky and got it out of the way early. Though it probably won't be your only story. Sorry to break it to you, but I refuse to give up hope that we will all find our person."

"It was just so disappointing after such great conversations, and I had high hopes. Seriously, I even started to let myself think about being able to get rid of the cobwebs down there!" I am a little surprised I so openly just said that. It is something that pre-Jake Carly would have said to friends. Maybe she is still here.

"I get it, I really do," Marti says. We all chat a couple more minutes about my date and then the conversation shifts to Lana mentioning she had a mediocre date last night. I am grateful the topic of the table shifted away from me. While it was nice to have been able to talk it out, it was also kind of mentally draining.

I turn my attention to what Lana is saying, "I feel like I have these exciting, whether in a good way or a bad way is questionable, dates with men. Then, I go out with women, and it falls flat, like I have no clue what to do, or we go straight to a hookup. Before I was married to my ex-husband, I had a couple girlfriends throughout college, but it was so much easier to meet people then. Now, between online dating or friends setting me up with any random lesbian they know, based solely on the fact that we both are attracted to women not any other shared interests, I can't seem to find a real connection on the female side of dating. Last night was no different. I met her online and the conversation was okay beforehand. Then we met in person, and it was like having a drink with a friend, no romantic sparks."

"It's hard to push that barrier down," Miles says to her, "Did I ever tell you that Cal is the first man I was in a serious relationship with, and I almost blew it completely?"

"No, I didn't know that, though it is hard to imagine there being a time you two were not together," Lana replies.

"Right? He is my soulmate," Miles smiles, "And before him I was still hiding in the closet. He is an angel for how patient he was with me. Anyway, my point of telling you this is because I was comfortable around girls, I had dated women since high school and even truly loved one past girlfriend. So, I knew how to flirt and act around them, but when I really began to let myself question my sexuality, I was lost around men. I did not know how to show I was interested or flirt. I questioned if I was gay or not, because I couldn't seem to figure out how to date guys to confirm it. I mean in hindsight I knew, but at that moment, I guess I had to prove it to myself.

Then one day in a Starbucks in Boston, I bumped into Cal. I mean like legit smacked into him, dumped both of our drinks all over him and the floor. Luckily, we were both in the mood for an iced drink that day but as I was apologizing profusely, I felt an attraction. I asked if I could buy him another drink and he was so gracious about the whole thing. He accepted my offer, as he was doing his best to clean off his shirt and pants. It was the end of the workday, so it was not a complete travesty. We ended up sitting at a table and talking for a while, yes despite the mess I made of his clothes. We realized that we had a lot in common and he told me about a free concert in a nearby park later that evening. He asked if maybe I wanted to go with him. I was in my head convinced that there was no way this man was asking me on a date. He seemed so, I don't know, like not gay, that I figured he just wanted to be friends and needed someone to hang out with. I agreed and we made plans to meet at the entrance of the park in a couple hours, as he obviously needed to go change."

I can feel my heart swelling as he tells his meet-cute story. I have not yet met Cal and really this is the first time Miles has talked about their relationship, all the conversation was on their twins. I know that they were carried by a surrogate and that there is some sort of biological connection, but not too much more. This was only the second time I have met him. I really am enjoying getting to know everyone in this group.

Miles continues his story, "I knew I was attracted to Cal, but had no clue what to do with those feelings so I packed them away and went in like a total bro. We hung out and enjoyed the concert from a couple of foldable chairs on a hill, not sitting too close. We went to order drinks and I ordered a beer, which I hate beer, but was trying to be a dude," he pauses to laugh and shakes his head at the memory.

"Cal ordered a nice red wine that I would have much preferred and then he insisted on buying the drinks. We went through the entire night of me being awkward and acting how I thought I should, so it made it weird, and he probably felt like you did, or your date did, last night," Miles says to Lana, "He asked if he could walk me home, since I lived nearby. That made me slightly question things, because guys don't do that for buds, so I freaked out when we got to my building. As we were standing outside, I punched him in the arm, yup punched him, just how I would with my guy friends back home. He looked confused and then said to me, 'Oh, sorry, I think I read the room wrong, I thought you were... never mind. Thanks for a fun night out though.' At that point he turned around and walked away. I yelled after him asking what he had thought. He turned around and said, 'I thought this was a date.' I froze in shock and did not stop him from leaving. I had been in my head so much about it and about him that I missed so many signs. More importantly, I almost missed out on him. Stop worrying about how you should act, what will make a woman know you are into her, what you have to say to sound more queer, etcetera. It will kill the mood and you will friendzone yourself."

"That sounds like sound advice for any date," Marti nods her head as she contemplates what Miles had just said.

"But what happened next that you did end up together?" I ask Miles.

"I let him walk away and felt pure regret in my gut for weeks after, months even. We had not exchanged numbers either, so I had no way to get a hold of him. I started to question why I was trying to force myself to not be who I wanted to be. I told one good friend that I thought I might be gay. She responded to me with, 'I know but didn't want to ask you until you got there on your time.' It was such a great feeling of support that I started thinking about what could have been had I just been honest with myself — and Cal," Miles shrugs with a half-smile. "I had started to go on a few dates with men over the next few months and it was just like Lana described. I was discouraged, thinking I was awful at being gay, but I kept pushing myself to explore this a little more. I had a couple guys stick around for several dates. I had a few hookups, which was an exploration of its own. One guy I dated early on was very honest in that he was not looking for anything serious and I really did not see him as a long-term relationship material, but he was kind and patient with me, which I will always appreciate.

But I digress, okay so about four months after our concert date, I was rushing through that same coffee shop we met at, and from behind me I hear 'Watch out folks, he is known to be dangerously clumsy with a drink in hand.' I stopped in my tracks, pretty convinced I was hearing things. I had not stopped thinking about him and our date. I slowly turned around and sitting at a table by himself was Cal with a grin on his face. I went over and sat down with him completely uninvited and blurted out that I never thought I would see him again but since he showed up in my life again miraculously, I was not letting the chance to say what I needed to say escape. I told him that I was first off, sorry that I acted weird on the date and froze at the end. I told him that I have done a lot of soul searching thanks to the night. And I told him that my biggest regret from that night was not kissing him on that street before I let him walk away. Then he reached across the little café table and put a hand behind my head to pull me towards him. That's where we had our first kiss and he's been it for me since."

Everybody at the table is silent. I am pretty sure we are all swooning over their story, even Dylan looks star-crossed. I think Gwen and Jayna are crying a little.

"Damn. Well, if it isn't like that, then I don't want it," Paula interjects through the silence, and we all agree.

I have seen love stories work out, like Amber and Paul, but Miles and Cal's story brings hope to my heart. It makes me want to keep trying on the chance I might meet my person to really, truly love me. At least it has to get better than having my face licked.

Chapter 10

❦

As I drive home from the café, I reflect on Miles telling us his story and Lana talking about her struggles with dating. I have only known this group of people for two weeks, but somehow there is an easy level of comfort with them. I feel part of the table and it has been a long time since I felt included. I am a lost cause when it comes to socializing. At the girls' schools, whenever I am around the other parents, I am so awkward. I feel like I cannot carry an adult conversation anymore.

The Café Club makes me feel seen and I do not feel like I am working so hard to make them like me. Talking to them comes naturally. If I had been left to overthink my awful date with Pete, I probably would have given up on dating all together. After sharing my story with them, I feel like I can either find a good guy, or at least have a good story for the next Café Club.

Turning onto my street, I notice the truck and trailer from next door out front again. Not surprising since I have seen it there a handful of times, especially on the weekends. As I get closer to the house, something feels different than the previous times. I crane my neck a little to get a better view and let out a gasp. It is parked differently than the other times. Normally he parks on the side of the driveway farthest away from my house, this time it is on the side by my house. His entire trailer is blocking my driveway.

"Well, that is just rude," I say to myself. The ramp was down on the trailer, so he must have noticed it when he took stuff off it. Normally, I would be mad but not say anything, however I feel brave today. It is my driveway, and this vehicle is illegally blocking it.

I park my car on the street in front of my house and march down to the other side of the truck to the front of the farmhouse. I can see a pile of stone next to the driveway where the truck normally parks, which explains why the truck is not there. I can hear some type of equipment in use around the side of the house and follow the noise on my search for Henry.

I find him on a small foot stool using some sort of electric trimmer to clean up the bushes on the side of the house that does not face mine. He does not see me come around the corner.

"Excuse me?" I say loudly. No reaction. I try again louder, this time waving my hands wildly, "EXCUSE ME!"

This time he notices. I must startle him because the next thing I know he is wobbling on the stool trying to catch his balance as the trimmer is still running. As he is trying to regain his center, the blades are cutting in the direction his arms are flailing, resulting in some avant-garde style bushes. He manages to stabilize himself, but not before destroying the bush he is working on and the one next to it. I gape wide-eyed at the damage.

He turns off the equipment and comes down off the stool. As he turns towards me, I try to defuse the situation with humor, "I'm not sure if that is the correct cut for the luck tree, but my bonsai skills are outdated."

He is clearly not amused, "Who are you and why are you startling a man with a sharp blade?"

I remind myself why I am there and that he is the one in the wrong, not me. "I live next door and your trailer is so rudely blocking my driveway."

"And?" He says disengaged.

"And I would like you to move it so that I can pull into my own driveway," I say with a growing sense of confidence as he pushes back.

"I am kind of in the middle of something," he gestures towards the chopped-up bushes.

"I know, it's my driveway that you are in the middle of. Please move your truck forward," I say firmly.

"I can't. The stone I ordered was dropped off this morning before I got here, and they dumped it where I normally park," he states like that made it okay.

"So, you decided to block where I normally park to have company in your misery?" I am getting fired up now.

"What? I didn't do it on purpose or think it was a big deal," his voice starts to lose its sharpness, but I am not ready to calm down yet.

"Oh, so you just go around accidentally preventing women from being able to use their own driveways without giving a shit? I think I saw an old woman with a walker down the street, would you like to kick that out from her too while you're at it?" I can feel how red my face was. I always blush when I get upset. I am internally cursing because I know that I am moments away from tearing up. I should find a way to cool off or I should turn around and just go home, but I do not want to concede. I feel a fight in me that has not been there in a long time. I never stood up for myself to Jake or to anyone else who has made me feel small since Jake came into my life. I have become complacent and I lost my voice. It is like I found a cough drop and finally I am able to speak up for myself. There is a sting in the corners of my eyes starting.

"Excuse me? Could you please turn the psycho down a little?" My face must be saying exactly what I am thinking because he takes a step back and holds his hands up defensively.

"Psycho?! Because I am upset that you are so inconsiderate? I think you need some lessons in being neighborly, sir," I step forward with this and poke him directly on the chest to drive the point home. I have no clue why I just did that but regret it instantly. Firstly, because I am not one to invade someone's personal space and secondly, because this man is pure muscle. I start to wonder what he looked like under the fitted t-shirt he is wearing.

He breaks my train of thought when he says, "Ma'am, I do not plan on being a neighbor. I am cleaning this place up enough to sell and then I will be out of here."

Did he call me ma'am? Now I am flustered, mad and feel old. Great.

"Okay, okay, I'm sorry. Can we just take a step back and start over?" He asks in a tone that is completely different than what he has been using. I envy his ability to control his emotions so quickly, "I will move my trailer out from in front of your driveway."

I am thrown off; I expected the fight to continue for a lot longer. Almost instantly my anger dissipates with the confusion, "Uh— okay thanks."

That is all I can manage as I watch him walk away towards the truck. I follow him up to the driveway. He gets into the cab and drives forward. For a moment it seems like he is going to drive away, then suddenly the truck and trailer start reversing into the driveway. They are moving in the direction of where I am standing, but I am still flabbergasted by this whole situation and still coming down from the adrenaline rush of this sparring match, that I do not move.

I see a head pop out of the driver side window and hear, "Can you please move? You are blocking my driveway."

He gives me a little smirk to show that he thinks he is being cute. It is not cute, but damn if he isn't cute. No, not cute, he is sexy. Before I can let myself get lost in those silly, pointless thoughts again, I walk over to the side so he can keep backing up. He parks the truck and jumps out, walking over to me.

"I think we got off on the wrong foot. I'm Henry," He holds a hand outstretched to me. I am still trying to figure out if I want to be nice or keep my attitude sharp and cold.

I decide to go with calm-but-guarded, and just respond stoically, "I'm Carly."

I put my hand in his to return the shake. His hand feels rough up against mine, like fine sandpaper.

"Well, Carly, I have to get back to work, the bushes are looking a bit misshapen," He raises an eyebrow at me, it feels almost flirty. I am sure I am reading that wrong though.

"Yeah, sorry I startled you, hopefully you can fix them. I don't know anything about landscaping, or I would offer to help fix them. I am clueless about gardening and anything in the yard, I manage to do a little inside but overall, I am not that very handy," I realize I am rambling, "Okay I should get going home. Thanks for moving the truck. Um… bye."

I turn to walk back over to my place. I sounded like such an idiot. How did I go from an angry force to barely being able to form sentences so quickly?

"Bye, Carly." I hear him say behind me as I walk away.

* * *

I try to distract myself for the afternoon. I do not want to think about Henry and the way that fighting with him actually turned me on. I felt a fire that has been extinguished and is now ignited once more. I have never wanted to punch someone so much while also wanting to touch every last inch of him. I am desperate, I decide. I need to get back out in the dating scene, even though the Pete situation makes dating seem questionable. Maybe looking for something serious was not where I should start, maybe I can try a little more casual to ease back out there. I don't even know if I remember how to turn a guy on anymore, much less how to have good sex.

Pete is obviously out of the running. There is no coming back from that date, but there are a couple other guys on the dating app that I did not get a long-term vibe from but that seem nice.

I open the messages in the app and scroll to the one guy other than Pete I have been going back and forth talking to. He is really cute but gives off total playboy feels. After last night and chatting with the Café Club this morning, it is starting to be okay to possibly not jump right into forever and maybe just have fun with someone. Go out for drinks, if it goes well maybe even hookup. I cannot believe that I am considering being casual about sex. It feels forbidden, like I am too old for that.

After Café Club, I chatted with Lana on the way out to the cars again. She mentioned that she would not be there in two weeks because her cousin's wedding was the night before and she had gotten a hotel room at the venue to get utterly intoxicated. She told me to take her number and just text her if I wanted to chat or hang out, before we see each other again with the whole group. Lana is around the same age as me, even though her kids are a little older than mine.

I need a sounding board to talk out my feelings. The idea of casual dating seems salacious and like something a mom is not allowed to do. I toggle my phone from the dating app over to the text messages. The first one on the list is Lana from exchanging numbers earlier.

Me: Hey, Lana. This is going to be super random, but can I ask you a question about this dating stuff?

Almost immediately I saw three dots pop up to indicate that she was typing.

Lana: Hi! For sure! What's on your mind?

I instantly start sweating and want to chicken out. What am I thinking? I am going to ask a near stranger about this? It is strange how comfortable I felt around her though, but this is too much.

Me: Actually, never mind. It's stupid and I am overthinking it.

Lana: Nope, don't talk yourself out of it. Ask away.

I just blurt out my question into the text box and hit send before I can delete.

Me: Am I too old to be dating not for a relationship? Like can I get away with doing casual things?

Lana: There is not any too old for sex and you do not need to be in a relationship to have it!

Me: Really?

Lana: Girl, I recommend it! Lol

Me: Haha – why?

Lana: Do you buy the first car you test drive or do you try out others first to make sure you know what features you want?

Me: [laughing emoji] It's not my first "car"!

Lana: Have you had sex with anyone since your ex? Our bodies are much different after kids and in our 40's... it's not a bad thing either. Just things you liked before may not be the same and men are a little more mature now... well at least more often than not.

Me: My standards at sitting low now, I just want a kiss on the lips not cheek!

Lana: That still makes me want to throw up for you. But that dude is definitely one of a kind... just not in a good way.

Me: Well, there's this cute guy I have been taking to on the dating app

Lana: Do it.

Lana: And by that, I mean do him!

Me: Okay I will try to plan a date, but I make no promises that I'm sleeping with him.

Lana: Exactly what you should be doing. Going out. Flirting. Doing what you want, not focusing on the "correct" number of dates before you get some!

Me: Ok... I'm going to meet up with him!

Lana: Get it, girl! You better text me and let me know how it goes!

I smile at my phone as I switch back to the dating app. I open the chat with the guy, Tim. We had started talking about a week ago. I had not put much into the conversation because he made it clear he does not want a relationship right now and I put a lot of hope into Pete. Maybe Tim the 47-year-old contractor is onto something.

A couple days earlier Tim had asked if I was interested in grabbing drinks. I did not say no, but I had not committed to plans. What the hell, why not? I send Tim a message asking if he still wants to meet up. Fully aware that he is probably not sitting on his phone waiting for a message on the dating app, I busy myself with laundry and other mundane tasks around the house. Every time I pass through the kitchen, where my phone sits on the charger, I keep checking.

About an hour later, there is a message from Tim. He says he would love to meet up and that he knows that it is short notice, but he is free tonight. My stomach feels like I am about to go bungee jumping and looking over the edge. I have one million reasons on the tip of my tongue ready to spew out an excuse to say I cannot go. For some odd reason though, I am motivated by being able to tell Lana that I pushed through the nerves and said yes. Then the idea of going on a date with no strings attached, it can be just one or two dates and that is fine, or maybe he does end up being my person. I am not feeling pressure either way and it feels so much freer than going into my date with Pete. I quickly say yes before the nagging Debbie Downer in my brain has a chance to wake up and make me feel like I am not good enough for someone as attractive as Tim, who hopefully actually matches his photo.

We plan to meet at a little distillery. He tells me that it is one of his new favorite spots with a great atmosphere and it is within walking distance to his condo. I am not sure if he is going in with intentions of making that walk back to his place together or if he just selfishly does not want to have to drive, but a shiver goes down my spine thinking about the possibilities. I have about three hours to get ready and meet him out there. I have been eating healthier and trying to do yoga after the girls go to school, so I feel pretty good about myself. At least better than I have felt in quite some time, there is still improvement that I want to see but the work I have done over the past few weeks helped my confidence a little. That is another round of Dr. Rose homework. During our second session she was practically bouncing off the walls when I told her the success her first homework assignment had been.

I can't wait for next week's session to tell her all about Carly's adventures in dating.

Chapter 11

⁓ஐ⁓

This winning outfit is a body-hugging little black dress with a pair of black high heel boots that stop just below my knee. I feel like a hooker, if I am being honest, but like the high-end escort kind of hooker. I don't think I hate it. This is much less like a 40-year-old mom of two that works from home in yoga pants every day and much more like Carly Neiman than Carly Kennedy. Nieman is my maiden name, I decided to keep my married name after the divorce. Tonight is a reminder that I am not a married woman. I am a sexy, single woman. Last time I was single, I was still a young adult, a girl. Lana's voice pops into my head about things being different, but not necessarily in a bad way, at this age.

On my way to the car, I see Henry at the end of the driveway packing up the trailer. He catches sight of me and freezes. My outfit must be working if even that grump is doing a double take. Or he is just surprised to see me out of my jeans and flannel with Crocs sandals from earlier. He recovers and returns to his surly self.

"You have a real good night, Carly," he says in a very drawn-out way as he looks at me from head to toe, pausing on the tight black boots for an extra second, and then back up again. All while fighting a smile, or something is tugging on his face. He starts putting the rake he has half on the trailer in again and the moment is over.

"Uhhh.. thanks," I say awkwardly with a weird wave. I get into my car before I can embarrass myself anymore.

* * *

Tim sends me a message that he is there as I am parking my car. I find a spot on the street quickly, which is a stroke of luck in that area. It might be, no it must be, a good sign that tonight will not be as bad as the previous night.

Walking through the front door, I immediately spot him at the bar with a sport coat draped over the one next to him. For some reason, the fact that he saved me a chair makes my heart skip a beat. It is nice to be considered.

Oh, thank God... he looks exactly like his pictures online, if not even more handsome. There is no question about it, this guy is freaking hot. Suddenly I am very happy that I gave online dating another shot. He spots me walking towards him and he stands up to greet me. As I reach him, I have to look up to meet his eyes. My goodness, handsome AND tall. He is a tall tree that I would not mind climbing.

"Hi, Carly? I am so happy to meet you," Tim has a deep, gravelly voice that makes me want him to read the closed captions on the sexy scenes of a movie. His eyes scan over me, and he grins like he is also glad we connected on that app.

"Hi, Tim! Thanks for meeting up with me." Confirming that I have no clue how to talk to a guy anymore, especially a man this handsome.

"Of course," he says as he grabs the sports coat and pulls the barstool out for me to sit down.

Soon after we get settled on our stools, a gorgeous blonde bartender walks over to me and says, "What can I get for you?"

As I give her my drink order, Tim's eyes never leave me as he tells the bartender, "I have a tab open, please put it on there."

There is nothing Temu about Tim.

Our conversation flows freely all night, he asks me a little about my kids, but not much. That is fine with me. I normally love to gush about them, but tonight I am not in mom-mode for once. We talk about our jobs; he owns his own business as a commercial contractor. It is the most mature evening I have had in a very long time. I feel important.

A few hours go by before I even glance at my watch. We have been talking, flirting, and drinking and it feels like we just got there. I still have my wits to me, but definitely have had one too many to drive. Our bar stools have inched closer throughout the evening, and his hand is resting on my bare knee. His touch sends shivers through my spine. I can imagine those hands doing a lot. I am getting the impression that our minds are on the same wavelength.

"Do you want another drink?" Tim asks me, pointing at my almost empty glass.

"I shouldn't. I am already considering ordering a rideshare to get home," I admit.

"If you want to let it wear off and just hang out with a movie, my place is around the block," he says. His voice is even and inviting, there are no expectations in it. He makes me feel safe around him.

"That actually sounds great. I would rather be able to drive my own car home plus I'm just not ready to call it a night," I say with a bit of liquid courage.

"Good, I feel the same," he gives me that one-sided grin again and my panties nearly jump off my body. He is several years older than me and the salt and pepper hair makes him look so dignified. He is aging in a George Clooney way; it is so not fair how guys can do that. The only wrinkles he has are around his eyes when he genuinely laughs.

They do not make him look older, rather just warm.

He closes out the tab and will not let me even leave the tip. I offer, but when he insists on paying, there is major mental clapping. He offers me his hand as I get off the stool as we are leaving and then puts his hand on my lower back as we walk towards the door. When we approach the door, he steps ahead and holds it open for me. Tim is a textbook gentleman.

He grabs my hand leading the way out of the crowd, but never drops it outside the bar. I start to get in my head a little bit about what may happen next. I have heard about what the younger generation calls Netflix and Chill, but I am not sure if my assumptions about what that entails are accurate. Maybe he really does just want to hang out since we had quite a bit to drink, and he wants to make sure I am okay. What if I make a move and that is not what he wants? Am I okay with this being a fling after our great date? He is very clear that he is not looking for a relationship and he is even clearer that he does not want children. I come already equipped with two of those.

I am startled out of my thoughts by Tim saying, "Here we are."

We walk into the foyer of a building of luxury condos. In the elevator, I can see there are 15 floors. He presses one of the middle buttons. Oh, thank goodness, I would not be able to contain myself on this dream date if he lives in the penthouse or something. This is all starting to get very real, but I have no desire to run out the door. I like this guy and whether we are going to watch the comedy movies we talked about and just hang out or something more, I am excited.

"Welcome to my crib," he says with his arms wide open in the style of the old show MTV Cribs. I laugh and appreciate him lightening the mood. "Can I get you a glass of water or something?"

"That would be great, hydration is probably the smart move," I laugh lightly, "Could I use your bathroom before we settle in?"

He points me down the hallway where I find an extremely clean and well-decorated bathroom. His hand towels, shower curtain, and wall décor all coordinate, but not in a way that screams that they were bought in a set from Kohl's. No, this is quality stuff. I pull out my phone and text Lana quickly.

> *Me: The date went great. Thanks for the push! I just got to his apartment to hang out and even though he seems super sweet, for my own safety here is a pin of my location, he's apartment 1106. If I am missing tomorrow, start there. LOL*

Then I do what I actually came in here to do. Before I even finish washing my hands, I have a response from her.

> *Lana: Yaaaaas!! Don't worry, I listen to true crime podcasts every day, so I am fully qualified to hunt him down if you go missing, probably faster than the cops can even get into their squad car. Now go get some and text me tomorrow to let me know how it went... well and confirm proof of life. [laugh-cry emoji]*

I send her a couple thumbs up emojis back and open the door to head back out to where Tim is waiting. The kitchen, with the beautiful man standing in it, is so stark white and clean. I cannot imagine that it has ever been used. The stove even has a faucet over it, that screams fancy in my book.

"Are you sure you are not married or something? Your house is so meticulously decorated and well thought out."

Tim laughs and shrugs, "You half caught me."

My eyes are wide as saucers but he quickly follows up with, "No! I am not married, but you are right about it being well thought out. I built this building for a client and from the beginning I knew I wanted to live in one of the units. So, the developer let me design this unit however I wanted. Plus, I work with a lot of people in the housing industry. While I would love to take credit for the décor, it is my interior designer's doing."

"Have I told you yet how amazing that dress is?" Tim's voice shifts to a more seductive tone. He makes his way over to me, looking at the curves of my body in the black fabric.

"I am pretty sure you did earlier, but please do not let that stop you from telling me again," I match his sultry demeanor. If I let myself think about anything besides this gorgeous specimen of a man in front of me, my nerves will consume me. But I am not thinking about anything other than how my body seems to heat up as he reaches me. He slips an arm around my waist loosely.

"You are gorgeous," Tim is so close now, "Can I kiss you?"

"Please do," I respond with a twinge of breathy desperation. His arm tightens around me and pulls me against him as his lips find mine. The kiss starts soft before intensifying as our mouths explore each other. He runs both hands along my sides, just ever so slightly grazing the side of my breasts. I cannot help but let out a little whimper of desire into his mouth. His hands continue down over my hips and to the hem of my dress. His fingers play under the hem for a beat.

I cannot remember the last time I have wanted a man this badly. He is not an amateur, which reminds me of what Lana said about older men in the bedroom. My body aches to find out if Tim falls into that classification.

He backs me up to the kitchen island until my spine feels the cold countertop. He breaks the kiss to grab my ass and lift me to sit on top of it. He is tall enough that we are now the same height. I push my fingers through his hair, which is so thick that I am able to grip it to pull his face back towards mine. My heart is beating out of my chest but I do not want to stop, not one little bit. At this point, I actually have a carnal need for him to continue.

He moves his mouth to my ear, nipping lightly at my earlobe as I feel his warm breath on the inside of my ear. Tim kisses down my jawline and my neck until he reaches the top of my dress, which offers a decent bit of cleavage. His mouth explores the top roundness of each breast, making my nipples hard against the dress that now seems like a straight jacket that I need to escape. I want to feel those lips go all the way down my body. He stands up and his dark gray eyes are practically black as he grins at me to say he is enjoying his exploration of my body. Who am I to stop him from his adventure, if it brings him pleasure? He is not the only one feeling it. He pulls my face back into his for another hungry kiss that is over almost as soon as it started. Ugh! I want more of him.

I still have my tight black boots on. Tim dips low, pulling one of my legs up on his shoulder. This offers him a view at the black lace thong I have on. With my leg still on his shoulder, his fingers find the zipper on the inside of my leg, and he brings it all the way down so he can remove the boot. As he drops it on the floor, he kisses my ankle and works his mouth up my leg. When he reaches the hem, again, he teases me by pushing it up just a bit as he kisses up to parts of my leg that are more and more sensitive. When he is so close to where I want to feel him, he backs away, putting my leg back down gently. My sigh of exasperation is louder than I meant it to be because he lets out a breathy laugh as he picks up my other leg onto his other shoulder. He repeats the process of taking off my boot and making his way up toward the hem again. This time he goes even higher so that I can feel him exhale through the lace. It takes everything in my power not to just push my center towards his face.

He backs away again to stand up and meet my lustful eyes with his own. He puts his hands behind me again, pulling me towards him. When I reach the edge of the counter, I am impatient. I wrap both my legs around him and pull him closer for another hungry kiss. His hands snake under me and he pulls me off the counter with my legs still wrapped around him. Tim carries me like I am light as a feather to the living room area. When we are next to the couch, I drop my legs straight and slide down him until my feet touch the floor. As I do, I can feel him bulging in his dark jeans. Feeling how much I am turning him is enough to drive me absolutely crazy. His fingers reach up the middle of my back until he finds the zipper of my dress, as he releases the pressure from the fabric it falls away from my body. Once he reaches the bottom of the zipper at my tailbone, he gives the bottom half a gentle tug down and the entire dress falls to the floor. He gasps slightly once he notices that I am not wearing a bra, leaving me standing there in only that black lace thong.

"You are so beautiful," he whispers in my ear, as I begin undoing the buttons of his shirt. Once I have a few unbuttoned, he steps back and grabs the bottom of the shirt to whip it over his head.

"Holy shit," I say out loud. He is a Greek god, dammit all. His skin is tanned and toned, with only a trail of hair heading to whatever is hidden under those jeans. He almost looks sheepish for a moment at my reaction, which makes me feel suddenly so powerful. I grab the top of the jeans and tug him back into my space, so our chests are touching. He shucks his jeans and boxer briefs aside. This man is completely naked in front of me. I have not seen a fully naked man in so long and I picked a great one to start with.

He gently lays me back onto the oversized couch and pulls the last piece of clothing between us away. As my thong hits the floor, he joins me on the couch.

Tim moves closer to where my knees are bent together and puts his hands in between to open my legs, exposing the most secretive part of me. He moved two fingers inside me and it feels like I am a musician, and he is the conductor of an amazing performance. My body molds around him and with every movement he brings me closer. In a quick movement, this thumb moves up to rub my clit with two fingers inside me still. Stars are forming in my vision and I let go loudly.

Before my body even finishes coming down from the high, he reaches over to the drawer on the coffee table to grab a condom. He rolls it over himself and immediately thrusts into me. The sensation after the climax is incredible. This time we share an orgasm, before he whisks me off to the bed for a repeat performance.

Chapter 12

After the third time, we both were spent and before we could even discuss whether I should head home or not, we had already fallen asleep. It feels very strange waking up in an unfamiliar bed in a strange place, but I quickly recover my memories, blushing at the vixen I became last night.

"Mm good morning, beautiful," Tim says as he stirs next to me.

"Good morning, I feel like I could have slept all day," I laugh and look at my watch. It is not as late as I thought. I still have plenty of time before going to get the girls, "So I should probably start finding all my clothes, it may be a scavenger hunt."

Tim laughs sleepily, "We sure did make our way through my house. I know what I will be thinking about while watching the football game on the couch later today."

"Oh yeah? I can easily say that last night will be living rent free in my mind for a bit. It was fun to just let go and not think," I say and then cringe, feeling like that is a little too much.

"So, I would love to see you again, but just want to be straight forward—I am not a relationship type of guy," he scratches the back of his neck as if he is preparing for a bad reaction.

I do not want to give him the wrong idea about me and my expectations, but I also want to be clear that we are on the same page. Except, while I do not want a relationship with him, for some reason it stings a little to hear he does not either... while we were in bed. Welcome, Carly, to more uncharted territory.

"I knew that going into last night. Everything that happened last night, us going on the date, the drinks, um—this," My hands circling over our naked bodies under the insanely soft comforter. God, does he own anything that isn't top notch quality? Honestly, how much do commercial contractors make? "Was just us being in the moment. My brain is foggy from lack of sleep—for an excellent reason—and lack of coffee, so words are not a strong suit right now, but I do not have expectations for a relationship. All that I expect from you is that on the times we do go out, if we decide to again, that you are respectful—which you most certainly were—and that we both are consenting to how far it goes."

He tilts his head to the side like he is trying to figure out what I just said before he replies, "That was perfectly said, and without coffee first, impressive."

I laugh and start to get up to get dressed. That is when it hits me that the sun has filled this room through the wall to ceiling windows and I am stark naked. I have no clue what my hair and makeup looked like right now. I am not sure how comfortable I am with him seeing my body in full light, plus walking around the house completely naked. I grab the throw blanket from the end of the bed and wrap it around me before standing up. Tim gets up and disappears into the large walk-in closet only to reappear wearing gray sweatpants that looked amazing on him. As he walks out, he is pulling a simple black t-shirt over his head. He notices me watching him and he grins at me.

"Come on, I will help you on the scavenger hunt for your clothes," he says as he reaches me. He puts his arm around me and leads me out to the living room. I catch a glimpse of my face in the mirror in the hallway. My makeup is surprisingly okay, but my hair is a lost cause of a mess. With my clothes back, I am incredibly overdressed, or maybe underdressed, for a Sunday morning. I remember my car is around the block near the distillery and I am going to have to do a walk of shame. There is a pair of ballet flats in my car, and I immediately regret not grabbing them before we came here.

"I'm going to walk you back to your car, I can let you wear one of my coats for the walk if you would like," As he looks me up and down in the dress, "Though it is a shame to cover up such a sexy dress. You really do look incredible in it, but it's 8:45 and there is a 9am mass at St. Mark's so I am guessing you would rather not get spit on by the little old women as you walk by."

"Thank you, that would be very much appreciated."

After I get everything gathered up, we set out towards my car, me wearing a long trench coat of his. Sure enough, as we turn the corner, we find ourselves navigating through a crowd filtering into St. Mark's while a couple priests stand at the top of the stairs leading into it. I blush a full red just thinking about the unholy things we did the night before, but I also smirk a little too. It was fun to be a little naughty.

We reach my car, and I hand Tim his coat back, "Thank you for this and for a fantastic night."

"No problem. I had a really good time with you, Carly," He leans against my car door, "I meant it, I would love to get together again. The next weekend you don't have your kids, shoot me a message."

"I will definitely do that. Have a great day, Tim," I go to give him a light goodbye kiss, but he reaches a hand into my hair and pulls me in for a deeper kiss. It brings me back to the night before and desire boils up in me again. There is no doubt I will be messaging him again.

"Bye, Carly," he says as he gently closes my car door. With one more wave, he turns around and heads back to his building. I tear off the boots and toss them on the passenger side floor for the replacement ballet flats.

* * *

Pulling into my driveway, I am calculating whether I have time for a nap. I need to shower without a question, plus a million other thoughts pull me back towards mom-mode. I need to race inside before Barb or any of the neighbors can see me. Shit, my boots. Last thing I need is Jake walking the girls out and seeing them in the car.

Going around sounds exhausting so, I just reach across. I can feel the hem of my dress scooting up as I stretch but can't grab it to pull it down while reaching the other arm out to the boots. I stand up quickly and fix my dress, grateful that Barb is not on her porch.

As I pull my dress back down as much as possible, I hear the sound of a man clearing his throat. I do not need to look to know who that man is, but slowly rotate towards the abandoned house with a driveway close to mine. As I expect, I find Henry just across the yard. I feel the red start at the tips of my ears and work all the way down my body. I am frozen, slightly willing myself to move.

Henry's face pulls again. I still cannot decide if it is a smile, or some other emotion. He is so hard to read. There is a hard exterior to him that made him appear cranky. However, when he softened for a moment the day before, it was noticeable in his body language, like a release of tension for a very brief second, I barely even caught it.

"Good morning, Carly," Henry practically growls. I sense judgement in his voice. There is no way he was not judging me. He saw me leave the house yesterday in this little black dress and now more than 12 hours later, I am returning in the same outfit. Plus, mooning him while grabbing the boots.

I open my mouth to say something as I gesture erratically from the boots to the car. All I manage are some rambling with miscellaneous words, "I just—my boots were—- I'm not—umm—Bye!"

Frantically, I flee into the house. I can recognize that this is not my finest moment, but Sane-Carly is not in control. I run right to my bathroom and strip off the black dress, ready to shower off the evidence of what happened at Tim's house. I am glad it happened, ecstatic really, but it is time to get back to real life and I need to shake off that Henry encounter.

A shower is just what I need to calm down. While I still am considering how I can climb out a window on the opposite side of the house to avoid seeing Henry, I have come to terms with the fact that it happened.

As I walk out of the bathroom I hear my phone ping with a text from Lana.

Lana: Sooo are you alive? If so, how'd it go?

It is strange how quickly she has wormed her way into friend status. I like having someone to, unapologetically and without much explanation, spill the tea with.

Me: Just got home. You were right about mature men... you were so right.

Lana: WTF a sleepover?! You can't stop there, I need details! I looked up that address—I'm nosey—and that building looks swanky!

Lana: Oh! And glad you are alive.

Me: It was so fancy! I am not sure I have ever been in a condo that nice. I barely recognized myself, it was like an out-of-body experience... x3.

Lana: Three?! Let me get this straight... you messaged this guy on a whim to meet up, which you do. Then you have drinks and then fuck him in his gorgeous castle multiple times. Okay, Cinderella! Please tell me the sex was mediocre or my jealousy is going to overflow. Just kidding! I hope it was amazing!

Me: Seriously though! I felt like a Disney princess... well like princesses gone wild.

Lana: I need all the details. What time do you pick up your kids? Do you have time to do lunch beforehand? I don't get mine until 4:30.

Her offer to meet up without weeks of planning and notice is so exciting to me. I have made a friend. Dr. Rose is going to be so proud of me, though I might filter out some of the dating details and give her the PG version. Lana, on the other hand, can hear the full R-rated version, mostly because I have to tell someone, and instinctively I know Lana is a safe space to talk about it.

Me: I get mine at 3:30, so if we pick somewhere that I don't have to get dolled up, then I have plenty of time.

Lana: Peppers in like 45 mins?

Peppers is one of my favorite places. It is just a dive bar, but they serve extraordinary melted sandwiches. It sounds amazing since the last thing I ate were 4 blueberries that garnished my last drink at the distillery.

> *Me: Absolutely! Their food will definitely get me to spill all the*
> *beans about my night.*

I switch gears to get ready to meet Lana. Peppers is about 10 minutes from my house, so I have a little time to throw myself together. Blow drying my hair would take too long, so up in a messy bun it goes. I throw on my regular outfit of jeans and a t-shirt with a cardigan over top. With a few minutes to spare, I add a touch of makeup. I look like Carly Kennedy once again.

As I grab my purse and keys, I swing open the front, then halt in my spot. The memory of getting home this morning is still fresh and humiliating. I inch forward until I can see around the door just a little, peaking over to see if I could tell where Henry is. I do not see him anywhere in the driveway, so I run to my car and drive away like I am stealing it.

There are only a few other cars in the parking lot when I get to Peppers. Just as I am getting out of the car, Lana pulls in and parks near where I stand. She gets out of her car and starts over to me. She is so naturally pretty. Lana looks like she belongs in the 1970's with her long blonde hair, jeans, fringe, and overall spirit.

"Hey, girl!" she says as she gives me a hug.

"Hi, Lana!"

"Let's go grab a table and food so you can tell me everything. I am dying to know!" Lana gestures for us to head inside, "Seriously, I need to know your secrets of how you landed high-rise-hunk!"

We sit down at a table far away from anyone else and I start telling her all about the night, pausing as our waitress comes by to take our order. Our food arrives just as I get to the couch part. In between bites I tell her the rest, and she asks questions intermittently but listens closely. I finish up the part of us waking up together that morning and end the story with a dramatic crunch of my pickle.

"Wow, that was quite the evening there, Carly," Lana says, fanning herself with her hand, "So, then you just got in your car and went home?"

"Yup, but then I managed to moon my next-door neighbor when I got home," I tell her, blushing. I had not turned red during any of the other stuff I told her, but for some reason the thing with Henry is making me want to crawl into my shell, "I was reaching across my seat in that damn little dress, and it bunched up over my ass. I did not realize that he was standing in his driveway."

"Oh no! Talk about timing. So, is the neighbor hot?" Lana asks, leaning forward with her head resting on her hand.

"What? Henry? No, he was a total jerk yesterday. He makes a lot of noise when he is there— he recently was given the house or something. His mom grew up there," I explain a little, "and he parked in front of my driveway yesterday morning. That was actually the first time I talked to him, and he's been coming around for weeks. Our other neighbor said he is an attorney, so it seems he only gets out to the house on weekends for the most part. He's just not very neighborly."

"I hear you that his personality sucks, but that doesn't answer my question... is he hot?" Lana pushes again.

"I haven't really noticed," I try to say, but I can tell that my face is crimson.

"Oh my god, he is hot!" Lana says, "Maybe we will have to hang out in your driveway next time. I can deal with a hot grump!"

"I mean, I guess he is attractive. I have no clue how old he even is," I ramble on.

"Age is but a number, I am happy to be a cougar if the prey is a sexy lawyer," Lana makes a cat claw motion with a purr.

I have no clue why I am getting flustered. I do not even like the guy, so if Lana wants him then she can have him. But then why does the thought of that tug at my stomach and make me a little envious? She is gorgeous. She can just look in his direction, I bet, and he would lose all the attitude to fall madly in love with her.

Lana stops with the teasing as she senses my emotional turmoil, "Okay, hands off the neighbor—I just am very curious as to why that makes you turn bright red."

"I think he is good looking, yes. But I know nothing about him," I say defensively and then pause before saying, "He was kind of fun to argue with though. He will be gone soon anyway. He said he's cleaning up the yard and house to sell. Once that is all done, he will be out of my hair."

"Okay, well never mind him. Let's get back to Tim, do you have a picture? Are you going to see him again?" she asks.

"I think so, we talked about how we are both good with a casual thing and that we want to meet up again," I say as I show her his dating profile photos on my phone.

"Holy shit, Carly. And you said he looks just like his photos?" She says, shocked by his photos.

"I actually think he is better looking in real life," I think back to the feeling of grabbing onto pure muscle on top of me.

"Good for you, girl. You should definitely hit that again ASAP!"

"I have every intention of planning something for the next weekend the girls are at Jake's to hang out and you know…again." She gives me a knowing look with a high five. I have missed having this kind of friendship with someone. Amber is so much like a sister and we just do not talk like this anymore, even though I can tell her anything. It's nice having both.

The conversation shifts to Lana. She decided to go out on a second date last night with the woman from Friday night. The excitement is a lot more noticeable this time.

"Something was a little different. I really had a good time." She has a big grin as she says it. "It was still a real slow burn, but it at least felt like a date. I even kissed her at the end of the night, and she is a really good kisser!"

"That's awesome! You never know, the slow burn could be a sign that this one is different," I encourage her. We talk more about that and chat about people at the Café Club until I have to leave to get the girls. As we get to our cars, I give her a big hug.

"Thank you for listening, it was so nice to have a friend to talk it out with!" I confess.

"Agreed! Anytime you need to chat, just let me know!"

"Same, if you need a friend to vent to or something."

I am in a very calm mood pulling up to Jake's house. The girlfriend's car is not in the driveway this time, so Jake walks out with the girls helping them with their backpacks. He tries to engage and get me riled up about something mundane, but it is not working like he wants. I can see the frustration on his face when I am not bothered or emotional. His control over me is weakening.

Chapter 13

The weekend after my date with Tim, the girls are with me. The weather is perfect for some yard work, so we head outside to rake up the fallen leaves together.

The girls are excited to work outside, though I know very well that it will be a lot of me raking and them jumping into the leaves, then me raking the same leaves again. As long as Millie and Remi had fun.

On the porch, I must audibly groan, even though I thought it was inside my head.

"What's wrong, mom?" Millie asks.

"Nothing, baby. The guy is working next door, and we had a little disagreement last weekend," I tell her.

"You want me to go pinch him, mama?" Remi asks, ready to fight.

"No, I do not want you to pinch him. Where did you even get that from?" I look at her in disbelief, "In fact, I do not want you going around pinching anyone!"

Remi rolls her eyes, "Ugh, fine."

She is such a fireball. Millie is always so mild and even keeled, while Remi is always ready to fight.

I don't see Henry anywhere but based on the trimmer disaster of the previous week, that does not mean much. There is a lot of work that needs to be done on the opposite side of the house—including fixing a few accidentally maimed bushes.

We grab our rakes and a couple of tarps to move the leaves with, then start in the front yard. Leaf season is in full-swing, and the yard is blanketed in them. I am working on getting the leaves out of the garden along the house when I hear Millie behind me.

"Remi, stay here."

My heart pounds out of my chest as I turn around so fast to see what Remi is doing. My pulse slows when I see her in the yard, nowhere near the road. But then, I realize that she is walking towards the property line—towards where I can see Henry coming down the wrap-around porch. Before I can react and catch up to her, she has stalked across the patch of grass in between the houses and has caught Henry's attention now.

"Well, hello there, miss," Henry says as he squats down to get to her level. His demeanor is much different than I have seen from him in our few interactions. Granted no one is mooning him today. Millie reaches them at this point, I am still making my way over. They had been raking along that side of the yard already, "And hello to you too."

"Hi, mister neighbor, I'm Remi and she's Millie," Remi points at her sister, "My mom says I am not allowed to pinch you."

I am contemplating all the ways I can crawl into a ball and hide but still retrieve my kids from in front of Henry. I make my way to them just as Henry speaks.

"My name is Henry. Remi and Millie, those are beautiful names! My grandmother's name was Millicent, she lived in this house once upon a time," Henry says in the softest tone. He is giving the girls his full attention, "And why did your mom tell you not to pinch me?"

"Okay girls let's go back to raking and let Henry get back to whatever he is doing," I say hurriedly, trying to get the girls to turn back to our house. I can tell Remi is invested in this conversation now and Millie is jumping ship too.

"Another Millie lived here?" she says pointing at the farmhouse, "There are never other Millicent's! Was she a really nice grandma? My grandma is cool. She lives far away, but always brings us presents when she comes here!"

"Well, I never met her unfortunately. My mom moved away before I was born, but I like to think she was a sweet woman," Henry's voice is laced with an emotion that felt displaced, "So, Remi, why were you going to pinch me?"

"Because you did not use your nice words with my mommy," Remi puts her hands on her hips like she had just remembered why she marched over here.

"I'm sorry, Remi, I didn't mean to upset your mom," He says to her, then his gaze slowly makes its way up to me, "But it is certainly interesting to see her all fired up."

He gives me an amused look with a raised eyebrow. My insides are mush with a mix of embarrassment and something else. It feels a little lustful, maybe a little attraction but that is crazy. I am not attracted to Henry; I have a thing going on with Tim— sort of. Tim is perfectly put together with not even a hair out of place, like he walked off the cover of GQ. Henry has dirt all over him and his hair looks like he ran his hand through it far too many times today. He does not have a clean-cut look, which is interesting given his line of work, but somehow, he makes this work for him. Dammit, Carly, stop.

"Okay, seriously girls," I regain my ability to speak, "back to work in our yard. There is some post-leaves hot cocoa for after I can see the grass again!"

The girls cheer.

"Lucky girls!" Henry stands back up. He gestures back towards the farmhouse, "I should get back to my work too. It is a pleasure to meet you, Remi and Millie."

He has my kids in the palm of his hand. What the heck? The grump next door is good with kids? Who would have thought that?

"Bye, Henry! When you finish your work, you can come over for a cocoa too if you want," Millie says to Henry. My eyes bug out of my head, realizing what she just said.

"What? Um—No!— I mean, I am sure Henry is very busy. Um—maybe another time or something—or not, because you are obviously a busy person but—" I start rambling again, I have no clue why this keeps happening around him. I barely manage to speak full sentences. He seems amused and more than happy to let me keep making a fool of myself.

Once I manage to get myself to stop talking in circles, I take a breath and say, "Bye, Henry."

The girls wave and we start to walk back to our yard. As we get to the property line, I hear behind me, "Bye, Carly."

I stiffen but keep walking, not daring to look back. I cannot let him see what the sound of his voice does to me. I don't even know him.

For the rest of the day into the evening, I cannot help but think about why I acted so weird around Henry. It must be because I want to see Tim again and I keep projecting my feelings onto the first man I see. I am subconsciously craving more of what I experienced last weekend.

Tim and I have sent a few messages back and forth since our night together. We loosely planned to meet up over the following weekend.

I send a quick message asking if he is free on Friday, and if he wants to meet up. I feel better taking the initiative and putting it out there that I want to see him again.

The girls are watching TV for a little bit while I clean the kitchen after dinner. I busy myself with loading the dishwasher, cleaning spaghetti splatter off the stovetop, and all the other simple tasks of my day-to-day life. My mind starts to wander back to last weekend with Tim. It is as close to an out-of-body experience than I can ever imagine having. I am standing in the kitchen in my baggy mom jeans with my hair in a messy bun remembering the way I was sexy just a week ago. I picture what it would be like right now to whip my hair out of this bun and have Tim bury his hand in it to grab me closer. My thoughts about finding time to go buy some sexier undergarments are interrupted.

"Um… mom?" Millie's voice jolts me out of my not-safe-for-mom-mode thoughts.

"Yeah, hon?"

"Why are you cleaning that same spot over and over? There is nothing even dirty there," I look down to where she is pointing. Sure enough, I have the sponge in my hand and I am mindlessly scrubbing one spot on the countertop, the sauce I originally went to wipe up is long gone.

"I was lost in my thoughts. What's up?" I brush it off, putting the sponge down and turning towards her.

"Can we have a snack?" And with that I am reminded of my real mom-life where I cannot finish cleaning up one meal before they are asking for a snack already. I shake my head as I reach into the pantry for some fruit snacks, tossing them over to Millie, "Give one to your sister, please."

Between this version of me and the new spicy side I have found, it feels like Dr Jekyll and Mr. Hyde. Balancing them both seems like a lot of work and exhausting to keep straight. Part of me starts to wonder if there is a version of me that I can find that falls in the middle.

Chapter 14

W alking back into the living room after getting the girls to bed, I hear my phone chirp with a message. I look at the screen to see a notification from the dating app that there is a new message from Tim. My entire body feels like it is suddenly heating up with excitement. I quickly open it up and have to stop myself from making too much noise as I dance around. He is free and would love to get the chance to take me out for a nice dinner on Friday, then a nightcap at his place.

Once I stop quietly swooning like a teenage girl, I start in with my response. I simply let him know that it all sounds great, and I am looking forward to seeing him again. The words "Tim is typing..." appear almost immediately after I send my message. When it arrives, my jaw drops open.

Tim: I am looking forward to it too. Especially if you promise to wear a sexy dress again so that I can sneak a finger inside of you under the table. I got hard at work the other day just remembering you and that black dress.

Whoa. One part of my brain is telling me that I should not go down this road. The other part of my brain wants to hear exactly what he wants to do with me on Friday. The problem is that I had never sexted before, even before my marriage. I take a deep breath and think about what I truly want him to do.

> *Me: I am trying to decide on some sexy underwear to wear under another dress, but that makes me think I shouldn't bother with any underwear at all.*

I feel like I sound ridiculous, and it is not as sexy as I mean it, but I hit send anyway. If that is the case, he does not seem to mind.

> *Tim: If I reach under that dress and there is nothing in between my finger and your clit I might just take you right on top of that table. I do know a great place with private tables and long tablecloths that give a lot of discretion... in case you drop your napkin and need to go under the table for it. I wanted to feel your lips around me last weekend, I am desperate to feel the back of your throat on my cock.*

Uncharted territory. I do not know where to begin to respond. I like how the things he describes make me feel so wanted and I feel sexually energized in a whole new way. I spent years in a marriage where my wants and needs were not important and definitely not met. The only time I have gone down on past partners is when it is someone that I was serious about. I have not done that since the beginning of my relationship with Jake. Could this new version of me be okay with doing it? I then decide to bring the sexy talk to a halt until Friday.

> *Me: I look forward to having your hands... and other things... all*

over me on Friday. Can't wait to see what surprises you still have left.

That seems to work to keep the spice alive, but we do not continue that sexual volley. The conversation ends when Tim says he has an early morning meeting and that waiting to Friday to touch me is going to be torture but so worth the wait.

I stand up and walk my water glass into the kitchen. I linger at the sink still thinking about the messages with Tim. That man is truly a sexual god, and I cannot believe I get to worship that body again. I know I am right; I am just desperate for more of that feeling with Tim. I have not thought about Henry once since I started talking to Tim. But why am I thinking about Henry right now then...

* * *

The week is moving along towards Friday. By Wednesday, my anticipation is overflowing. I have been texting Lana about my excitement and planning my outfit.

My work day finishes up with a little bit until I have to pick up the girls. At around 5pm, I hear my phone ringing.

Lana is calling me. We have never actually called one another. Strange.

"Hi, Lana."

"Carly, turn the TV onto the Channel 4 news right now. Quick!"

"Lana, what are you tal—"

"NOW!" She sounds frantic and I know from her tone that I need to listen. I go over to the TV and flip it on. I am greeted by Sponge Bob Square Pants' opening song on Nickelodeon.

"Forget the pineapple under the sea, dammit, and turn the channel! It's the first story they are covering after these twits at the desk stop talking about their fucking days! They had a snippet of the upcoming stories in the very beginning."

"Okay, okay, I'm going!" I switch it to 4 to see the anchors transitioning from their welcoming piece for the 5 'o'clock news to the actual newscast.

"... we will now go over to Naomi for our top breaking story."

"Thank you, Clint and Ashley. I am here at the Sander Building downtown where the story all began. Shortly before our broadcast this evening, a group of local professionals were brought in for alleged money laundering and additional illegal activity. We will continue to report on the actual crimes that they will be charged with as we get more information."

"Lana, am I on the right channel? Did you mean Channel 2?"

"Shh— we need to keep watching because I am really hoping I am wrong and overreacting right now."

"There were 10 men and women taken into custody Wednesday afternoon following an FBI investigation. The developer that owns the Sander building, Lawrence Palen, and three others from Palen Development were allegedly working alongside of a local contractor to hide funds from tenants leasing business space—"

The TV moves from the reporter to a video of a group of mostly wealthy looking people in handcuffs stepping out of police cars and heading into the Court Building downtown. The first two are older white-haired men who look like they will grab your ass and call you baby then expect you to thank them. Next is a woman who looks completely terrified. Then there is a slightly younger man with salt and pepper hair... I gasp and drop the phone.

"Carly! I heard a bang, did you faint?! Oh my god tell me you did not fucking faint. If you don't make some noise, I'm coming over there right now!" Lana says on the phone on the ground. She is practically yelling, and I could still hear her. I scramble to pick up the phone and bring it back to my head.

"That's Tim. The guy that is planning on fucking me senseless on Friday is on TV getting arrested."

"Commercial Contractor Timothy Griff is thought to be the mastermind of the operation by coordinating all of those involved with an additional cut of the falsified profits for himself. A source tells us that the whistleblower in this case was part of his company."

The reporter rambles on about the details, but I am in a permanent state of shock that I am not even listening to her anymore.

"Carly, I'm so sorry. I don't even know what to say. I just saw the preview of the story and the guy looked just like the photos you showed me. Then they said something about Timothy whatever and I knew I had to call you."

I start laughing, not because it is funny, but more manically. Tears are forming in my eyes from this fit and then I suddenly stop, "I think he's going to have to cancel our reservations."

"I would say so. He seems to be otherwise detained and unable to break free to make it on time," Lana matches my tone and adds to my insane thought process.

"Maybe we can try to meet up again in 20 years, 15 for good behavior, if we are lucky." We both burst into actual laughter now, "God, I really know how to pick them."

"If I didn't see it for myself, I probably would have thought you were full of shit," she says to me.

"This sucks. I am finally getting back out there and after one night together, he is arrested for some serious shit. I don't want to go back to sitting home alone on the weekends." My voice shifts to show my sadness. I am afraid this will knock me back in all the progress I have made to hide in my little cocoon of fear.

"Carly, don't let this halt you. First off, you have us in the Café Club now! I will talk Marti into holding the club meetings in your front yard, if you stop coming. And you said yourself that he is not a forever thing, I mean I get that you weren't done with him yet but at least it is not something that a boyfriend is doing behind your back."

"Yeah, you're right. Honestly, I didn't even know his last name until that reporter said it." I start feeling better, but I still do not want to be alone all weekend. Lana must sense how I am feeling.

"I have a great idea! Be my plus one at my cousin's wedding on Friday! I thought I would have a date by now and the only potential date I have is that girl I went out with, but that is not serious enough to meet family," She quickly adds, "But for real, it would be nice to just have a friend there, not a date to babysit. It's a wedding so there will be a bunch of single guys there! My cousin's fiancé has some sort of fancy job and a rich family, I've only met him a couple times. I bet his fancy job hot friends will be there too!"

I think about what she is proposing. My whole body is telling me that I want to hide inside my house with my two boyfriends, Ben and Jerry, while watching Christmas Hallmark movies in Fall. As I am about to say no, I hear my own voice from Dr. Rose's office saying that I want to be social and go out more. This is perfect to have a no pressure night out, right?

"Yes, okay I'll go! Text me the details so I know what to wear. Thank you, Lana, seriously I need a fun night out." I say, proud of myself for doing it. Then jokingly I continue, "But for real, please do not get arrested before Friday night."

"I make no promises! I am a scandalous woman, don't you know? If you don't, you'll hear just how scandalous from my uncle's newest wife," Lana replies.

"Sounds like fun," I laugh lightly. Then like a freight train a thought smacks me in the face, "Oh shit! Lana, do you think that they will go through his phone and see those messages from last weekend??"

"Oh, shit," Lana does not even try to sugar coat it.

Chapter 15

⚜

By the time Friday rolls around, no one has contacted me about Tim. The story is all the buzz in the area, and almost no one knows that I am connected, if only briefly, to the supposed ringleader. As more details are released, it becomes crystal clear why his condo is filled wall-to-wall with luxury. He managed to arrange for all the other people who were arrested to do the hard work of the con, but then he took more than the rest. Allegedly.

The news says that all the people that were arrested are out on bail waiting for their court hearing. Even so, I have not heard from Tim. I do not expect to, nor do I know what I would say.

Lana's cousin's wedding is at a nice hotel about 45-minutes from where we live. Lana already had a hotel room booked but she called there to request two beds so we could have a girls night slumber party. She is insisting that I am not allowed to pay her for a bit of it. I am looking forward to a night with a friend getting drunk and dancing.

The girls are at school and Jake will pick them up from there for the weekend, so I am off the mom-clock until Sunday. We had decided to go over right at the 3pm check-in so that we could blast some music and get ready in the room together before the 5pm ceremony.

I am getting everything gathered up when my phone pings with a text. I check it quickly to make sure it is not Lana. It is not, but instead a beautiful 3-day old face. Amber and Paul had their baby, Paul Jr. or PJ, on Tuesday.

I felt guilty that his birth was overshadowed in my mind by the craziness that happened the day after he was born, but then I went to visit Amber and meet PJ yesterday. Amber could tell that something is on my mind, and I spilled everything. I told her all about my date with Tim and what happened, with details. More than once I covered PJ's brand-new ears before telling her some of it. When I told her about him taking off my boots, she screamed with shock so loud that she woke up PJ and we had to halt the story while she got him situated with nursing. She is invested in the whole story.

When I got to the part about turning on the television to see him in handcuffs, she dramatically and not quietly said, "No! No way!"

This again woke up PJ, but this time it did not stop her.

"I have been following that story! I am so bored lately that I have soaked it up for the local reality TV that it is! Which one is he?"

I did not mention his name and a couple of those arrested are around our age. I was curious if she thought it could be Tim, so I asked, "Which do you think he is?"

"Hmm... I am going with the accountant for the contractor's company? I could see you going for another accountant," she guessed.

"Do you think an accountant is capable of those things?"

"Hey, who am I to judge? And the accountant did not look like any of the male accountants you've introduced me to. I don't know if it is just the handcuffs, but he has a bad boy look," she laughed, "So, not the bad boy accountant. I definitely do not think the old man developer, I feel like old-balls there could not accomplish all that in one night."

I cringed and laughed at the imagery.

"That guy who orchestrated it all looks like a naughty boy, but he's not really your type."

"Why do you say that?" I asked, curious of her answer, even though I knew she was right. He is not like anyone I would have considered in the past.

"His demeanor screams fuck boy. He is not the guy to seriously date someone. He's the type to just—" I watched as she processed what she was saying in comparison to the story I told her, "—he's the type to just throw you up on the counter to have his way. Or take you right on the couch and have condoms all ready-to-go in every room... like the living room coffee table. Oh my god! Carly!"

"Yes, I have a night of wild sex with the guy that is facing the most number of allegations against him and is the reason that it all happened," I confirmed.

"You hooked up with Timothy Griff!"

"You did what?!" We heard behind us as Paul walked into the room. He had been at the gym, and we did not hear him come into the house.

"Babe, you are not going to believe this!" Amber said excitedly, as she gave me a look to tell the details again to Paul. I shrugged, because the friendship between the three of us is like that even after they got together, we just told things to both, not just one.

"Well, you walked into the punchline of the story, so it won't be as dramatic," I said jokingly rolling my eyes, "But here's what happened—"

I proceeded to tell him the story, I started to hold back on the spicy details, but Amber was not having it.

"You missed the boots part! Tell him the boots part! I'm hoping he gets some ideas," Amber quipped at me.

So, Paul got the full story and in all the years I have known him, I have never seen him unable to find something to say until that moment. A day later I am still laughing over it.

* * *

Lana and I both are racing around the hotel room trying to get ready on time. When we arrived at the hotel at check-in time, they told us they did not have our room ready just yet. Logical answer was to wait at the bar, of course. That left us slightly buzzed with barely enough time to throw ourselves together.

I am doing my makeup sitting on the floor in front of the full length mirror. Lana is sitting cross legged on the bathroom counter in a pair of tiny shorts and her strapless bra. She is so confident in herself in a way that I envied.

"Shit! Do you have pink or nude lipstick? I only grabbed a bright red one and my dress is dark green. I will look like a fucking Christmas tree if I wear this," Lana asks me. I laugh and toss a mauve colored lip stain that will compliment her dress perfectly, "Lifesaver! Thanks!"

We finish getting ready quickly. Lana is wearing a long green dress with off-the-shoulder straps and a slit on the side that went dangerously high. I have only one option, it is my go-to for nicer weddings, such as this. The floor-length, navy-colored satin dress hugged my body. The neckline is a tasteful square cut with cap sleeves that cover my shoulders. I do not say anything to Lana, but I feel frumpy, and the dress feels a little restricting. The sexy confidence I experienced with Tim seems to have gone away and now I see all the lumps of my not flat stomach. I should have brought some shapewear to put on under the dress, but I did not even think about it when gathering up my stuff.

I must be wearing my concern in my facial expressions because Lana pulls my hand to make me face her and not the mirror. She then says to me, "Stop it right now. You look stunning, that dress is fantastic, and it makes your ass look awesome! Tonight we are not tired single moms. No, tonight we are a couple of sexy mamas ready to party, so own it!"

Her speech works for the most part because by the time we are entering the large room that is set up for the ceremony, I feel a little better. I still am not having a sexy night, but I feel pretty being dressed up. We take seats up towards the front. Lana's parents are already there, along with her two brothers and both of their wives. We sit down in the row behind them, and Lana makes the introductions. Back in the hotel room I asked Lana if her family would think that I am a date. She laughs and says that they might have, except that she told her mom and most gossipy aunt that she is bringing a friend who is not a love interest. She makes it seem like telling them is filtering information throughout the entire bride-side of the room.

We did not have much time to talk because the ceremony started exactly on time, these are my kind of people! The bridesmaids in stunning blush-colored gowns and groomsmen in black tuxedos walked down the aisle, it is clear that this is not a low-budget, DIY wedding. I always wanted a wedding like this.

As the music shifts and the bride comes into view with Lana's uncle, we all stand up. She is stunning and I could see the family resemblance to Lana. As she approaches the front, my eyes shift to the groom. He is enamored by his bride and trying, but failing, not to cry. I don't even know these people, in fact I do not even remember their names, but I can tell without a doubt that they love and respect each other. I feel myself longing for a connection like that.

The rest of the ceremony is short and sweet. After a dazzling dip and kiss at the end, they head down the aisle. We all stand up to filter out to the ballroom where the reception is to be held. Lana mentioned that they did pictures before the ceremony so that they could start the party as soon as possible. We pause and wait patiently because everyone is trying to crowd into the aisle toward the exit. They finally start to clear out enough that the crowd could move smoother.

On the far side of the crowd, coming from the groom's side, I caught a glimpse of the back of a man's head. For a fleeting moment, he reminds me of Henry. Why do I keep thinking about him at random times?

That man is probably here with the shockingly perfect woman that is next to him. She mostly is blocking him with long red hair that has volume that is almost as unnatural as her breasts. Holy shit why am I getting jealous about a gorgeous woman across the room because she is with the guy who's back of head makes me start to think about Henry again. Something is definitely wrong with me.

"Carly?" Lana gets my attention, and by her curious tone, I can tell it is not the first time she has said my name, "Let's go! There is a bar and an extremely overpriced meal calling our names!"

I laugh and reach down to grab my clutch off the chair. When I look up, the couple had made their way through the double doors. The irrational disappointment sits in my stomach, which makes no sense. I am now projecting Henry onto strangers—I am nuts.

By the time we make it to our table any and all thoughts of Henry are long gone from my mind. The ballroom is immaculate, from the massive chandeliers to the waiters walking around with trays of champagne and hors d'oeuvres. I glance at the seating chart on the way in and see that there are 49 tables for guests in the room, plus a head table for the couple and the 16 members of the bridal party. I am not sure if I know eight women, much less eight women that I would ask to stand for me in my wedding.

"Your family is loaded," I whisper to Lana matter-of-factly.

"Meh, my uncle definitely is," she shrugs, "My part of the family is just normal."

I have doubts that her definition of normal matches mine, but I just let it go as we find the bar and then our table. We are seated with her parents and siblings at a round table. The bridal party is introduced, and all come in doing fun dances, then all break out into a choreographed dance with the bride and groom as they are introduced. I have never seen anything like this in real life, it is TikTok worthy.

The basic wedding things are done in quick succession. The couple has their first dance. The best man and maid of honor give their speeches. I do think that the best man could have been a little more tasteful about their college conquests, but overall heartfelt. Once dinner is finished, the tables are being cleared for dessert and the dance floor is beginning to fill up.

"I have to freshen up my lipstick and break the seal, do you want to come with me to the bathroom?" Lana asks, grabbing her purse. I am having a conversation with her sisters-in-law about kids, they have a son and daughter the same age as the girls.

"No, go ahead, I am fine here," I tell her honestly.

Shortly after she leaves the table, the conversation all seems to quiet down, and Lana's parents decide to head out for a dance. Soon after the other two couples go for a dance as well. I am at the large table watching the couples dancing, lost in each of their own little worlds. I am bewitched by them, when a tap on my shoulder brings me out of my trance.

Before I can turn around, I hear, "Excuse me, miss, would you like to dance?"

I freeze. I recognize that voice.

Chapter 16

I swivel around in my chair, and it is confirmed. Henry is standing there with a hand, palm up, reaching towards me. He is wearing a blue patterned tuxedo jacket that somehow is almost the exact shade of my dress. I thought he was hot in the lumberjack look when he worked around the house, but this is a whole different level of hot. Henry always has a little facial hair and wears flannel shirts with dirty jeans. While I hadn't pictured him dressed up before, I could see that I was missing out on that image. It fit him well.

"Henry?!" It comes out squeakier than I hoped for.

"Hi, Carly," The pull of his smile that I have often noticed is nowhere to be found. No, tonight he gives me a smile that reaches his eyes, "So would you like to dance? Or at least give me a high five here so I can save some face as to why my hand is out."

I laugh at this, unsure what to say, and I give him a little mischievous look. I reach out my hand to give him a high five as a joke, but when I do his hand grabs mine and when I attempt to lift my hand up, it does not move. He moves so quickly that I am trying to figure out what to do next. I do not get a chance to think too hard because he has some sort of spell on me. He pulls my hand up a little and I raise to my feet automatically. His hand is so soft and so worn at the same time. I cannot explain it, but his hand feels tender holding mine.

I follow him to the dance floor, and I am still trying to figure out what is happening. Did someone drug my drink and I am dreaming? If so, why am I dreaming about Henry? He guides me onto the floor as an up-tempo song ends. Something in his face gives way and I can see that he is nervous too. It helps relax me a little bit and my heart rate starts going down—until he guides my hand up to his shoulder and then his hand goes to my waist. There is nothing particularly sensual about this, but somehow it feels intimate. The DJ is talking about slowing it down a bit, I only heard a few words he says before he plays, All of Me by John Legend.

I have not said anything except his name. I need to speak, or this is going to get even stranger. Right now, it was a 'she-is-surprised' strange but inching towards 'this-chick-is-weird' kind of strange quickly.

"Why are you here?" I say way too quickly.

"Because I was invited. Why are you here, Carly?" He says far calmer than me. Why does the way he says my name make my insides heat up every single time.

"I came as a plus one," I whisper.

"Oh my god, I'm sorry, are you here with a date? I just saw you sitting at the table with some people and when they all left, I just acted before thinking that you are not alone," Now he is the one talking too fast and stumbling over words. I laugh softly at this.

"No, no, don't worry. My friend, Lana, is a cousin of the bride and she asked me to come with her for a girl's night after—" I trail off, "What about your date? Is she okay with you having a pity dance with the neighbor you saw sitting alone?"

"I am not here with anyone. I decided to fly solo tonight," he said and before he could keep going, I butt in.

"What about the gorgeous red head you were with at the ceremony?"

"You saw me at the ceremony, huh?"

Oh, shit. I just outed myself with no turning it back around.

"I thought I saw you but then when I looked again the crowd had shifted. I figured it was a mistake, apparently not," I say honestly.

"Interesting…" he says with a smirk, "To answer your previous question, the woman with red hair is not accompanying me but rather she is the wife of one of the other partners at my firm who would have been on her other side. We are all here because the groom is our third partner's son."

"Oh, I see," I do not know what else to say. I wish I could control my blushing, but I know I am turning red.

"And as for your other statement," he paused to spin me out and twirls me back to him. As I return to him, he pulls me closer than we were before. Our bodies are now touching, and I am shocked by how much I like feeling his warmth. He leans in closer to my ear, "There is not one second, I have taken pity on you. I have seen firsthand how wildly independent and confident you are. I saw you sitting alone as an opportunity."

I move backwards just enough to look him in the eyes. I am in shock.

"Me? Independent? Confident?" I pull in again to hide my face.

This time he moves back so that we make eye contact.

"Need I remind you of my bushes and the fiery woman that came storming at me while I massacred them? For the record, I tried to fix them and have discovered I am not a bonsai artist," He gives me a look like he is confused by my confusion.

"That day was an anomaly. I never do things like that. I am the quiet, people-pleasing accountant, Carly." I shrug and my face falls at that truth.

He is back in my ear and whispers in his husky voice, "There was nothing quiet about that black dress with those boots."

I gasp loudly and he laughs menacingly into my ear. He pulls back again, pauses for a beat, then spins me before pulling me back in. He looks at me up and down while I am spinning out, his gaze seems to linger on my lips for an extra beat.

"However, I kind of like this dress better. You look beautiful tonight." He brings me back in close to him once more, like he wants to say something else but then he just breathes deep against my neck like he is keeping that thought locked away forever. We sway in silence for a little bit as I ponder that comment about this dress. Somehow it feels comfortable and familiar, like he knows that the black dress was not really me.

The song ends and neither of us stop dancing, I get a sense of relief when another slow song comes. I can't explain why, but I do not want to leave this little bubble with him on the dance floor.

Henry breaks the silence first, "Your girls are adorable, by the way. They seem like great kids."

"Thank you, they really are incredible. I am a lucky mom. Do you have any kids?"

"No, thought about it at one point, but I couldn't imagine doing the newborn stage at 45 years old now."

So, Henry is appropriately older than me. Seriously, why am I even thinking that? It does not matter how old the grumpy neighbor is. The hot, grumpy neighbor who does not seem very grumpy at all right now.

"What grades are the girls in?" Henry asks, genuinely paying attention.

I answer that question timidly, not wanting to dominate our conversation with talk about the kids, but after that question he asks another which leads to another. I stop holding back my responses once the urge to gush over them takes over.

"They are lucky to have a mom like you. It is really incredible."

"What is incredible?"

"The way you light up every time you talk about them. I could keep asking you questions all night about them just to watch that sparkle in your eyes keep coming back."

I don't know how to respond. I am not sure how to take that, but I know it feels special to have someone I have barely met see that.

Just as I was about to say something, anything, to fill the space, the DJ comes back on the microphone.

"Alright folks! Let's get this party started!! Everyone get up for the Cha Cha Slide!"

"I can manage to not step on your feet with a slow song, but organized dancing is not my strong suit," Henry gives me a look that tells me he really does not want to try this dance. Lucky for him, that makes two of us.

"I could really use a drink. How about we let them shuffle and shake or whatever it is, and we hit the bar?" I suggest. It is becoming easier to talk to him without tumbling over my words.

"Fantastic idea," he says as he places a hand on my lower back and guides me towards the closest bar in the ballroom. The warmth of his hand gives me that internal surge again and I shiver just a tad. I try to hide it but when I look at him, he's smirking again.

We order our drinks and as they are being made, I try to think of conversation points. I want to know so much about him without sounding like a stalker. Before I get a chance to, Lana comes gliding up next to me like a green goddess.

"Carly! There you are," Lana turns her attention to Henry, "And hello to you too, mystery dance partner. I am Lana, Carly's friend, or if she signals that she is trying to dodge you this is where I tell you I am her lesbian lover, then snatch her away forever."

My eyes go wide, ready to make excuses for my insane friend, but much to my surprise Henry let out a huge, genuine laugh at this.

"Thank you for warning me about that, Lana. I'm Henry Reid, I have been working on the house next to Carly's for the past couple of months."

Almost instantly I see recognition strike Lana and the next words tumble out before she thinks to stop them, "Oh! You're the hot grumpy neighbor!"

I want to hide in my shell and never come out. I think my jaw is actually on the ground now. Lana puts a hand on her mouth when she realizes what she just said and gives me a "sorry" look.

Henry does not miss a beat and replies, "That is me, I think, except I swear I have been all sunshine and roses. She's the one who yelled at me and destroyed my bushes. She even almost sent her daughter to come over and pinch me!"

I gasp and he smirks with one side of his mouth. Even though he is talking to Lana, he is staring right at me. He is enjoying this and the redder I get, the bigger he smiles. Our drinks are put in front of us at some point, so I grab mine to take a huge sip. Lana looks between the two of us and laughs. I can see the gears turning in her mind through the smirk she is giving us.

"Well, I think I am going to go with a friend over lesbian lover tonight. There is a chick over there that has been eye fucking me all night, so I am going to go ask her to dance just to piss off my uncle's homophobic third wife," Lana subtlety points to a stunning woman sitting at a few tables away with skin that looks as smooth and dark as expensive brown silk. She is one hundred percent giving Lana all the eyes.

"Please don't ruin your cousin's wedding with drama," I scold, always the mom.

"Oh please, my cousin would love nothing more than for me to torture her dad's new supply. This step-monster is a born-again Christian and tries to pour holy water on my cousin every time they see each other because they lived together before marriage."

"Wow," I say as Lana is already slipping away, "Make good choices!"

She gives me a quick look back and shakes her head to say no, with a devious shimmer in her eyes. I envy how carefree and easy she navigates life, maybe it will rub off on me a little, because I feel so out of my element. Henry lets out another laugh next to me. God why does he have to even have a sexy laugh?

"So, you told your friend I'm hot?" My hopes that Henry did not hear that part were squashed. I down the rest of my drink and signal to the bartender that I need another.

He is enjoying this a little too much. He is letting me squirm in my embarrassment. Then, Henry leans in so only I can hear him and says, "Don't worry, I get it. I also have a hot neighbor. Though mine is less grumpy and more powerful- standing up for herself."

I take a sharp breath at those words. It is another reminder of how little Henry knows about me. First it was confident and independent, and now I am powerful. I honestly do not know how to handle what he is telling me. It is nice to be told these things, but it feels like he is lying to me for whatever reason. Like maybe he *is* showing me pity for being the little single mom in the tiny cottage next door who is just trying to make ends meet day to day. I have so much pressure on me constantly and I never feel like I am hitting a milestone of progress. My chest feels tight, my eyes sting, and I am having trouble breathing.

"Will you excuse me for a minute?" That is all I can manage as I run towards the ladies' room about to hyperventilate. I push open the door only to find several women crowded in the bathroom waiting for stalls to open. Always a damn line. Some of the women turn around to look at me with looks of concern.

It feels too crowded, so I head back out of the women's room and run right into a man's chest, as his arms shoot out to catch me from going down backwards. I smell the same scent of sandalwood that I had smelled on the dance floor. I look up and find myself staring at Henry. If I was close to hyperventilating before, I am now full blown doing so. I try to turn to run away again but Henry's hands are gently around my arms holding me in place.

"Come on, Carly. Let's get you some fresh air," he guides me out the front doors into the cool Fall evening. Immediately I shiver and before I can even fully process that I am cold, there is a tuxedo coat around my shoulders.

The openness of the outdoors starts to help control my breathing, as Henry leads me to a bench off to the side in one of the hundreds of gardens this venue was known for. It is away from the others lingering out front, which I am grateful for.

"Big, slow breaths, now," He coaches me while rubbing circles on my back. I do as he says and start feeling better, "There you go. Now tell me what happened? Are you upset about what Lana said? If that's it don't worr—"

I cut him off with a half-hearted laugh, "No, not that. I mean look at you, obviously you're hot. Like seriously, aren't lawyers supposed to be preppy looking pricks? You look like you fucking split logs with your bare hands."

Now he looks a little embarrassed with a slight flush on his cheeks.

"It was you calling me all those things. Independent, confident, and powerful. You said it so assertively, like you did not doubt it at all."

"Because I don't doubt it."

"What do you mean? You just met me, and we've had minimal conversations. No one would use those words to describe me after getting to know me, especially not in the last ten or so years."

He cocks his head to one side and gives me a look like he is trying to figure out all the secrets I bury down deep.

"What happened in the past ten years that you weren't hearing how strong you are?"

"Oh my god, there! Another one! I am not strong, Henry." Why does he keep toying with me? We both know I am none of these things and if he is just trying to be nice, it is having the opposite effect.

"I am going to ask one more time, Carly, what happened?" His voice takes a new commanding, stern tone. It sounds protective.

"My marriage happened. My long, drawn-out marriage, which gave me the two best things to ever happen to me, but it also damaged me in a way that feels like I'm beyond repair. Most times I can hide away my insecurities that my ex-husband drilled into me, but tonight was not one of those times. I'm so sorry! I'm so embarrassed!" I answer, hiding my face in my hands.

"I have an urge to kick the ass of anyone who makes you feel like that. You do not deserve that, especially not from your partner!" He gently grabs my hands and peels them from my face. When they come down, he does not let go of my hands. His voice then softens, "It is so clear that you are all those things and more. Do not feel embarrassed, please. You are safe here, understand?"

I just nod. I am still embarrassed that he saw this, but I am starting to breathe normally again.

"Come on, let's go for a walk around these gardens before heading back in there," Henry puts a hand under my arm and stands us both up.

"That sounds really nice, thank you."

"No biggie, you are actually helping me by hanging out here. If I go back in there I will be fed to the wolves. The other partners' wives are always trying to set me up. They mean well but they have no clue what my type is."

I laugh as an image of women lined up waiting, like he is Prince Charming at the ball.

"So, what is your type then?"

He stops walking and turns to meet my eyes, "You want to know my type?"

There is something deep in his eyes that makes me just whisper a meek, "Yes."

"Powerful like a storm."

He turns forward and starts walking down the pathway again. I take a moment to recover then fall into step next to him.

Then, like he did not make a profound statement to me, he changes the subject completely and asks, "Did you grow up around here?"

I must be drugged and making this whole night up. I shake my head to collect my thoughts before answering him. Talking about where I grew up brought me back to reality. For the rest of our walk, it was an easy back and forth of questions about life, work, and even more about the girls. He seems to avoid talking about his family and the house, though.

We loop around the gardens in the front of the building. As we approach the entrance to the venue again, I start to walk toward the door.

"Carly?" I stop and turn to look at Henry. He put an arm around my waist like he did while we were dancing.

"Yes?"

"Thank you for going on the walk with me, I enjoyed getting to know you better."

"I enjoyed it too."

We stand there looking at each other, and it seems time stands still.

He steps into the hold his arm has around me. He stares at my lips again and begins pulling me closer to him. My breathing grows ragged as his line of vision moves from my lips up to meet my own. I feel him start to lean towards me, our lips just hovering above each other, when the door flies open. We both jump backwards a little and I look over to the people.

"It's time to send off these kids," an older man says walking down the sidewalk, wiggling his way right through us, depositing sparklers in our hands.

Henry shakes his head and looks at me. He apparently has recovered from the trance we were in.

"Perhaps it's for the best." He grabs his jacket off my shoulders and walks backwards to the other side of the walkway just as the sparklers are all lit. There are sparks flying everywhere and I cannot see through them. The bride and groom race down the path heading towards a waiting Rolls Royce with a Just Married sign on the back. When the sparklers all die down, I look across and Henry is gone.

Chapter 17

~~~

After the sparkler send-off, I go back into the ballroom. I look around trying to find Henry, but he is nowhere here. I spot the table with the redhead from the ceremony, I am figuring that is where he is seated. There are only a few people left at that table; Henry is not one of them. I get to the table where Lana and I are seated. Lana's parents are just getting up to leave and her siblings look like they are gathering their things as well.

"Carly," Lana's mom says, walking around the table to me. She grabs both of my hands in hers, in such a motherly way. It makes me miss my mom, "It was so nice to meet you and it was lovely to chat. Please feel free to come with Lana for our weekly family dinner! We would love to have you and your girls join us. There are tons of kids running around for them to play with!"

"Thank you, Mrs. Harrington," I reply, genuinely touched by how welcoming she is.

"Please, call me Betty. Mrs. Harrington is my mother-in-law and well…" she trails off but points to an older woman a few tables over yelling at a waiter then stuffing everything she can find off the table into her purse. Betty sighs and shakes her head, "The woman is worth millions and not a single roll, fork, or salt shaker is safe around her."

We both laugh and I am grateful for getting to talk with her before I left. She is centering me again after the abrupt ending to the walk with Henry. I look around the ballroom again, but this time not for Henry.

"Betty, have you seen Lana recently?"

"Last time I saw her she was bumping and grinding to some pop song with a gorgeous young lady, who I honestly think is too young for Lana," Betty rolls her eyes ever so slightly. I laugh but love that she is only concerned about the age of Lana's partner, not gender, "They were dancing up near where my brother-in-law's newest wife was seated. I thought they were going to give that awful woman a coronary."

My hand goes to my mouth to stifle a laugh.

"Oh, no don't worry, it was hilarious, but I am sure we will hear about it later," Betty says with an amusement in her eye that I can see exactly where Lana gets her spirit from. She continued a little louder and to the entire table, "Well us old folks are heading back to our room for comfy PJ's and bedtime."

Betty is dressed in a designer gown that probably costs more than I make in a quarter, but she has such an approachability to her. In fact, the whole Harrington family does. They are obviously extremely close-knit.

"Sounds like Dad's fun stops here! Pops, the bar is still open, see if another martini helps you get lucky!" Lana's brother jabs at Mr. Harrington. My eyes must be like saucers, I am in shock to hear him say that. The whole table is laughing, then they see my expression and laugh even harder. I join in the laughter because I have to say, it is contagious. They may all look like a bottle of champagne on the outside, but they are all cracking a beer on the inside.

As we all disperse, I head off to find Lana to head back to our room.

I have a key and can text her that I'm leaving but I figure I will give it one lap to see if she is nearby. Plus, after all that laughing I need a bathroom. I head back to the bathroom I tried earlier and there is now a line out the door. There is an employee walking by, so I ask her if there is another bathroom somewhere. She points down a quiet hallway and tells me there is a smaller one that way that usually is not as busy.

"Great, thank you!"

I head where she directed me and thank God, there is no line spilling into the hallway. I push the door open and immediately see that there are people on the far side where there is a countertop vanity and mirror. It takes me another second though to recognize that green dress.

"Lana?" I say as I now register that she is sitting up on the counter and the girl from the ballroom's head is under her dress between her legs, "Oh my god, I am so sorry!"

Lana points to the girl nodding her head with a look that says she's proud of herself for making this happen. I laugh under my breath. The girl's head starts coming out when she hears me.

"Oh no you don't, you stay down there until you know I'm done. We don't leave things unfinished," Lana says, commanding her situation, as she pushes her head back closer to her. I should feel way more uncomfortable right now than I do. I have only known Lana for a short time, but she has quickly engrained herself as one of my best friends and this carefree attitude is part of that. At least someone was getting lucky tonight.

"I'm heading back to the room," I say, shaking my head with a smile. Lana just gives me a thumbs up and I hightail it out to give them their privacy.

Lana's new friend starts coming out again when I spoke and as I slink out the door, I hear Lana say, "Be a good girl and get your fucking

132

tongue back up there until I come on your face."

Sometimes I wish I could be as bold as her. I cannot imagine being able to talk like that during sex. Even with Tim, it was mostly sounds, you know groans and moans, or saying what felt good, but not this kind of unapologetic dominance.

As I step into the hallway, I see a pair of women walking towards the restroom.

"Oh, you do not want to go in there!" I say plugging my nose, "Something did not agree with someone's stomach in there right now."

The ladies both gasp and put a hand on their chest. They look from me to the door and back to me. I am trying hard not to laugh.

"Thanks for the heads up!" They say as they turn around and we start to walk down the hallway.

From behind us, I hear Lana scream and yell, "Oh my fucking god!"

The women look behind them at the bathroom, wide eyed, and the one says to her friend, "I hope it wasn't the clam dish!"

And now I officially lose my battle of trying not to laugh.

* * *

By the time Lana comes up to our room, I have changed into pajamas and taken off all my makeup. I am just climbing into my bed to check out what is on TV when I hear the beep of the door being unlocked.

"Well, hello there, out past your curfew, huh?" I say jokingly.

She laughs, "Not my curfew, but maybe hers."

"Oh no, Lana, how old is she?"

"She's legal. I checked. She is actually 25. But damn, she is experienced beyond her years. She may look tiny, but I think all her muscle is in her tongue."

I shake my head, "I envy you sometimes."

"Me? Why? Oh my gosh, Carly, are you wanting to experiment with a girl? Or have you before? I mean obviously I am not meaning me, I don't blur friendship lines, but I can find you someone." Lana sits on the edge of my bed. She babbles quicker than I can process it.

"Jeez, Lana, stop talking," I say laughing hard at this conversation, "No I have not hooked up with a girl and no I do not want to. Just not my cup of tea. I just mean how outgoing and confident you are."

"Really? People usually complain about how bold and crass I can be," Lana's voice is softer than before. It is clear that she is thinking about something and trying to piece words together carefully, "I tried to change myself for someone before. My ex-husband loved the idea of me being with women in the beginning, but I did not realize that it was like a pornographic fantasy to him. It soon became something that embarrassed him, and he would call it a phase, like he saved me from being bisexual and I was now cured of homosexual thoughts."

"Wow, I am sorry he treated you like that. It is not okay," I put a hand over the one she has closest to me propping herself up. She looks so vulnerable, like admitting how her ex acted is not something she has fully healed from. I need to bring her spirits back up and get the regular Lana back, so I say, "You might be crass, but I freaking love it. You say what we are all thinking. But the thing I do need more about, how do you talk like that during sex? I am nervous to even say that something feels good, much less tell him what to do to me! I mean, I failed at just sexting."

It works because she cracks a smile, a devilish smile, "You have no idea what you are missing out on then! Let me get changed and I will help you with some basic things you can try next time, after you fill me in about hot neighbor Henry and if he's going to be the next time."

"Definitely not," I say looking down at my hands and picking at my nail polish trying to hide my disappointment of how the night ended. I do not know why I am disappointed, kissing him would have been weird and complicated.

Lana goes off to the bathroom and returns in record time. She is wearing a silk pajama set and her long hair pulled up on the top of her head in a messy bun. She did not even bother with taking off her makeup, so she still looks glamorous in this get-up. She sits on my bed with me again.

I ran through everything from the beginning, starting with how I thought I saw him at the ceremony into him asking me to dance.

"Damn, he sounds so yummy, and I agree he is really hot," she says and then scrunches her face, "Sorry about saying that. I totally forget how to take my foot out of my mouth sometimes."

"I mean I wanted to kill you on the spot, but it led us to eventually heading outside for a walk where we almost kissed," I hid behind my hands, peeking out between my ring and middle fingers to see her reaction.

"Holy fuck! You kissed him?" She was jumping on my bed now.

"No, almost kissed," I correct her.

"What the fuck does that mean?"

"It means that we were just about to when the entire wedding poured out of the building to do the sendoff. The moment was broken and all he said was, 'Perhaps it's better this way' and moved to the opposite side of the walkway. Then he was gone when the crowd started to clear, I couldn't find him inside either." I shrug my shoulders, because ultimately it is what it is. There is nothing I can do about it now.

"Carly, there is obviously something there. You should march up to him next time you see him and demand an explanation of what that means."

"We both know I will not do that. I am way too chicken."

"Did you want him to kiss you?"

"I mean, we probably just got caught up in the moment of the beautiful wedding and everything."

"You need to stop deflecting questions you do not want to answer because you might be scared of that answer. It is your defense mechanism."

"Does my therapist know you're coming for her job?"

She laughs and shrugs, but then repeats herself emphasizing each word, "Did you want him to kiss you?"

I sigh and close my eyes real tight. I do not open them when I say, "Yes."

"Well, then it sounds like you need to have a chat with dear Henry, or I can come over and do it for you?"

"Oh god, I can only imagine what that would sound like!" We both laugh and it breaks the seriousness that we can move on.

"So, you never told me, how did he end up being at the wedding?"

"Your cousin's new husband is the son of one of the other partners at Henry's law firm," I recall.

"Other partner? Are you telling me that he is a partner at Edward's dad's firm?"

"I didn't think about it when he said it but yeah, I guess so."

"Carly, his firm was ranked as the number one personal injury law firm in the city for like a bazillion years in a row. Henry is fucking loaded, girl! You should definitely lock it down with him."

"Not that how much he is worth matters to me, but I doubt it. Maybe I heard wrong, because the truck he drives is for sure not new, he dresses like a lumberjack most of the time, and if he is so rich, why is he doing the work on the house himself when it obviously annoys the crap out of him."

"Maybe you should find out more about him then," she grins, "Like if he's a good kisser to start and then find out what else he is good at. I bet he has a huge di—"

I gasp and say "Lana!" before she can finish that thought. She falls over in my bed in fits of laughter.

"Well, let's get you ready for when you do realize that you are badass, and you end up dancing horizontally with him. We will get you out of your shell and find a whole new world of enjoyment in sex. I know you said it was great with Al Capone," I know she is trying to avoid saying Tim's name tonight, or at all, "but until you learn to tell them exactly what you want, then how do you expect them to know."

"Okay…" I am skeptical that I will ever be able to participate in dirty talk.

"Like tonight, the more I told Shay exactly what I wanted her to do and made it a command rather than a request, she responded by listening and working harder at it."

"You sounded like a damn dominatrix in there. Are you going to see Shay again?" I ask, desperately wanting to change the subject. As much as I want to know, I am also nervous to talk about my own dirty talk.

"Oh god no, she's way too young for me." Lana shakes her head dramatically, "I didn't even ask for her number. Honestly, I think her name was Shay, but I really am not totally positive."

"Lana!"

"What? It was just for fun. So back to what I was saying to her. Even if you don't use it, your partner might and you need to be ready to not freak out or squash the mood," Guess I am not getting out of this lesson. Lana goes into different levels of dirty talk both leading up to and during sex. I am blushing hardcore at some of the things she says but it is not as embarrassing as I thought it would be. Some of it is rather mild, but she's right I would freak out about what I should do or say.

At some point we grab the bottle of wine we have in the mini fridge and pour some in the plastic water cups. We get pretty drunk by the end of the second bottle of wine. Between that and us being exhausted, our sentences barely make any sense, and it just causes us to erupt in laughter over and over.

Aside from the weird encounter with Henry, this has been the type of night I have needed so badly. I do not remember the last time I got drunk with a friend and laughed until our abs were sore. Eventually, we are both asleep on my bed, I have no clue when though. Lana passes out first, with her feet up towards my head like she laughed so hard that she fell backwards but never came back up. I put a pillow over her feet, so she did not kick me in the middle of the night. Wait, it is the middle of the night. I laugh at myself so hard that I fall backwards onto my pillow. I remember nothing after that.

Chapter 18

ᐁᐧᐤ

Beep, beep, beep.
Quack, quack, quack

"What the fuck is that noise?" Lana is face down on the bed talking into the mattress.

"Shit, the quacking is my alarm to wake up for Cafe Club. I forgot to cancel it! I don't know what the damn beeping is." I open my eyes and am hit with light on my eyeballs. Every light in our room is still lit up like Christmas.

"That's my alarm. Which means it is only 6 in the morning. We need to go find our phones to shut them up."

"Yeah, we do. Am I moving yet?"

"No, how about me?"

"No, be careful when you do. It's like a fucking interrogation room out here."

"What does that mean?" Lana lifts her head off the mattress to look and I hear the regret, "What the shit, who installed the sun's surface in this room?"

The quacking and beeping are still going, so we both roll out of the bed. I look in my clutch and realize my phone is not in there.

"Fuck, I think I left my phone at the wedding!" I shriek.

"Then is there an actual duck quacking in this room?" Lana says as she makes it to her phone that is sitting on her discarded dress on the floor. She has a solid point.

The quacking gets louder when I open the closet door, I cringe at the noise coming from the pockets in my dress.

"Found it." I say grumpily as I switch off the alarm.

"Ah silence once again," Lana says.

We both slump into the chairs around the little table.

"I feel like hell, but now I am awake," I say.

"Same, I need coffee and a hydration IV."

"Well, are you still drunk?"

"No, does that matter for whether or not I get coffee?" Lana pinches her face with confusion.

"It matters if we want to drive to get coffee this morning."

"Ugh, are you suggesting we show up at the club like this?" Lana opens one eye to give me a look like I am crazy talking.

"I think we take showers and get dressed in whatever, you know no one will care. We are at a coffee shop on this side of the city now, that 'You're Grounded' shop on 72nd Street. We can even leave our stuff here and come back for it after."

"Ugh, that is really close." Lana pauses like she is evaluating herself to see if she can do it, "Fine, but I am showering first while you make us pregame coffees. I doubt my ability to operate a coffee maker right now."

"Deal!" Lana winces at how peppy my voice sounds.

A little over an hour later, we are both dressed in gym leggings and baggy t-shirts heading down to the car.

* * *

"Whoa, I did not expect to see you this morning," Miles looks at Lana up and down, then turns towards me, "And you look just as rough as her."

Our eyes are hidden behind our oversized sunglasses and neither of us bothered to dry our hair. We are definitely riding on the hot mess express today.

We are actually a little bit early, and Miles is sitting at a large table alone.

"Thanks, jerk," Lana says, playfully smacking his shoulder as she plops down on the chair next to him. I sit in a chair across from them.

"Do I want to ask, or should we wait for the whole group?"

"Group. Only telling once." Lana has her head laying on Miles' shoulder. Miles is laughing at her with his shoulders moving up and down, "No, no, no. No moving, making nauseous."

Next to show up is Marti and the rest of the group follows quickly after. At one point I think Lana is snoring on Miles' shoulder.

"Okay the gang is here, spill, girls!" Marti says not hiding her desperation for the tea.

"Carly. Hot neighbor. He has cute butt." Lana starts.

"Lana!" I snap playfully at her, "And his butt? Really?"

"Don't act like you didn't notice. You tell your story while I nap," she says, not incorrectly. Dammit, Henry does have a great ass.

Everyone's eyes double size, they are practically salivating for details. I tell them my story about my evening from Henry asking me to dance to the interrupted ending.

"Perhaps it's better this way?" Gwen repeats.

"What the fuck?" says Jayna.

"Dyl, you're the token dude around here, what does that mean?" Paula says to Dylan.

"Seriously, we need more straight guys around here. I hate telling you the shitty things guys do," Dylan shakes his head, "That sounds like he has some demons he needs to work out and he may have done you a favor. Take caution getting involved with him."

"Don't worry," I say with a sigh, "I don't foresee any 'getting involved with' happening. Okay, enough about me. Why don't you ask Lana about the time I walked into a public restroom to a girl going to town on her pussy?"

A few of them gasped and they all looked at me, not Lana.

"Carly, why does the word pussy sound so strange coming from you?" Miles asks. The whole table erupts in laughter before Lana spills the details of her night with Maybe-Shay.

***

Lana drives me home after we go back to the hotel to pack up our things. We are just singing along to the radio together and not talking about much of anything.

Instinctively, we both look next door when we pull into my drive. There is no truck on the street or in the driveway. The slump in my shoulders must be noticeable because Lana gives me a sorry look.

"He was out late last night too, so maybe he will be here later," Lana offers as an excuse. It is not a big deal; it does not matter whether he is there or not. There is nothing between us.

I plaster my best smile on my face and say, "Maybe it's better this way."

I am trying to just be funny, but Lana's look deepens, "It's okay to admit that you feel something, Carly. It's okay to admit you wanted that kiss to happen."

My eyes are fixed on my hands where I am picking at my nail polish. It is a nervous habit; I don't even know why I bother painting them anymore. My body shows my give-in, even though I do not reply. Looking over to Lana, I give her a half smile that shows the resolve. She understands because she reaches over and squeezes my hand.

I get out of her SUV and go to the trunk to grab my overnight bag and dress bag. As I close the trunk door, I nearly fall over. Lana is standing there on the side of the car, even though I did not hear or see her get out.

"Holy crap! When did you get over here? I need to put bells on you, I swear," I am still clutching at my heart dramatically.

She does not say anything but instead she pulls me into her for a hug. I return the hug as she says, "Thank you for coming with me. You were the perfect date, and I think I had the hottest date there!"

She has broken the gravity of the moment and we both giggle a little.

"I am serious! You are a badass and I am glad it was me going home with your sexy ass," She reaches down and smacks me right on the butt.

"You are so weird," I shake my head humorously at her, "But for real, thanks for bringing me. It was nice to get out and I had a lot of fun. Your family is awesome, too! Your mom even invited me to family dinners, which was so kind of her."

"She did? Whoa, she really likes you then! She does not mess around with our family dinners! For real, any time you and the girls want to come for a delicious home cooked meal, courtesy of their weekend chef of course because my mom is as skilled in the kitchen as Moira Rose, you are always welcome!"

"Weekend chef?" I squint my eyes at her and pause. She returns it with a shrug and a sheepish look, "I knew you were freaking rich!"

She laughs as she gets back in her car. As I walk past her window towards my house, she whistles at me, "Hell yeah! Look at that sexy ass of my hot date!"

Shaking my head, I throw up a hand and wave, not looking back at her, "Goodbye, weirdo!"

I make it all the way to my front door before I cave and sneak a peek to check for Henry one more time.

He is not there for the rest of the weekend. The house just looks even more empty than it did before Henry started coming around.

Chapter 19

I spent the entire weekend pretending to myself that I was not moping. Every time I heard a vehicle, I convinced myself it was a truck with a trailer, and I ran to the window to check. Seriously, what is wrong with me?

I pull into Jake's driveway behind the little sports car. Great, Riley was in the house again. No… wait, a teensy woman that I presume is Riley walks down from the house holding hands with both Millie and Remi towards my car. Jake is walking a little in front of them.

No, this cannot be happening right now. Please tell me I am not going to meet his new supply in her painted-on jeans and shacket that made her look like a Taylor Swift album cover. I look down quickly to check myself out. I am rocking frumpy sweatpants and a t-shirt from one of my clients that I have worn so much that it is not white anymore. My hair looks like I may be living in the jungle and there is not a swipe of makeup anywhere on my face.

Jake reaches the car first. He gives me one look and scoffs. He legit just scoffed at me. I have now accepted my fate and figured I should just get this over with so I can go home and call Amber to vent about it.

"Hey, Car, this is my girlfriend Riley," he gestures towards her. Riley and the girls have now reached the car too, "She is going to be around the girls, and she wanted to introduce herself."

"Hi, there, Carly. I have heard so much about you," Riley says, breaking the bond between her and Millie's hands to reach it out to me.

"All good things, I hope," I say as I shake her hand and give Jake a knowing look. Lord only knows what that asshole has told her.

"Of course! And the girls just gush about their mom," she says with a sweet naive smile, like she has no clue how harsh the world can be, "I know if I was their mom, I would want to meet someone who is around them regularly."

It stings when she says, 'if I was their mom.' It sounded too much like longing for my comfort. But play nice, Carly, play nice. Riley is being polite, and she has not given my primo outfit any judgmental looks, yet.

"Well thank you for that. Do you have kids too?" I ask, seizing the opportunity to pry a little.

"Oh no, not yet but I definitely want to! But there is plenty of time for that someday!" she exclaims enthusiastically. I raise an eyebrow and give the 46-year-old Jake a look so quick that Riley misses it, he does not. Jake coughs, borderline chokes.

"Isn't that nice?" I say through a thin smile, "Well it was so nice to meet you, Riley, but I need to get the girls home so we can start making dinner."

"Oh! Of course! I was so nice meeting you too," Why does she seem so damn sweet? I want to warn her to run away from him as fast as she can. She waves one more time and heads back up to the house while I get the girls buckled in. Jake is still standing near the car and says a last goodbye to the girls.

"Nice sweats, Carly. You've really embraced the spinster look," Jake says low enough so that the waiting Riley cannot hear him.

I keep the smile plastered on my face, "Good luck with the next round of babies, grandpa. Riley will be done with baby diapers just in time to have to start changing yours."

I give Riley one more overly sweet wave and get in the car. Jake is looking shocked by what I said. I keep my expression solid and get in the car. I do not think I breathe until I am like two houses down. Then I finally let out a huge breath and now get mad. I am having a battle inside my head over his jerky comment and having Riley thrown at me unexpectedly. The girls do not seem to notice. They are chatting about the Barbie Dream House that they have at their dad's. I do not miss the innocent comments they make about Riley playing with them and how they think she looks like a Barbie doll. I just sigh and drive in silence not trusting myself to say something kid-appropriate, if I were to try talking.

When we pull into home, I glance slightly over to the farmhouse next door. Still dark and lonely.

* * *

Our week went along as normal. Girls go to school, I work, rinse and repeat for 5 days straight. I try to force myself to not look at the empty driveway next door and I try even harder to not care.

We made it to Friday and the girls are with me this weekend. I wanted to do something fun and get out of the house a little bit, but Mother Nature has other plans. There are weather warnings all over the news. We are about to get our first early snow fall and it does not sound like only a light dusting. New England is fierce that way sometimes. One day you are wearing shorts and flip flops, then the next snow pants. It is supposed to start mid-morning tomorrow.

We have not really experienced much snow in this house, by the time

I moved in we did not have any more storms. I am not complaining about that at all. Luckily, it is the weekend, and we can hole up in the house. I bought tons of snacks and stuff for meals plus wine for me, because priorities. We are going to watch movies, play games, and hang out all weekend inside.

The girls are excited to build a snowman. Me, not so excited about the idea of going out in the snow. This week I have been kind of gloomy and I am not sure if I have the amount of energy playing in snow requires, but I will muster it up for the girls.

I grab a glass of wine out of the kitchen after the girls go to bed. I need to shake this slump I am in, but it is tough. A client meeting caused me to cancel my therapy appointment this past week, which I was kind of glad to have to do. I am struggling with being forced to face how I am feeling. If I start talking about it, then I will probably end up admitting things that I am denying to myself.

With a big gulp, I empty the glass. Wallowing in my own self-pity, I pour another glass of Merlot.

I sit back down, and shift focus to Jake and Riley. He was so awful to me for so many years. It does not seem fair that he gets to move on, and I am stuck. My self-confidence has been inching upwards lately, but it was still below average. There have been some moments lately that I felt like I could figure out how to heal, but this week has not been a forward moving one.

I must have fallen asleep on the couch because the next thing I know, Remi's face is over mine and it is light out. I am blinking, trying to gain traction on where I am and what day it is, all with her giving me zero personal space.

"Mommy, can you make breakfast finally?" she says in her cute little girl voice.

I look at my watch. It is only 7:00am, what does she mean by finally?

"Rem, can you give mommy a few minutes to wake up? Then I will make something. Is your sister awake yet?"

"No, she was snoring really loud. Mommy, is Millie an elephant? She sounds like one." She was on roll now. Remi moves away from my face and bounces over to the window, "Mommy, I thought it was going to snow. Where is the snow? Maybe we can build a snow elephant instead of a snowman. Do elephants like snow? No, it's too cold for them. I like snow. No, I love snow. Do you think Henry loves snow too?"

I had my arm over my eyes still trying to wake and keep up with her, but the last bit got me to bolt up on the couch and look over at her.

"What did you just say, Remi?"

"I love snow."

"No, after that."

"Oh, do you think Henry loves snow too?"

"What made you ask that?"

"Because I see him, and I want to know."

"You see him?"

"Yes, Mommy. He is right there."

"He is right there?"

"Yes, right there," she groans and rolls her eyes at me, "I'm done with questions. Can I watch TV now?"

"Uh huh," I say in her direction, but my eyes are on the window she was just at. I get up slowly from the couch and walk over there. I vaguely hear the television start playing Peppa Pig behind me.

When I reach the window, my stomach flips over like ten times in a row. He is there. I am not sure what it matters, it is not like I plan to race out there and demand answers, or something. Answers to what really? I don't even know the questions I would hammer him with. I am staring out the window at him unloading some things out of the trailer, busy with making a pile next to the truck. He takes the last item off the back and closes the little tailgate on the trailer. He looks like he is frozen in place in that spot, then suddenly he moves again. His shoulders go up and down like he just took a deep breath, and he turns around towards my house. Towards the window I am standing gawking at him from. I should duck or run or something, but I am a deer in the headlights. He gives me a sad look, or maybe a pitiful look, I am not sure what he is trying to convey. His hand lifts in one solemn wave before he goes over to the pile and starts carrying things inside the house.

My trance breaks and I run away from the window before he comes back out. I try to refocus on Remi and "finally" make her breakfast, but my mind is mush. I tried putting a banana in the toaster and the bread in a smoothie. Okay, maybe the bread really did make it in the blender, and I realized it only once it was getting pulverized.

Millie eventually wakes up and I shake off the weird state I am in. We start hanging out together and my attention is recalibrated to be on them.

It is around 3 'o'clock when the snow starts falling, and it is coming down hard. The wind is blowing fiercely, creating little snow gales with it. I look out the window to check out what is happening out there. The girls have asked only about 50 times to play outside in the snow, but it looks too nasty to let them. I have not seen Henry again today, but the truck is still over there. I feel suddenly protective, hoping that he gets on the road soon, so he is not driving in this increasingly awful weather. I shake that feeling, he is a grown man who can make his own decisions. I have my own snowy day to worry about and keep the girls entertained.

* * *

The girls and I ended up doing two art projects, baking 2 dozen cookies, and playing 4 games of Candy Land. It is dark now and the storm is only worse. I cannot check to see if Henry ended up leaving even if I wanted to, because the visibility is non-existent outside. The wind and snow are pelting against the windows.

"Mommy, I don't love the snow right now. It's being loud," Remi says, looking stressed by the sounds of the storm.

I remind myself that I am the grown up and it is my place to keep them distracted from what is going on out there, even if I don't love the snow right now either.

"Okay, who is ready for a movie and snacks?" I hope I sound cheery for them. It must work, because they are jumping up and down excitedly. We head into the kitchen to pop some popcorn and grab all the candy we can fit into our arms. I set it all up on the coffee table while the girls go get blankets and stuffed animals.

Once we have ourselves nice and comfy, we start our movie decision making. Remi wants to watch Frozen and Millie wants to watch Beauty and the Beast. Personally, I want to watch Frozen as much as I want a root canal. Remi plays it on repeat and when she is not watching it, she sings the songs from it on repeat. I place my vote on Beauty and the Beast and talk Remi into wanting to watch it too. She likes the household items being alive in the movie, so I tell her that I will make the objects around our house talk tomorrow. As much as I hope she will forget that promise, I know she will not. Wonder what our mop might have to say to his brother the broom.

I have one low lamp on and the bathroom light for the movie. The girls are watching intently. There is a tree branch hitting the side of the house and my heart rate is running a little higher every time it does. I tell myself it is just a storm. I am brave. I am not going to let this storm bother me in front of the girls.

I pull my attention onto the movie, and I start to relax. The girls are curled up on either side of me. I start to forget all about the storm and soak up this moment with them. The movie gets to the part where

151

Belle's dad is riding through the forest, lost and a storm is brewing around him.

The storm on the screen gets more intense and I can hear the storm outside matching it. I hear a big boom outside. The entire house suddenly goes dark. Both girls scream and, while I hate to admit it, I let out a surprised yelp too. I am struggling to think right now. I know I need to calm down the girls but inside I am freaking out too. I cannot remember the last time I experienced a power outage.

"Mommy, what is going on? I can't see."

"Mommy, I'm scared."

"Mommy, when will the lights come back?"

"Mommy, why did the TV turn off?"

I can barely hear them through my panic. I am trying to gather my thoughts and think about what to do next. I can't even think of a single flashlight or candle anywhere in the house, pretty sure I do not have any.

Knock, knock, knock.

The girls scream again. I almost do too but catch myself this time.

Knock, knock, knock. It's coming from the front door. Shit! I take a deep breath and try again to pull it together.

"It's okay girls, it is probably just the scarecrow decoration hanging on the door getting blown around," I smooth my hands over their hair to try to calm them down.

Knock, knock, knock. Louder this time. I shuffle around until I find my phone and turn on the flashlight.

"Stay right here, girls. I am just going to take that down so it stops knocking."

As I stand up, I feel them crowd together and Millie puts her arms protectively around Remi.

I am just about at the door when I hear, Knock, knock, knock, "Carly! Carly, are you in there?"

152

I swing open the door and gasp loudly. There is a snowman at the door.

Chapter 20

❦

I stand in the doorway with snow blowing around me but I think I forgot how to speak. My brain finally catches up with my eyes and I process what is going on.

"Henry! What are you doing here?"

"I don't know, the power went out and I was worried about you and the girls. Before I could think, I was grabbing my emergency bag and walking through the snow to come check," Henry says through chattering teeth. He is covered in snow and his eyelashes look like ice.

"Oh my god, get in here. You are going to get hypothermia!" I grab his arm and pull him inside. I shut the door behind him, blocking out the angry storm. He sighs as the warmth hits his face.

"Mommy?" Millie says timidly from the living room. In the light from my phone and the lantern style flashlight Henry is holding, I can see both their eyes peeking over the back of the couch. They look terrified, but then they look over to our visitor.

"Henry!" Remi jumps up and races off the couch to come over to us. Millie is not far behind her, "You look like Olaf!"

"I look like a snowman made by two sisters who were the best of friends and loved each other so much?" he says in the same voice he used with the girls last time when they met in the yard. Well, kind of. This version was a little shaky with cold. I gave him a perplexed look about the Frozen knowledge. He catches my eye and shrugs with a small smile. I could stare into his eyes all day and night. Dammit, Carly, stay in the real life.

"You look freezing, come on in and get warmed up," I say hurriedly. I realize that the snow is melting off his hat onto his face. It takes everything in me to not reach up and wipe away the droplet of water on his cheek.

"I won't stay, I just want to make sure you were safe and that you had candles or flashlights."

"Really?" My face softens and I feel my insides get warm. I know he does not want to kiss me or be involved as more than neighbors, but it is nice to know that he is a good guy that looks out for his neighbor.

"Of course, Carly. I am sorry about last weekend. I care about you–" he coughs and notices the four little eyes looking up at the two of us. He changes his demeanor ever so slightly, but I notice, "I mean, I care that you are okay, especially being here alone with the kids. Who knows when they'll be able to get trucks out to fix the power. I saw the transformer blow over the hill on the other side of my house."

"Oh shit!" I say.

"Bad word, mommy," says Millie. Then she gets a conspiratorial smile on her face, very similar to when she is trying to trick me into saying yes to ice cream. She turns towards Henry, "You can't walk back to your house! It is scary out there, I mean it's really scary in here too, but scarier outside."

"Oh no, Millie, I didn't come over to impose. I just brought some supplies in case you needed it," Henry lifts up the bag in his hands. Millie gives me a look with big eyes and gestures her head towards him, as if to tell me to step in here. She is something else.

"You aren't driving back to your regular house in this, right?" When we were walking at the wedding, he had mentioned that he owns a house closer to where the wedding was held on the other side of the city.

"No way, I will stay in the farmhouse until the weather lifts. Here take a couple of these and some of these," he says as he hands me two flashlights and a handful of tea light candles. Millie deepens her look towards me. I give her a look right back because I know what she is silently saying to do, but she does not know the whole story... and she's only 7 freaking years old!

I crack first.

"Henry, please stay. I—," Millie coughs at me, so I try again, "we would be very worried about you just walking back, and even more worried about you alone in that old house."

"Seriously, I don't want you to think that's why I came here. I was the one worried and I couldn't stop thinking about that night at—" he trails off and looks down at the girls, but I know he was going to say the wedding.

"Let's not worry about that and just join forces to stay safe. We have a wood burning fireplace here. While I have wood for it in a little woodshed on the side of the house, I have no clue how to use it. If it gets cold enough though, I will figure out. We have plenty of food and drinks. Please stay."

His eyes find mine and he looks conflicted but then they soften and he nods his head. "You're right. But before I get out of my get-up here point me towards the woodshed. I will bring some in before the snow gets any deeper."

I nod and tell him where to find it but tell him not to fret if he can't get it open or something. We can make do with blankets and layers. He shakes his head at me and heads back outside.

About 5 minutes later, he is knocking on the door again with an arm full of wood plus the bag that is kept in the shed, full of wood. He rushes in with it and puts it down next to the door.

"Holy shi—shoot," he corrects himself looking at the girls, "It is only getting worse out there. But luckily the woodshed is on the side opposite of the wind and wasn't too buried yet. I grabbed as much as I could for now. Let me get my snow clothes off and I will take a look at the fireplace to make sure it's in working condition before we light it."

"Sounds good, it should be, the guy I rented the place from had a fire going when he was showing it. I think he was creating ambiance or something," I walk over to the back of the couch and grab a handful of clothes, as he takes off his outer layers and sweatshirt. His jeans and t-shirt are soaked, "Here, I do not know how well they will fit but at the very least they are dry."

"Thanks, Carly, but I really do not think your clothes will fit me," Henry says with a laugh, "I'm almost a foot taller than you."

I laugh because it's more obvious now that I am not wearing high heels that he is much taller than me.

"They are not my clothes," He gives me a curious look like I am giving him an ex's clothes as he takes them from me, "One of my clients is an athletic clothing producer and they sent me a thank you package for catching a major problem before the IRS. They must have assumed that I was still married or something, because they included a whole bunch of guys' clothes too. So, pick through it and see what works."

"Oh cool! Thank you for this," He picks up one of the flashlights and points down the hall to ask where to change. I direct him to the bathroom and watch him walk down. Even in the limited lighting, I can see how toned his back is with the shirt clinging to him. I am still thinking about it after he slips into the bathroom.

"Mommy, what are you looking at?" Remi shakes me out of my thoughts.

"What? Oh, nothing, honey," I am glad it's too dark for them to see my face getting red.

About a half hour later, the four of us are all warm in front of the fire Henry built. I have no clue what he did, but he pulled on levers and blew on something and put his head in to look up the chimney. It was all far more than I would have done, but I am glad he seemed to know what he was doing. The girls are under their blankets on the couch while Henry and I sit on the floor on either side of them. Remi is telling us a long-winded story of all the preschool drama going on. Just when she stops to take a breath and I am about to redirect the conversation, as to not bore Henry, but he beats me to it.

"So, what did Mckayla do after she found out that Noah buried her teddy bear in the ball pit?" I laugh because he sounds invested in her story. I shift, trying not to over analyze the situation. I am glad the girls feel so comfortable around him, because I am a nervous wreck. I am freaking out and trying to not text Amber or Lana. I would lose that battle if I was not trying to conserve battery on my phone.

Remi continues on with her story which basically ends with her and her friends having to sit in a friendship circle to discuss how we are kind to each other. I am barely listening because I cannot stop watching Henry take in the whole conversation.

The room comes to a little lull after Remi's vibrant storytelling.

"Do you want something to drink? Like an adult drink?" I ask. We had made hot cocoa with tons of marshmallows, thanks to the gas stove, but those are empty mugs on the coffee table now.

"Sure, why not, we are not driving anywhere any time soon," He replies. Suddenly, I panic wondering whether he will go to walk back to the farmhouse to sleep or stay here. It scares me how much I want the answer to be the latter. He stands up first and holds his hand out to help me off the floor. I put my hand in his and it feels electric, like I can feel his touch through my whole body. Once I am standing, our hands linger a second longer than required before we drop them to our sides. He follows me into the kitchen.

"Do you drink wine? I also have vodka or tequila. Sorry, I do not have any beer though," I am looking at my liquor cabinet and when he does not answer me, I turn back to him. He is staring at me with so much emotion on his face. It is the first time tonight we have been alone without the girls in the room.

"Carly..." he starts but trails off, "Carly, about last weekend..."

"No," I interrupt, "Henry, we can't right now. I am very happy you are here, because this storm and power outage had me low key freaking out. You have helped immensely tonight. So, we can't go down that road right now. We are locked into riding out this storm here together, so please, let's just act like last weekend did not happen. So, wine or no?"

He looks like he wants to say something, lots of somethings, but then I can see his face shift to agree with what I said and with a sad smile, he just says, "Wine would be wonderful."

I pour two glasses of red wine and hand him one. We walk back into the living room, he is leading. He stops just over the threshold and looks back to me. With his free hand, he puts a finger to his mouth to tell me to be quiet. I look around him at the couch to find both girls fast asleep at either end.

"Aww, I could tell they were working hard to stay awake to keep spending time with you. They adore you, and you are really good with kids, you know?" I say to him, as I set my glass on the table.

"Thanks, I have a bunch of nieces and nephews, biological and through friendships, I have always been around kids," He explains, "Plus they make it pretty easy. But are you really sure Millie is only seven?"

I laugh quietly so I do not wake them up, "I know right? I have counted the rings and confirmed seven years."

I move around to pick up Remi to take her back to their room, "I am going to put them in bed quickly, it should be warm enough in there with their comforters. Let me just take Remi back and I will be right back for Mil."

I start walking away with Remi when I notice him put his wine glass down on the table next to mine. Then he goes over and picks up Millie with ease and follows behind me. I just smile at the thoughtfulness.

We get the girls tucked in their beds, which is strange to have someone doing so with me. The room is not cold at all. I had opened the door while the fire was going hoping that heat would make its way in there. I shut the door behind us so that us talking in the living room would not bother them. Talking... I really hope we can just make it through the night without talking about last weekend. I start feeling the pull down again with the embarrassment of how I thought there was more between us than he wanted. He just wants to be friends, or just neighbors, acquaintances, whatever.

Henry goes over to the fireplace to feed it another log and I sit on the far end of the couch, with my back against the arm rest and my legs pulled up into my chest, facing where he is. I watch how carefully he puts the log in the right spot to not diminish any of the other logs that are already on fire. He stands up straight and stares at the fire for a while to watch his handiwork. From my seat, I can see the side of his face glowing red and orange from the flames. He looks so peaceful and so beautiful. I know guys are not supposed to be called beautiful or whatever patriarchy bullshit, but this man in my house at this moment is nothing other than beautiful. I am memorized.

After watching the newly added log for a bit, Henry slowly starts to turn back towards the couch. He catches me staring at him, with the flames now reflecting in his eyes. I do not even try to look away from him. He is a witch's spell of a man. I notice he is staring just as intensely right back at me.

160

"What?" I ask, shyly. The eye contact is too intense, and I am the first to break away. I look down and pick at my nail polish nervously.

"You look like an absolute goddess, especially with the fire dancing on your skin," He starts walking towards me. Even though I am not looking, I can tell he is still staring,

I have never been told anything like that. I feel those words in every way, from my heart to much lower. I cannot let myself get turned on by him, we are just friendly, nothing more.

I see his body reach the couch and expect him to sit down across from me, but he doesn't. When I look up to see what he is doing, I am met with his stare again.

"Henry," I say weakly. He is moving towards me still in what seems like slow motion. He does not say anything back until he is next to me and squats down to be at eye level. Our faces are so close that I can smell the wine on his breath.

"You are truly a goddess," he reaches a hand out and tucks it behind my neck, pulling me even closer so our foreheads are touching.

"Henry," I say again, I have lost the ability to come up with anything other than his name to say.

"My goddess," he whispers and before I can overthink the moment, his mouth is on mine.

Chapter 21

I t is a soft, slow kiss like Henry is worried about scaring me away. Then I open my mouth in response to him and that sets something off in him. His tongue breaks the barrier into mine and he deepens the kiss. His hand moves from the back of my neck up into my hair, and my arms find their way around his neck.

He moves up from the spot on the floor, without ever breaking the kiss. Everything in me is pulsing and wanting him. Right now, I want him near me, on me, in me. All of it. I can feel the need for him between my thighs. He is moving to pull himself over me. He breaks the kiss and I whimper a little. His gaze is smoldering with want and my nipples are instantly puckered knowing that it is me that he wants.

With one leg moving over me, he moves to place himself on top of me. He is holding himself up to keep his full weight off me, but when he kisses me again his hips come down and I can feel how badly he wants me. He is hard against my leg and the sweatpants I gave him to wear are doing nothing to hide it. I am desperate for more of him. I push my hips up against him and then there are only a few layers of clothes in between my pussy meeting his cock. They are like magnets gravitating towards each other.

When his hardness grinds against my center, he lets out a moan into my mouth. In response, he puts his hands back into my hair and pulls me in as he breaks from my mouth to kiss along my jawline. At my earlobe he sucks slightly and intentionally lets a breath out into the inner ear. Such a simple thing and I thought I was going to come from that alone, but then he moved to my neck.

My hands move around his back, up and under the t-shirt he is wearing. He sucks on a particularly sensitive spot between my neck and shoulder, I react with a jolt and my nails dig into his back quickly. His breath hitches, he liked that... noted. He comes back to my mouth with another feverish kiss as my hands play on the waistband of the pants on his back. As I get more of my hand up underneath the fabric, I can feel him more against me. His pelvis gives another good thrust into me, and I let out a little noise of pleasure, but then he is moving his weight off me to shift to lay more on his side. He has broken the kiss too with this. I pout at him which earns me a little laugh and another light kiss.

"You really are incredible, my goddess," Henry says while taking in our bodies lying together fully clothed still but reacting so clearly to each other. His hand is tracing the outline of my body, starting at my hip and moving up. As he moves up, he is pushing the hem of my t-shirt too. He reaches the swell of my breast, and his thumb moves away from the invisible line he has drawn up my side. It sneaks under my bra, and he is now tracing the bottom roundness. I am aching for him to touch more, he must see it in my face because he starts kissing me again, pushing his tongue in, hard. At the same time, his pointer finger moves to join his thumb, as he pushes my bra cup up completely, and the fingers work together over my nipple. My body jolts at the touch and I just want more of him. I reach my hands up and twine them into his hair. I pull playfully, but hard enough to make him pinch my nipple hard. I like that reaction, so I do it again and am rewarded with more playing.

I am so wet now I cannot even think about anything other than what it would feel like with him in between me thrusting into me. At this thought, I force the kiss harder and faster while pushing my chest into his fingers. His hands come off my breast and he moves the hand to be a flat palm on my exposed stomach. The want for him to keep that hand going south is almost more than I can take. As if he had been inside my mind, his hand goes closer to the elastic band around my waist. He reaches down farther, bringing his fingertips over my clothes not where I need him to touch me but around the side of it, down to my inner thigh. He works his fingers back up soft but with enough pressure to know he is there. His hand goes to the center, and he pushes the heel of his hand up against my clit. I lurch and gasp, breaking my mouth away from his. This makes him chuckle and he does it one more time with a similar response. His hand comes up to my head again to pull my face back towards him for a desperate kiss that is almost as effective as the hand against me. With our mouths put back together, his hand returns to my stomach and then begins even more of a descent.

I might burst with anticipation and want. I am not the only one either, I can feel his erection against my leg. I have an urge to help him with that. He begins playing with my waistband again, grabbing it to pull me into him, letting his finger tease underneath it but not going as far as I want. I am losing my mind, and I am desperate for him. I want to tell him what to do but I cannot think of any of the things Lana and I practiced, not in this state of mind. I am just about to beg him to touch me, when we hear the click of life returning to the household. As quickly as things were escalating, things have now ceased as the entire room lit up like a tanning bed.

The veil of darkness lifts and we are both staring at each other, silently begging the other to say something. Then words were unnecessary because we both started laughing. Henry slowly backs up from me, but he does not scurry to the other side of the couch. He picks up my legs and sits under them, then stretches them out over his lap. Ever so gently he moves his body towards where my breast is exposed. He grabs the bra cup, with a light flutter of his fingers on my still hard nipple before pulling the bra back down. Then he straightens out my shirt for me.

I sit up a little bit, just looking at him. I am not sure what to say right now. I am not totally sure what just happened. My self-doubt is starting to flood in faster than I can control it.

"Wow, okay, I am so sorry. I am not sure how that happened but I'm sorry, so sorry," I ramble.

"Oh my gosh, Carly, what are you sorry for? I am sorry if I pushed that too far, I don't know if I would've been able to stop if the lights did not come on so brightly," His face looks like something just clicked in his mind, "Oh god, I am an idiot. Your girls are here just down the hall and here I am groping you all over. I'm the one who is sorry."

"I'm sorry because you made it clear last weekend that you are not really interested in me. Obviously, the storm got to us, but I'm sorry, it can't happen again," I say, shaking my head.

"What?" Henry looks at me stunned and confused.

I take a deep breath, pushing through the nerves to say what I need to say, "I can't just be a hookup, Henry, not with you. Somehow in the brief time I have known you, I have developed feelings. I have tried to ignore them, but tonight, well I just couldn't help it. Since you are not interested, then I do not want to blur the lines."

Henry does not answer right away, but he leans towards me and cups my face in his hands. He kisses me deeply again. This is not fair, but I find myself wanting to take the last few bits I get from him. Then he surprises me completely.

"Carly, I have wanted you since the moment you blazed into my yard," He pauses to look into my eyes to make sure I am listening, "I tried staying away and not letting myself get sucked in, but I have failed. What just happened was not causal in any sense for me."

"Oh."

"Oh?"

"Yes, oh. I have no clue what that means for us, and I am afraid to dissect that right now. Because, as you mentioned, my girls are here and I am afraid I will not be able to stop, if it were to happen again. So, yes, oh."

"But you want it to happen again?" He is probing for confirmation, but I can tell by his look that he knows already.

"Is it going to happen again?" I ask, deflecting.

"Unless you pointedly tell me that you for certain do not want it to happen again, then it will most certainly happen again, and then some," his voice is husky with exhaustion and pent-up desire, "but when it is just the two of us."

Then before I can answer, he kisses me. Not the hungry emotion from earlier, but a kiss almost like a promise. He grabs a bunch of pillows to build a spot to lean on at the other end of the couch. Irrational disappointment strikes immediately once I realize he is moving away from where I am. Once he is settled in, he looks at me.

"Hey Carly," he says with a finger beckoning me to come closer to him. I oblige while scooping down to the floor to grab a blanket for him and press the remote for the lamp in the room to turn off. We are back in a mostly dark room with the fire going, but not completely dark anymore. When I get close enough, he grabs me by the waist, and I almost let out a yelp. He turns me around, so I am sitting in between his legs with my back against his chest. He pulls me in tight and I feel his chest bouncing up and down with amusement. He puts his lips to my temple, sweet and light, then moves his lips to my ear to whisper, "This is where you belong, in my arms."

I lay my head back on him and feel how tired I am. As I drift off to sleep with his arms hugging me from behind, I hear him almost silently say, "Goodnight, my goddess."

* * *

"Mommy, are you awake?" Remi's little voice says dangerously close to my face.

"Remi, what are you doing in my room this early?" I rasp out.

"Um, mommy, you're on the couch... with Henry. Why did I have to sleep in my bed if it was a slumber party?"

Slowly I start opening my eyes and gathering my bearings. I am indeed on the couch, and the heat behind me is definitely not coming from the back of the couch. Plus, there is an arm wrapped around my waist holding me close as the little spoon. Just as I fully confirm to my brain that Henry and I were just caught by my 4-year-old cuddling on the couch, I hear his breathing change. He's awake.

Remi notices this too, I can't see his face to know if he opened his eyes or something, but she knows somehow.

"Oh, hi, Remi."

"Hi, Henry. The lights are back on," she says like seeing me on the couch with a guy doesn't phase her at all, "Can I watch TV, mom?

"Sure, baby, why don't you go watch the TV in mommy's room?" I suggest. She seems to accept this and pads off down the hall.

Once she is out of ear shot and we hear the sounds of Bluey distracting her, I flip over to face him. I am not sure which direction this is going to go, but I am scared the answer is regret. Except I am taken by surprise instead. He is smiling sleepily with his eyes half closed.

"Good morning," he pulls me in closer to him, so my head is in the crook of his neck. His leg swings over me and he pulls my bottom half into him too. I can feel his morning greeting against my leg. Trying to not think about it, I sink into the embrace instead. I should get up before Remi comes back or Millie wakes up. What does Remi think about seeing me on the couch with him? What do I think about falling asleep with him on the couch? Shit, this is too much thinking before coffee.

"I can feel the gears turning too fast in that beautiful mind, you're freaking out inside, aren't you?" Henry says into my hair.

"Yes." I do not even try to lie.

"About Remi seeing us or about what happened last night?"

"Yes." I say again. He laughs at this. He starts to move to stand up, but as he does, he peeks down the hall to make sure it was empty. He has one hand on either side of me to hold him himself up as he moves over the couch to the ground. Except when he gets one foot on the ground, he is suspending himself over me and he stops. He carefully closes some of the space between us, just enough that I can feel my body crying out for him to touch me more. His lips meet mine for a slow, deep kiss before he lifts himself up and off completely. He saunters off to the bathroom.

I sit on the edge of the couch cushion for a moment. I am willing myself to stand up, but my legs may be jelly. Finally, they seem steady enough to go into the kitchen. I start a pot of coffee and stand there lost in thought while watching it drip. I hear Henry come into the room, but I do not turn around, I am still staring at the brewing coffee maker.

I can sense him coming closer and feel his arms wrap around me. He drops his head down and kisses my neck, "Stop overthinking. We will find a better time to talk about it, just the two of us."

My stomach flutters at him planning on having time with just us.

"But for right now, I promise to start behaving and keep my hands to myself until we can talk more," Henry says this but then he is spinning me around to face him. His lips find mine again for a hungry kiss and as he does, his hands explore under my shirt and play with the underwire of my bra. I let out an involuntary, quiet moan. He ends the kiss. While he straightens my bra and shirt, his smile looks purely devilish. "Okay, starting now. Sorry, I couldn't resist that last one."

That kiss shocks my system in all the best ways and it takes me a few beats to recoup, "Umm… coffee's ready."

He chuckles and moves away from me to fill the mug I put out for him. Much to my surprise, he grabs the second mug and pours coffee in it. He looks over at me to ask, "How do you take your coffee?"

"My coffee?" I stutter out. I am really not doing great conversationally this morning, "Oh… I like just a splash of oat milk creamer. I'll grab it."

"Nope, you sit at the table. I will get it and bring it over to you. If I make it wrong, feel free to yell at me so I know better next time."

I give him a raised eyebrow look but listen to his instructions.

"Next time?" I ask as he preps both coffees and returns the creamer to the fridge. He grabs both mugs, setting one in front of me very carefully. As he bends down to do so, he kisses the top of my head and then moves to his own chair.

"Yep, next time. I have no intention of this being the last morning coffee we share."

Chapter 22

❦

H enry is in the kitchen with me helping to clean up after our pancake breakfast. He has found little moments to subtly touch my shoulder or waist, even sneak a kiss when the girls went to wash their sticky hands. I am trying hard to not like this as much as I do. I also am not immune to a lot of other concerns. I always said that when I started dating again, I would keep it away from the girls' life until I was very sure it was serious, but here I am having sleepovers on the couch with my—well, I don't even know what to consider him, we have most certainly graduated from just being neighborly, but I do not want to assume that he is on board for the long haul.

The girls are looking out the front window. The wind has calmed down now, so they can see the fresh snowfall better. They have been asking to go outside since the moment they woke up and I have been pushing them to wait a little longer, so they do not wake up the entire neighborhood.

"Mom," Millie calls over to the kitchen, "When we go outside, can we use all the fallen branches for the arms of our snowman?"

"Those are way too big, you can't lift those," Remi says to Millie.

Henry and I give each other a confused look. We walk into the living room to check out what they are talking about.

With all the wind drifts stopped, we can see all the branches on the yard, plus it looks like an entire tree is going across the road between our houses going into Barb's front yard. I stretch my neck to see how far the tree went and am relieved to see that it is not touching their house.

"Oh shi—oot, that wind really made a mess out there," Henry remembers the tiny ears mid-word again, "I need to go over to the house and make sure none of the trees in the back or other side did any damage."

"No! Don't go!" Both the girls start to panic. They are already attached to Henry; I can see that clearly. It was nice playing house with him through this storm, too, too nice, but I need to be more cautious of involving the girls. I understand this was a crazy event of Mother Nature, but I need to figure out what this is before I allow any more nights like yesterday.

"I won't leave without saying goodbye, I owe you gals a big thank you for letting me come over last night and stay warm," Henry says, squatting down to their level.

"Okay..." the girls say solemnly. Henry gives them both a little squeeze on their shoulders before standing back up.

With all his snow gear back on, Henry heads out the door to go back over to the farmhouse. The girls are perched at the front window watching him go through the snow. I need something to cheer them up, so they are not moping until Henry gets back, if he is definitely coming back. He might come to his senses about getting involved with the single mom next door.

"Girls, what do you say that we get our snowsuits on and go build that snowman?" Their moods turn up instantly. There is cheering and Remi is running to the kitchen to hijack a carrot for their snowman.

We bundle up, then unbundle again when Remi realizes she has to pee. I am excited to see the girls have fun, but damn I hate being out in the snow. We start towards the center of the yard, moving slowly at first but then we find our footing in the heavy boots.

The girls go right to rolling snowballs for their snowman, or elephant—I am not sure what snow creature we decided on. I am looking at the tree in the middle of the road, this will definitely need to be removed before the road is plowed properly. I don't even know where to start on something like that. As if he was reading my mind, Henry is trekking down what I think is his driveway, even though the snow is the same height across the whole yard and driveway, except for where I could see the truck and just the top of the metal trailer. He is carrying a chainsaw and heading towards the tree.

I warn the girls quickly to stay where we are because Henry is using something dangerous to move the tree. I can imagine them seeing him and running over to where he is working. They both nod and go back to their attempts at a snowman, they are having difficulties getting the snow big enough for the base.

Within a few minutes of Henry starting the chainsaw, I see Bud coming out of his house geared up heading towards Henry. Barb is in the doorway and gives me a wave, she watches the girls playing for a moment and shuts the door with a smile. When I look over to where Henry and Bud are working, I see two more guys have joined them. I do not know their names but recognize them from the neighborhood. The four men make quick work of cutting up the fallen tree and moving it out of the street. They also moved the part that was in Bud's front yard, so he did not have to deal with it later. That all happened so quickly that it feels like it's only a few minutes later that they are now dispersing after gloved handshakes and pats on backs. Henry is walking back to the house and my stomach drops with envy as I see Barb welcoming Bud home. She puts her warm hands on his red face, and he gives her a quick kiss before they shut the door. It must be so nice to have a person and be someone's person.

"Whatcha looking at?' Henry says next to me. I am so startled by him that I fall into the snow. He laughs as he reaches a hand out to help me up.

"Where did you come from!? Last I saw you were up at your house!"

"You were watching me huh?" He pulls me in a little closer to speak low enough to avoid tiny ears, "Checking out my snow pants ass, huh? Did the abominable snowman lumberjack look do it for you? I will keep that in mind."

"Can I compare it to the shirtless lumberjack for research comparison purposes?" Did I really say that out loud? I must have because his eyes are on fire.

"Hmmm, I think I can make that happen," he winks at me. Then, his whole demeanor changes like a switch, and he turns towards the girls, "Do I get to help build this snow person?"

I can't even hear what they are saying because they are talking over each other, but it sounds along the lines of extremely excited. We spent the rest of the afternoon building something that resembles a snow creature, not sure which one we were aiming for still. We are heading inside once it is finished to warm up and get some hot cocoa.

As we reach the door, I hear a loud noise down the hill on the other side of Henry's house and driving into view is a huge snow plow clearing the snow off the road.

Henry looks over, he hears it coming too, "Guess I will be able to get on the road tonight to go back to my place."

The way he says it does not match the sinking feeling I have in my stomach about him leaving today. It feels like at any moment he will repeat the wedding and tell me it's better this way, then go back to just being the guy fixing up the house next door.

"Yeah, it appears like it." I try to hide any traces of my internal dialogue and give him a little smile. I follow Henry and the girls inside the house.

***

We have an early dinner with Henry so that he can get on the road before dark. He has a plow on the front of his truck, so getting out of the driveway is not tough for him. He unhooked the trailer to leave that at the farmhouse and avoid driving home with it. Home…

It suddenly feels strange that he is only an occasional visitor to the house next door, even if he does own it.

I watch as he makes it out of his driveway. He is only a few feet from the farmhouse before slowing down. My heart is beating rapidly wondering what he is doing, did he forget something at the farmhouse? Is he coming here to say that he can't leave and needs to spend another evening with us?

His truck turns towards Barb and Bud's house, where Henry proceeds to plow the snow from their driveway, including getting out to shovel the snow in front of the garage door. Then he leaves their driveway and comes to mine. My heart beats fast again. While I am trying to telepathically beg him to get out of the truck and come inside, he clears my driveway of snow just like he did across the street. Once it is finished, he catches me watching in the window and he gives me a wink before leaving the driveway. This time he really heads down the street and out of the neighborhood.

What did I expect? I am not sure. Logically, I know he had to leave, and it would not have been appropriate for him to stay at the house with the girls without extreme reasons, like last night. But I may finally be admitting to myself what I am feeling and that I do not want to let Henry go.

* * *

Henry: Hi, I just got home.

My heart flips when I see a message from the newly acquired phone number. I had asked him to let me know when he made it back safely. I thought he forgot because it has been awhile since he left. The girls are watching the rest of Beauty and the Beast that we never got to watch due to the power outage.

Me: Hi, thanks for letting me know! How were the roads?

Henry: Not too bad, but I took it slow just in case.

Me: Gotcha, glad you were able to make it home safely.

...

The three dots of him typing pop up and disappear a couple times before the message appears.

Henry: I'm happy to be safe but really not happy that I don't get to sleep with you in my arms again tonight.

I squeal. Like legit squeal with glee. The girls turn to give me a confused look.

"You okay, mom?" Millie asks, sounding half curious and half annoyed that I interrupted their movie.

"Sorry, baby, I'm okay. Go ahead and finish your movie. Once it's over, bedtime," I say, remembering to put on my mom-hat. They murmur something and turn back to the screen.

Me: It was nice... sorry about the 4-year-old alarm clock

Henry: She's fine, they are such fun kids! I really cannot remember the last time I played in the snow just for fun.

Me: That was so much fun, even if you tried giving the snowperson boobs. LOL

Henry: I may look like a grownup, but it's all a facade, I have the mind of a teenage boy sometimes.

Me: I must be a teenager too then... It made me laugh my butt off.

Henry: Well, if we are both teenagers at heart, should I take you to the homecoming game so we can make out under the bleachers for our first date?

Holy shit! First date! Okay, I need to play it cool here, even though I want to tell him yes to anything.

Me: First date? Hmmm... I don't remember getting asked out.

Henry: Good point.

Good point? That's it? There are not any typing dots or anything like he is going to say more. He is going to be the death of me with the mixed signals. Fine, two can play that way.

Me:So, I guess I do not have a date... perhaps it's better that way.

I instantly regret sending that. What if he takes that poorly and not as a joke? We had talked about that night at the wedding a little more this morning and he told me that he chickened out. We even joked a little about that phrase, however, I still feel like he was leaving something out. Maybe a recent breakup or something. The three dots pop up.

Henry: Disagree. That's not accurate.

Me: What isn't?

Henry: Both. You do have a date on Friday night. And it would not be better that way. You are too irresistible, there is no way in hell I would be capable of walking away again.

Henry: That was not my best moment.

Me: Hope you don't go running when you realize you are building me up higher than I actually am.

Henry: Not a chance. You are stunningly beautiful, you have a huge heart, and you are the best mom to those girls.

Me: Thank you. <3

Henry: So, is that a yes then?

Me: To what?

Henry: You are going to make me work for it here, aren't you?

Me: 100%.

Henry: Okay... then I have something very important to ask you.

Henry: Carly, my beautiful goddess, would you honor me by accompanying me on a date this upcoming Friday evening? I would be the luckiest person in the entire restaurant to have you on my arm.

Me: I would love to.

Me: Even though I was kinda into the bleachers idea... I was even thinking about letting you get to second base... third if you gave me your letterman's jacket.

Henry: *mentally scouring my parent's house trying to remember where my high school jacket is* ...but then I remember that my letter is for bowling and have a feeling that might take me back a base.

Me: The teenager half of me is trying really hard not to make a comment about bowlers knowing how to put their fingers in the holes... Must. Be. An. Adult.

Henry: HAHAHA... Carly, I did not expect that from you! You never fail to surprise me.

Me: I hope that is a good thing! I'm looking forward to Friday.

Henry: Me too. It will be the only thing I can think of until then.

Me: Gotta get the girls to bed, good night, Henry.

Henry: Tell them goodnight for me, and goodnight to you, my goddess.

I have a date with Henry! I have a date in like 5 days with Henry! My face hurts from smiling right now. I need to say, well type, it out loud or I'll burst. I change my text message chains and click on Lana.

Me: Hey, hope you and the kids were all good during the storm. We were good. Got snowed in with no power last night. With Henry.

Lana: Hi, we were good, just bored kids, mad that the wifi wasn't working. And EXCUSE ME?? Please elaborate on the Henry part. Was I right about his eggplant??

Me: Lana! I can tell you that he is a very good kisser, and we have a date scheduled on Friday...

Me: If you want to know about the eggplant, I have more investigating to do. Even though it greeted me on full salute this morning and through clothes I was not disappointed. For more information, you'll have to meet me for lunch tomorrow!

Lana: Holy shit! I need to know exactly how it got to the point of you being that close!! That man is an absolute stud. Peppers at noon work?

Me: That works! See you then... and remind me to tell you about the kitchen make out session this morning.

Lana: UGH!! Killin' me!

And the next day we are at Peppers, and I tell her the whole thing. By the end of the story, I am in disbelief that it all really happened to me, and Lana is speechless. I am still waiting for the other shoe to drop. The more I analyze what happened, the more I am certain that it was a fluke.

After I leave Peppers, I stop over to Amber's house since she is still on maternity leave. I tell her the whole story. She already knew the wedding part. I had told her about that when I called to tell her about meeting Riley.

I am starting to see the balance between having Amber and Lana both to lean on. Lana helps me be more impulsive and push my boundaries, within reason. Amber is the voice of reason and a true sounding board. Amber and I don't talk much about sex, especially not in depth about her and Paul's bedroom life. I think the story about Tim was the most in depth I have ever been about my sex life, but it is also the most adventurous I have ever been. A part of me feels more complete with my childhood best friend supporting me on one side and a new friend to help me bridge into this new chapter. They both are helping me to come back stronger.

Chapter 23

At least twice a day every day leading up to Friday, I almost text Henry to cancel. I am trying to not have expectations, or more so, not wonder what Henry's expectations are. The snowstorm slumber party got pretty heated, and I know it would have gone further if the lights did not come on and the girls weren't asleep down the hall. There are no kids around tonight.

It's almost time to go. Henry is picking me up in about 15 minutes. He insisted on driving me, since is not telling me where we are going. When I asked how I should dress, he said, 'Nice, not casual, but not really fancy either."

I still have no clue what that was supposed to mean. I opted for a black pleated satin maxi skirt with a dark purple blouse that gave enough cleavage to stay on the classy side, but also slightly sexy. I frost the outfit with a simple bar necklace and matching earrings, plus a couple bracelets. I had them on both wrists, but they reminded me of handcuffs. Which then started my mind down the gutter of what kind of non-criminal activities could involve handcuffs. I finished the outfit off with a pair of suede stilettos with a scallop cut in a purple almost spot on to the blouse.

I give myself one last look in the mirror. I do a little spin and love the way the skirt circles around and out. I look up from my skirt to check the rest of the outfit.

"Oh shit!" I say out loud to the empty house. I still have a curler in the back of my hair. I have no clue how I managed to miss that. I am scrambling to fix it and work the curl out with my fingers to match the rest of my head. I get the last strand done and I hear a knock at the door.

"Coming!" I yell through the house, as I stuff random things I might need tonight in my purse. I need to calm down and look cool before I let Henry see me. I stop in the hallway right before where I know I am visible from the doorway. Breathe in, breathe out. I have to center myself before I go any farther. It only takes a couple seconds before the frazzled feeling is gone.

I take a step out of the hallway and turn towards the door. My heart dances as I open the door. He is wearing black pants with a long black coat buttoned up with a simple blue plaid scarf tucked in around his neck. Wow, he is handsome. He dresses up so nicely, but still nothing compares to him dressed down working around the yard. Though I bet completely dressed down to no clothes at all might compare...

"Hi," is all I manage to squeak out, bringing myself to the man in front of me instead of the version of him I was creating in my mind.

"Hi, you look beautiful," he replies. He grabs my jacket out of my hand and holds it out for me to slip in. Such a minor gesture, but it makes me want to melt, "Shall we go?"

"We shall," my brain and speaking abilities are finally on the same wavelength, "And where are we going?"

He grins boyishly but does not answer. Instead, he offers an arm for me to walk down the pathway with him. I loop my arm in his. We start walking, then I stop abruptly.

There is a sleek black sedan in the driveway. It was sporty, but practical. I am not great with cars, but I think it is a Mercedes. I had expected to see his truck in the driveway. Did he borrow a car for our date to seem fancier?

He stops with me and follows my gaze.

"I figured the dirty, old truck was not the best option for tonight," he explains.

"Did you borrow a car just for our date?"

"No, this is mine," he says, "I have the truck for projects like the house next door or when I am working on projects in my own house, or I need the plow or trailer. This is my normal day-to-day car, even though I think I prefer the truck. I work in the city, and this is so much easier to park. I wouldn't want the truck blocking anyone's driveway, now, would I?"

He gives me his devilish look and it breaks the nerves a little more. I laugh at this and say, "No you do not. And I can't have other crazy women coming out yelling at you, which turns into you taking them on mysterious dates."

"Crazy women would not get a date, I promise," His eyes locked with mine, "I only ask out the powerful goddess that scolded me and then surprised me by infiltrating my mind 24/7. And just to be clear, she is you."

Before I can try to say anything, he puts his hands on both sides of my face and meets my lips with his. The kiss is so intentional. I can feel that he meant those words through his lips. Whether or not I believe that it is true, he makes me want to believe it.

He breaks the kiss but keeps his hands on my face. He gently pulls me forward and kisses my forehead before dropping his hands to his side. The hand closest to me effortlessly finds mine and his fingers interlace mine.

"We better get going, we don't want to miss our reservations."

He leads me out to the car, still not giving me any more information than that. When we reach the car, he opens the passenger side door for me to get in. After I do, he carefully shuts the door. In the couple seconds that he is walking around to the driver side, I try to take in all that I am feeling. I have never had a first date quite like this. Granted this was a first date with someone that has had his tongue down my throat and his hands on my boobs, plus met my children. This was not a typical first date by any means. I decide to just go with what feels right tonight. I will not obsess over what order things "should" go. This is different from my last first date. I never intended to have anything serious with Tim. It never felt like our connection would have taken a more serious role. However, here with Henry, I can see how he would fit into my life, mostly because he has organically done so in many ways. The most surprising part of it all was that I wanted that.

Henry sat down in the driver's seat and backed out of the driveway. His hand reaches over the center and finds mine like they are magnets drawn together.

"So, how was your day?" Henry asks me as we ease into small talk for the drive. It is natural like we chat about our days every day.

We chat for about 10 minutes before we slip into a comfortable silence. I do not feel required to fill the silence with him like I would have with Jake. Silence with Jake always felt like a judgement or a punishment. It was a tool he used to make me stew in my head about what was wrong with me, or he would just stay silent and ignore me whenever I spoke to him. Only if talking to each other was his idea were we allowed to, otherwise it was not worth his time. This is different. It is a peaceful silence.

A couple minutes later, we pulled into a parking lot that I know well.

I turn to Henry and ask, "Are we going to Pacino's?"

"Oh, wow, where did that restaurant come from?" Henry cues the theatrics, "Well since we are here and it is your favorite restaurant, then I guess we will stay for dinner."

"How did you know that it is my favorite?"

"You told me," He turns to look at me with amusement all over his face, "At the wedding, we were talking about how good the gnocchi they were serving was. You mentioned that they were almost as good as your favorite Italian restaurant..."

He gestures to the building in front of us. I had completely forgotten about that part of our conversations that night, but he did not. He remembered and he brought me here because I said I liked it. Pacino's is one of the busiest Italian places in the whole city. I realize something at that moment, and I jarringly turn back to him.

"Are we getting take-out? That is the only way we can get dinner here. Reservations have like a 6-week lead time, and you only asked me out Monday." I am certainly confused and frazzled. He mentioned reservations earlier, but he must have something else planned and we are taking food from here to-go.

While I sit there stunned, Henry is laughing at me, like full chest laughing. He just shakes his head and gets out of the car. He walks around to my side to open the door. He offers me his hands.

"Come on, Carly. Let's go have some dinner," I take his hand, still wondering what is going on. People sell reservations to this place on Facebook Marketplace, it is impossible to sneak in without one. There is a whole lottery system for getting a table from cancelled reservations. He pulls me up by the hand until I am standing right in front of him, closely. He puts an arm around my waist and pulls me in closer. "The look on your face right now is so sexy and a whole lot of fun. Remind me to surprise you a lot, I like this."

He kisses me deeply before I can even respond. He breaks the kiss and starts to turn but I pull him back to me.

"If I forget to tell you, I had a really great time tonight," I say quoting the movie Pretty Woman, then I give him another kiss.

"Okay, Vivian," he says, referencing Julia Roberts' character in the movie. I am shocked and I must look it. "That is my mom's favorite movie, I have seen it a million times."

He's laughing as he takes my hand and loops it through his arm to escort me to the entrance. The smell of garlic is strong as we walk in, but incredible. I am reveling in the atmosphere when we make it to the hostess. She looks like she could not even be out of high school yet, but handling the waiting guests like she was born to do so. She looks right over to us, and a smile breaks out on her face. She whispers something to the second hostess that just walked back from seating people.

"Uncle Henry! You're here! I was so excited when I saw your name on the VIP list tonight," the girl runs over and gives Henry a huge hug.

"Franny-pants, look at you running the show up here tonight, where's your mom tonight?"

"She took Vinny to his hockey tournament in Hartford, so they are letting me take care of the front tonight. I have your table all ready for you, this doesn't look like your normal business dinner, Uncle Henry," she says looking at me with a big smile.

"Oh my god, I am being rude. Franny, this is Carly. Carly, this is Franny Pacino—"

"Uncle Henry, please!" she gives him a look that could kill.

"Sorry, this is Francesca Pacino, my beautiful goddaughter," Henry corrects himself. I am overwhelmed and excited by this information. Henry knows the family that owns my favorite restaurant.

"It's so nice to meet you, Carly. Since I am not three anymore," she shoots a look at Henry, "everyone just calls me Frankie."

"It's so nice to meet you too!"

"We are super busy tonight, so I will get you guys set up at your table before my dad comes out to see the line building up." Frankie grabs two menus off the hostess stand and leads us over to a table along the wall. It is in a perfect spot to be slightly tucked away from the mass crowd.

"Shannon will be your server tonight, she'll be right over with water and bread to start," Frankie says like she probably has a hundred times already tonight. She sets down the menus and smiles again, "I'll let Daddy know that you are here, and with a very pretty date. I am sure he'll be around soon."

With that she turned on her heels and headed back up front. I look at Henry, still trying to place all the pieces of the puzzle.

"So, the daughter of the owner of my favorite restaurant is your goddaughter?" I lead with this question.

Henry laughs with a smile that fully reaches his eyes, "Yes, she is my oldest godchild."

"Oldest, how many do you have?"

"Four. One of my nephews, plus I have a core group of friends from college, there are 5 of us guys in total. They have all gotten married and had multiple children, who all call me Uncle Henry, and godfather to three of them, including Franny."

"So, Frankie's dad is—" I trail off.

"Dominic Pacino, 3rd generation owner of this very restaurant. And my college roommate." Henry just shrugs at this tidbit. "So, when you mentioned that this was your favorite, I stored it away in my back pocket for when I stopped getting in my own way and asked you out finally."

"Wow, just wow," I start to say, "I am in awe of this all right now. You are full of surprises, aren't you, Henry Reid?"

"I sure hope so, because it'll get really boring really quick if I use them all by an hour into our first date," Henry jokes and I can't help but laugh with him.

Our server, Shannon, comes up to the table at that point. Henry orders us a bottle of wine and we agree on an appetizer to start. All the nerves I had felt are practically gone and I am enjoying this moment with him. We chit-chat about details about ourselves, nothing intense or deep though.

"So, how are things coming along with the house?" I ask him after he asked me about how I like working from home.

"Good, now that the weather has started to turn, I have been focusing a lot more on the inside. It is in pretty good shape in there, much to my surprise. It is definitely outdated, and the furniture must be over a hundred years old. I am going to have an antique dealer come out soon to give me an idea of what I have in there."

"That's so cool. I always wondered what it looked like in there. I think I imagined more of a haunted mansion with floors missing and cobwebs everywhere."

"Trust me, I did too. There were definitely plenty of cobwebs, but structurally good. I am getting to the point where I need to bring in outside help, like an electrician to check the wiring, a plumber to check the pipes, a realtor to access the value of the property, and so on." Henry makes a gesture with his hand making it seem like the list was endless.

"That's a lot to go into it. So, a realtor? Does that mean you plan on selling the house?" I ask him. I figured that would be the case since he owns a house already, but it is still nearby. It will be disappointing to look over and see someone else in that yard, but it does not mean that Henry and I can't still see each other.

"I'm leaning that way. The house does not hold great memories for my mom, so I don't want to hold on to something that may upset her. But speaking of the house, Carly, there's something I need to tell you," Henry takes a deep breath, "If I decided to sell, ther—."

"Reid, who let you in here?" A big booming voice interrupted his sentence. I look over in the direction of the voice. As a round Italian guy comes towards us. Henry stands up and is about 4-5 inches taller than him. They meet with a big guy hug. You know, where they shake hands while hugging.

"Frankie told me you were here with a pretty date," he looks over at me. He is handsome with dark features. Not to stereotype but he seriously looks like an actor in Sopranos. He grabs my hand and places a kiss on the back of it, not in a creepy way. "And she was not wrong. Hello there, I'm Dominic Pacino, welcome to my restaurant! Sorry, you're stuck with the legal department all night."

I laugh at this and add, "Well, he's stuck with accounting, so it's probably even. It's so nice to meet you, I'm Carly Kennedy."

Dominic looks pleased that I joined in the joking around. He gives me a hug, which is warm and inviting. I have seen him walking around greeting tables when I have been lucky enough to dine here before, but never a greeting like this.

"Thanks for getting us in tonight, Dommy," Henry says.

"Bro, you know you always have a table here. Unless Taylor Swift is in town, then it goes to her, or Frankie would murder me with her Swiftie friends. Even though it might be worth it to see you actually bring a date in."

Henry's cheeks turn a little crimson.

"Does he bring all his lady friends in here to impress them?" I ask, which makes Henry blush a little more.

"No, you're the first one. Business associates and coworkers, yes, but someone special, never." Dominic outs Henry.

"Oh, is that right, very interesting," I say to Dominic, but I am staring at Henry.

"This place and these people are very personal to me. But you brought me into your house and let me around your girls, so I wanted to show you a piece of my family," Henry says while returning the stare down.

"Hmm, well this is a different side of you, Reid," Dominic said in a serious tone, "I like it. I wish Sonya was here tonight to see this, she'd get a kick out of it. Sonya is my wife; she went to college with us as well. Poor Reid had to put up with us constantly canoodling in the dorm room."

"And unfortunately, they still haven't learned how to keep their hands off each other."

"Not denying it. Twenty-some years married and she is still one hot mama!" Dominic's smile while talking about his wife is so sweet, "Alright, you two, I have to get back in the kitchen. Don't leave without dessert! Sonya made your favorite tiramisu when she heard you were coming in."

"Yeees," Henry said dramatically, his eyes rolling back a little. I let out a laugh, "Wait until you try it and then tell me if you disagree."

Dominic laughed and headed back towards the kitchen. As he walks away, Shannon is back with our appetizer and wine. The rest of the night is a series of food, wine and lots of laughter. It is a perfect date.

Chapter 24

⟨⟨⟨⟩⟩⟩

Henry is not wrong about the tiramisu, it is incredible. We say our goodbyes to Dominic and Frankie before heading back to the car. Henry opens my door and lets me in again before coming back around to his side.

"Carly, I enjoyed sharing this piece of me with you," he said as he started the ignition.

"I had a great time tonight. I think I even managed to not fangirl about meeting the Pacino family after so many years of coming here!"

Henry gives a throaty laugh and shakes his head, "You did great, I had no clue, and I was staring at you all night."

"Stop, you are so flirty," I say to mask how gooey that made me feel. Henry starts the drive back towards my cottage, but as soon as the car starts going forward, his hand finds mine in the dark.

On the drive, we talk mostly about our dinner. He tells me a little more about the guys he and Dominic are close to, including their wives and kids. It sounds like they get together often, and the kids all play, while the adults hang out.

At my house, he gets out to open the door for me again. Except this time when I stand up, he does not pull me in for a kiss again. I thought we had a good time, but he is acting a little weird right now.

He walks me up onto the porch and we stop at the front door. I turn towards him, but I am avoiding meeting his eyes. I am looking at the keys in my hand, fidgeting with them. His finger finds my chin to gently bring my face up to his. When I am looking at him, he does not take his finger off my face, instead he traces along my jawline. He makes it to the sensitive spot behind my earlobe and it sends a shiver down my body. I meet his gaze again, which, much to my surprise, looks a little nervous. I know for a fact that my face is not hiding my nerves.

His finger leaves my ear and traces along my cheek to my lips, where he switches out the pointer finger for his thumb. It is sandpapery as he drags it along my bottom lip with a little more pressure now. I feel all the heat in my body bubbling and since I do not know what to do with that, I try to break my eyes away from him, but he doesn't let me. The rest of his hand comes up to my chin to pull my gaze back to his. He does not say a word. He just keeps exploring my face with his fingers. After my lips, he goes back to the pointer finger to trace a similar path on the other side of my face.

I am soaked just thinking about how those fingers made me react to them on my face, I can only imagine what they could accomplish elsewhere. Once his finger has finished its path, his hand snakes around to the back of my head. He twines his fingers through my hair and pulls me in so close that I can feel his breath on my tongue.

"You are so beautiful," he whispers. I shift under his gaze and closeness with my uncomfortableness with the compliment. He puts his other hand around to my lower back to hold me in place, like he fears that I will bolt. That is fair, it has crossed my mind in these last few seconds.

"Thank you," I squeak out. It almost does not sound coherent. He has a spell on me at this point and I do not know how I will function when he takes his hands back.

"Carly," he says my name in a husky, strained tone, "I should go."

He unlaces his hands from my hair and slides his other hand off my back. There is a sudden breeze of cold air as he takes a step back, away from my body.

"What?" All my self-doubt tendencies start bubbling to the surface. I must have heard him wrong, because there is no way he can leave me like this on my doorstep. He has not even kissed me since we got out of the car, and he is saying goodbye. I start to get annoyed at this, at him. "Well, okay if you want to leave then go right ahead."

"Carly—" he starts to say with apologetic eyes.

"Henry, stop," I hold up a hand, "I thought we had a good time tonight, but maybe you're just getting a friend vibe, or even temporary neighbors vibe."

"Carly, it's definitely not that," he reaches for my hand, but I cross my arms with my hands out of his reach before he can.

"It is 8:30 on a Friday night after a nice dinner. I had hoped you would come in for at least a glass of wine, but you look like a retreating puppy dog. You look sad and guilty, for what? For not getting the same feelings from our time together?"

He breaks into the conversation, "Carly, there are things we still need to talk about."

"And there are things I need to tell you too, Henry. We can't know each other's life story after one snowstorm and one date. But you are clamming up and that is not what I need—I need someone who will step up and tell me what they want." I do not know where this is coming from. It feels like the out-of-body power I had when I yelled at him for blocking my driveway. I don't even know why I was getting so upset at him, other than I had looked forward to his flirty texts all week about how he can't wait to make out again, or how he enjoyed wrapping me in his arms. They seem like just words now.

I turn away from him with a huff and put my keys in the lock. He has not moved since pushing away from me. I push the door open and before I walk through, I turn back to him and say with a strong confidence I did not know I had, "Thank you for a nice dinner. Don't worry about it, we can still be cordial when we see each other outside. It's fine, Henry. Goodnight."

Inside the house, the warm air feels inviting compared to the coldness of the outdoors and of this conversation.

I swing the door shut, but to my surprise it does not close. Henry's foot is jammed in the door keeping it from closing, followed by the rest of him entering through the door. He has fire in his eyes now. I do not know if he is mad or something else completely, but the heat is unmissable. Before I can say anything, he turns to back me up towards the door with an arm on either side of my head. The door slams shut with the force of his hands.

"What the hell do you think you are doing?" I demanded, returning his stare with an anger of my own. I may not know what his face is saying but I know that I am both turning and seeing red now. I have more to say but am silenced by his lips crushing into mine with a hungry force. I do not think I have ever been kissed like this before. There is pain and passion interlaced with the force of it. I want to punch him and undress him at the same time. I am pissed off even more now. I push him off me.

"What the hell do you think you are doing?" I repeat like he did not hear me the first time. This time my voice is breathy and tense.

"It's not fine, Carly," he says sharply.

"So, are you just proving a point here? Because you stopped making sense a while ago," I challenge him.

"It is not fine," he continues like I did not just ask him a question, "I do not want to be just cordial with my temporary neighbor. I will not let that door close behind you with me on the other side without making it very clear that I do not see you as just a friend."

"Then what do you want, dammit," I am practically yelling at him, tears are stinging my eyes from being so mad, "Because I am not looking to be toyed around with. You're hot then you're cold and I cannot keep up with you. I need a man that knows what the fuck they want."

I stare him down with this declaration and I can practically feel his skin boiling. At least a minute passes of neither of us speaking, just locked eyes waiting for the next move.

I break first and look down towards my shoes, then in a more defeated tone I say, "I think you should leave."

I expect him to back away and let me move away from the door for him to leave, but that does not happen. One of his hands does move off the door and grabs under my neck, almost around my throat. His hand pushes up to force my eyes to meet his, when I meet his glare, he does not let go of my throat. His hand is not tight enough to hurt me or make it difficult to breathe, but there is possessiveness in the pressure. This should scare me, but it does something else completely to me. I am conflicted and even more angry by how I want to show him how wet he is making me right now, but at the same time I want to push him outside and slam the door with all this adrenaline.

"Look me in the eyes and tell me that you want me to leave, and I'm gone," his voice is demanding and forceful. He moves forward to press his body against mine. His hand adds the slightest bit more pressure around my neck and I have to bite my cheek a little to keep from letting out a noise that would show him that I like it. This is not anything I have experienced before to know, which adds an extra layer of conflict. "If you want me off you and me away from you, tell me to go."

I stay still not breaking the connection but also not saying a word. I have used all my words, and I was not ready to stop this. I want to further challenge him. It is electrifying to feel his entire body react to me, to this emotional hunger. He is close enough that I can feel how hard he is against my stomach. I never imagined that he had this domineering side to him. But I want it... I want to let him control what happens next and just submit to him.

"I am giving you three seconds to tell me to leave before I just take the answer I want." His hand around my neck loosens a little and I don't let him see my disappointment, but he must sense it somehow because he lets out a single laugh from his throat.

"Three." His hand tightens up again, just a little. I react this time by moving my chin up and closing my eyes at the ecstasy of the pressure. His hand forces me back roughly. "Eyes on me, Carly."

"Two." Even tighter and his body presses harder into mine, pushing me roughly against the wooden door. "Tell me to leave now before this goes any further."

I focus on the center of his eyes with a look of both anger and desire. I answer him with a whisper, "One."

Chapter 25

⎯⎯ ❧❦❧ ⎯⎯

A s soon as the word escapes my mouth, his lips are on mine. I am still royally pissed off and want to be mad at him, but my body is driving right now. His hand moves away from my neck and is replaced by his lips moving down. I can feel his warm tongue licking where it is probably a little red from his hand.

I move my hands out to grab him but, in a blink, he grabs both wrists in one hand to pin them against the door above my head. His body is still pressed against me, I could not go anywhere, if I wanted to. I let out an exasperated grunt at my lack of movement and he laughs against my jawline. He is enjoying watching me squirm. He squats down a little then stands back up pushing harder against me, as he does, I can feel his cock push against my clit even through all of our clothes. I let out a little gasp which is rewarded by him doing it again before loosening the force he has pushed against me.

With his free hand, he reaches behind me at the elastic waistband of my skirt. He easily dips his hand into the skirt and his sandpaper palm is on my bare ass next to the thong I decided on for tonight. He groans when he realizes that he is not touching fabric, but his hand and my cheek are skin-to-skin. His hand moves back to the band of my skirt, and he yanks it down. It easily floats to the ground with far more gentleness than we are giving each other right now. His hand is back on my ass cheek, and he grabs hard enough for me to let out a little sound. Which he seems to like because he pushes his length against the front of the thong in response.

My arms are getting sore from being above my head, but I do not care. There is not a chance that I am breaking the trajectory of this. I have never been with a man like this, even with Tim it was hot and really good sex, but not anything out of the ordinary. But this is different, Henry was fully clothed still, and I was still mostly clothed, but it felt primal. I want him to use my body for his pleasure. I want him to tell me exactly what to do. And I have a feeling that is exactly what he likes.

He brings his fingers over to where my thong is wedged between my ass and he frees the thin material with his hand cupped over the center. He is not touching my entrance there, but the heat of him over it makes me moan slightly. The sound I am making deepens as his hand moves forward to cover my bare pussy with his entire hand. He pulls his middle finger through my folds, and I push towards the sensation. He takes his finger away to return it to the rest of his hand still cupped over where I want him to touch.

"Fuck, Carly, you are so wet for me," he says into my ear. He takes my hands down from above my head and places them on his shoulders. The relief in my muscles causes me to push towards him again. He nips at my earlobe and says with a warm breath, "So eager, so ready."

With no warning, he pushes a finger inside of me and I gasp loudly. The sudden intrusion nearly makes me come apart right there. But as quick he is to enter me; he quickly withdraws his finger and this time his entire hand leaves its spot in my panties. He is teasing me. He got me angry, then took control by seduction, and now I am getting mad again. Henry must see it in my face, because he laughs at this.

"There she is, my powerful goddess," he says to me as he puts the finger that was just inside me to his mouth and sucks, "A goddess that tastes so good."

"Are you just going to tease me all night, or are you going to fuck me already?" I challenge him with anger from earlier finding its way forward again, mixed with my need for him. He pulls us away from the door and smacks a hand on my ass cheek just hard enough to sting, before pushing me back against the door again.

"Such a dirty mouth," he says before grabbing my face and kissing me hard, "If you don't want to do it my way, all you have to do is look me in the eyes and tell me to stop. Then we can stop and have some nice missionary sex, or is that what you want? Another boring guy to jackhammer into you grunting while sweating all over you, not bothering to worry about whether or not you are taken care of?"

His description hits so close to what I have had in the past. Words are not forming in my throat, so I just shake my head to say no. I really do not want that, I want whatever Henry wants to give me and I want to give him whatever he is going to let me give him.

"I need to hear you say it, Carly, do you want to switch gears and have basic vanilla sex with me?"

"No," My voice catches in my dry throat, but I look him straight in the eyes, "I want you to ruin me, use me, take me."

He groans with pleasure, "Good girl."

His hand moves back to my center, but from the front this time. He pushes aside my thong and slips a finger back into the wet folds. His mouth takes mine in a deep kiss, our tongues wrapping around each other. He puts a finger inside of me again. He pumps it in and out a few times before he adds a second finger. I moan at this sensation. I can feel how tight I am around his rough fingers. He repeats the pumping slower this time, giving my body a chance to adjust then he moves faster. Suddenly, his thumb reaches up to rub my clit and I start to see stars. I am going to come quickly if he keeps doing this. Almost as though he can hear my thoughts, his fingers move out of me, and his entire hand is away from the only place it should be right now.

"No, please don't stop, I am so close," I whimper from the edge I am on.

"I know you are," he says back, pleased with how undone I am. I move my hand down, determined to get my orgasm, even if I must do it myself. But my hand snatched away and brought up over my head. "You don't touch yourself unless I tell you to. Understand?"

I nod quickly.

"Now, do you want me to help you come?"

"Yes, yes." I beg.

"I think the words you are looking for are yes, please." He says while gently caressing a finger over the front of the thong, a touch that makes me buck with need.

"Yes, please," I beg.

"You really are a good girl," He smiles and kisses me hard while pushing the heel of his hand against my clit. I nearly scream, I am so damn close to coming apart. "I want to taste the first time you come for me. Do you want that?"

"I do want that." I say with desperation, but he gives me a waiting look before I realize what he is waiting for, *"please!"*

He let go of the arm above me as he kneels in front of me. He starts by grabbing my ankles and moving his hands up slowly until he reaches my waist. He loops a finger on either side of the soaking wet thong and pulls to the ground as I step out of it. I am standing against the door still wearing my blouse and stilettos. I had managed to take my jacket off earlier before Henry's foot stopped the door. Right now, my entire bottom half is fully exposed to him.

Henry takes one of my legs and drapes it over his shoulder, which opens me up right in front of him.

"You are so perfect," he whispers as his fingers slide through my wetness again. He already has me so close to the edge that I jump at this feeling. Those fingers come back to open even more for him. He stares at my pussy for a beat before I feel the warmth of his mouth in front of me. His tongue starts at my entrance as he gives me a long lick towards the front. I make a noise of approval and of need for him to give me more.

I can still feel his breath on me when he says, "I want you to scream my name with you fucking come, Carly."

And with that his full mouth is on me sucking and exploring with his tongue. He fucks me with his tongue and takes more full-length tastes, but his tongue keeps flitting over my clit, not staying to play. I am so close to the edge, and he is keeping me there on purpose. Finally, after what felt like forever, his mouth comes over my sensitive spot and his tongue flicks with precision while he thrusts two fingers inside me.

"Yes, Henry! Oh my god, Henry. Harder, don't stop!" And then it hits, and I am almost instantly catapulted over the edge; my entire body is screaming through the orgasm. I keep yelling his name as my body is convulsing and shaking involuntarily. He stays there licking and sucking right through the climax and as I come back down. Once my body is still, he gently kisses the soft skin above my clit and sits back against his shoes to look up at me.

I am still in a state of euphoria. He gently takes my leg off his shoulder and helps guide it to the floor before standing up.

"Carly, that was so fucking hot. God, it should be illegal to taste that good." And like he wants to share the secret he kisses me hard. I can taste myself in his mouth which reminds me what just happened and while I just came down from a mind-blowing orgasm, I felt the tingle between my thighs wanting more of him. I reach forward and start undoing his belt buckle, wanting to have access to him. I feel his dick twinge to tell me that he wants it, but Henry pulls my hands away. My face falls instantly, I cannot figure out why he doesn't want me to touch him. Is there something wrong with me? Self-conscious Carly is creeping up and I start to feel a little panicky. I am so far out of my comfort zone here. I feel the reality of it all creeping up like the blush up my neck to my face.

"Carly, baby, what's wrong? I'm sorry, did I hurt you or something?" Henry softens immediately and puts my face in his hands. As soon as he does this, I lose what little control I had left and the tears that were threatening to fall now do. He scoops down to grab my skirt off the floor and holds it out for me to step into. I cannot tell if he is doing this so he can get out the door that I am still backed up against or if he just does not want to look at me naked anymore.

"No, I am not hurt. I just have never done this before," I say weakly through my tears.

"You've never done this before? Like you are a virgin? Wait, you have two children. Wait, what?" Henry is perplexed and extremely confused.

I cannot help but give him a sad little laugh, "Not having sex. I've been doing that for nearly half my life, but this—er—- style of control is new to me and I don't know why you pushed me away and it made me realize I am in so far over my head."

"Oh god, I shouldn't have come on so strong without asking if you liked it like that first," he says and pulls me into him.

"If you asked, I would have said I wasn't into it, but only because I didn't know how much I would like it. I would have talked myself out of it just because of fearing not knowing what to do or say," I admit. Henry pulls me back a little to look at my face. He raises his brow with a smirk. Why is he so attractive? That little smirk he does gets my lady bits tingling every damn time.

"You liked that, huh?"

"I think I did. It was fucking hot, and I didn't have time to overthink everything for once. But like I said, I am inexperienced in that realm of sex."

"Okay let's take a little step back," Henry says as he grabs my hand to guide me over to the couch. He sits me down and then takes the spot next to me, holding my hands in his, turning slightly towards me, "First off, trust me I want nothing more than your hands all over me but I was going to burst just from feeling you anywhere near my cock. I'm sorry I made you feel like anything other than desired, because you are incredible.

Next, sorry if I got carried away. You looked so sexy while you were mad at me and drove me insane. I just wanted to punish you for yelling at me. I was either going to make you scream my name or put you over my knee for a spanking—or both."

I gasp and cover my mouth with my hand. My eyes go huge with surprise, but my body is heating up, telling me that I know I liked the first one and that I might even like the second one. Henry notices my reaction with a small grin.

"I'm serious that I am so lost with all of that. I have never had a partner concerned about me being, like you said earlier, taken care of. And I definitely do not want that—um, jack hammering vanilla sex." I know the blush is deepening now, "I get embarrassed easily and am not good at verbalizing things. I recently asked Lana for a dirty-talk crash course."

"You did? I'm intrigued." Henry chuckles.

"Well, remember when Lana left us at the bar at the wedding to talk to that girl?"

"Yes…"

"After we separated, I went to find a restroom and walked into her under Lana's dress and the things Lana said to her were spicy. And that was only a couple seconds of it before I got out of there. So, when she came back later that night, I asked her how she does that, and she explained." It hits me what I am telling him right now. I need to stop talking.

"And what did she tell you?" That smirk again. Without even thinking, I roll my eyes at him, "Excuse me, did you just roll your eyes at me?"

"I definitely did. But it was because of that freaking sexy ass smirk of yours."

"Ooo you think I'm sexy?"

"No, not all of you, just the smirk. The rest is kind of meh," I joke. His mouth gapes and he pretends to be mad.

"Well, I think the over-the-knee punishment may not be right here, but I definitely think I need to get you to remember how overall sexy I am."

"How so?" My insides do a flip in anticipation.

"There is really only one solution," he says as he moves in closer to me. He kisses my neck and I moan slightly. His hands go above my hips and he whispers, "I need to tickle you until you concede."

"Wait, what?" But I am not quick enough, and his hands squeeze my sides. Unfortunately, I am indeed extremely ticklish and do not stand a chance against him. I am a goner and laughing too hard to even possibly tell him he wins.

Chapter 26

"He tickled you and you made out for the rest of the night?"

"Pretty much."

"No more sexy time?" Lana asked exasperated. We were in my car on the way to 'You're Grounded' for Early Bird Cafe Club. Lana texted me this morning saying that she was so hungover that she may still be drunk but did not want to miss the tea about my date, so I am obligated to pick her up. Her house is somewhat on the way, so I did not mind. Also, I did not want to go into the story of the date with the whole crew, but one hundred percent needed to debrief with Lana.

"The making out was pretty heated."

"Okay, but you're saying that you still have not seen his wiener?"

"Lana!" I playfully hit her shoulder, before saying, "But yeah, no. No wiener sightings."

"But why?" She says dramatically, dragging out the why part.

"After I had yet another mental breakdown in front of him, we did not take it that far again in the evening. I think it ended okay, and I certainly hope that he was still into me at the end of the night." Seriously though, I hardly ever cry, and Henry has seen me do so at least twice in the short time we have known each other. He must think I am a completely unstable wet blanket. Jake left me damaged and I have worked hard to heal, but the insecurities sneak in still.

"Do you have plans to see each other again?"

"We do. The girls go to Jake's for dinner on Wednesday nights, so Henry is going to meet me at Lakeside Park for an early dinner at that little diner there and if we have time, for a walk along the water. Jake's house is about two minutes from there, so we can maximize time this way."

"That's sweet... but that leaves no time or place for you to suck his salami or him to plant that eggplant in your garden!"

I look over at her quickly, shocked with her—um, imagination.

"What? Don't you want to have him fill you like a gas tank with his premium grade gasoline?"

"Where the fuck do you come up with these things?"

"I am one sick mother fucker, I tell ya." She laughs at herself, and I can tell there is way more in that head of hers. She is like Truck Stop Barbie. Built like a supermodel, but the things that come out of her mouth could make a sailor blush. And I love her for it.

"How did your date go last night?" I ask, shifting the subject to her. We are only a couple minutes away from the cafe and I really do not want to talk about my date anymore.

"I'll save my date story to share with the whole class. We do not have even close to enough time to unpack it before we get to the cafe." Well, color me intrigued.

We went into the cafe and ordered drinks before walking over to the table Marti reserved. We are a smaller group today with only Marti, Dylan, Jayna, and Gwen plus us.

"Hey, where is everyone today?" Lana asks as we sit down.

"The twins are sick, so Miles stayed home, but not too sure on everyone else," Marti responds.

"I know Talah has been on a business trip all week and will not get home until this morning," Jayna adds.

"You two rolled up together, anything fun happen last night?" Marti asks.

"I woke up questioning my sobriety and Carly was sweet enough to pick me up," Lana responds. I shrug nonchalantly, not wanting to add much. I love this group and how quickly they have all become integral parts of this new chapter I am in, but I just do not feel like revisiting my date again. I am still processing it myself.

"Where were you that you drank so much?" Gwen asks.

"I had a date. I was not driving, and he was incredibly boring. So, every time he mentioned his cat's name, I did a lemon drop shot. After about 9 shots, on top of the regular cocktails I was drinking, I had to quit the game and suffer through hearing all about Lemonade, the bestest cat ever without additional alcohol. I made a tally though; I would have had another 14 shots." Lana cringes and I can visibly see her turn a little green.

"Oh, I get it! Lemon drop shots for Lemonade, that's crafty," Marti laughs at the connection.

"I had to get my kicks somewhere. My drinking game could have been based on either Lemonade the cat, his mother, or his love of all things tennis related. I hate tennis, I did not want to insult a woman I don't even know, so Lemonade it was."

"How can you hate tennis? You are a country club baby. I wouldn't be surprised if your mom didn't go into labor on the tennis court," Gwen says.

"While my parents are doubles champs at the club, I was not born on the court. However, she did go into labor with my brother, Jackson, at the club Halloween party. Everyone thought it was part of the schtick as a pregnant nun and she ended up winning the costume contest."

The rest of the meetup I know I am being quiet and not adding a lot to the conversations. I am listening to everyone else talk while retreating into my own thoughts. I cannot help but overthink my date. I never thought of myself as inexperienced, but I really am. The last time I was out dating, there was no such thing as Tinder or other hookup apps. I am also not mentally prepared for how my feelings are developing.

* * *

Wednesday comes around with rain. Not just a slight drizzle, but torrential downpours. Henry is meeting me at the diner as planned but any chance for a walk is impossible.

I walk in and he is already in a booth by the windows. He waves me over and the way his smile reaches his eyes when I start walking over has my inside fluttering. He is so good looking but in such an approachable way.

"Hi, there," he kisses me quickly on the lips and helps me out of my raincoat. He hangs it on a hook on the wall for me. Such a small gesture, but I have to pause for a moment because it is nice to have someone who cares that I am taken care of. He certainly made sure I was taken care of the other night when his head was in between—my thoughts are interrupted by Henry's smooth voice even though I have no clue what he said. My ears are a little pink, like he could have known what I was just thinking.

"Sorry, what was that?"

"I asked if you have ever been here?" He repeats, apparently, as we slide into the booth across from one another.

"Oh, yeah, um, I bring the girls here sometimes," Why am I so nervous right now? "We love their milkshake menu. Um, there are, um, like, um, 40 flavors or, um, something."

Henry raises an eyebrow at me and gives me a little confused look,

"Am I making you flustered, Carly?"

"Why are you smiling when you ask that?" His teasing snaps me out of the stuttering fool I just was, and I give him an incredulous look.

He leans in close so no one near us can hear and says, "Because I like being able to get as much of a reaction from face-to-face as I do when my face is elsewhere."

"Henry!"

"What?" He laughs, "Maybe it is a good thing we are somewhere with a table in between us. We can have a real conversation without ending up making out."

A throat clears next to us, and we look over to find our waitress at the edge of the table. We both look a little sheepish as the woman who looks old enough to our moms' ages gives us a knowing smile.

"Alright, love birds, what can I get you to drink?"

* * *

The rest of the night was easy. We talked about our workdays and the girls, plus Henry told me a little more about his work life. We were stretching our time together as long as possible until I had to head to get the girls.

By the time I was pushing ketchup around my plate with a french-fry without actually eating it, the conversation came to a mild lull after I told Henry about my mom retiring to Tennessee and that we are still very close, but distance is tough.

"So, what is your family like? Your mom grew up in the farmhouse, right? Is she excited to see it restored?" I ask him and notice his body goes rigid. I am not sure why, but it feels like I asked the wrong question. He has mentioned his mom in the present tense and instances recently that he has seen her, so I know it was not mentioning her post-mortem or anything like that. I stay quiet to see if he will fill the void with an explanation.

He breathes in slowly through his teeth and pauses for a long moment before answering.

"My family is amazing. My parents are celebrating 49 years together on Christmas Eve," he says this all with ease but then he stiffens again. Another long pause.

"Wow, that is incredible! Such a long marriage," I offer in the break.

"And my dad still calls her his bride, and they are like teenagers. Sometimes I will still come around a corner and catch them making out. So gross, but also so inspiring. My parents are a great influence to me and my siblings."

"How many siblings do you have? Brother, sister, mixture?"

"One brother and one sister, both younger than me. My brother is 4 years younger and my sister, well, my sister was a pleasant surprise to my parents. She is 15 years younger than me." He laughs a little and he is defrosting. But as the thought is going through my mind, he goes back to seriousness, "The rest of your questions are complicated. Yes, my mom lived in that house until she was 18 but she left and never came back. Her father, my grandfather, did not believe women belonged outside of the home, unless with permission from her husband.

My mom secretly applied to college without telling her parents and was accepted to Columbia, well her father forbade her from being allowed to get a degree, especially not one in a 'man's field' like engineering. He said she needed to get married and support a husband in the home. She said she tried reaching out a couple of times after she left, but his attitude never changed. My uncle would come to visit us occasionally when we moved back to the area.

She is still an Engineering professor at the university, and she mentors young women in the industry. After my uncle passed away, she inherited the property but I guess did not want to go anywhere near it. Honestly, I suspect there are parts of the story I have not heard about her and her father, and I would never push. So, she let the house sit for a long time until I was doing some estate work for my parents' will and this came up. I didn't even know my mom owned it, anything needed done with the property, she had just hired someone to do it. Apparently slacking on the landscaping help. When I asked about it, she said if I wanted to take care of it, she would sell it to me for $32.00."

"$32.00? That's an odd amount," I sneak in while Henry takes a breath. He let out a single chuckle and a weak smile.

"It's my birthday, March 2nd. She has always had a thing about our birthdays being our lucky numbers. Like my t-ball jersey was always number 32," Henry explains, "So, I bought it from her. I did not even have to take out a mortgage on it."

I reward his joke with some light laughter, but I can see something else on his face. This is not the end of the story. I am quiet to let him finish.

"When I drove by the first time, I could not even see the house through the weeds that were overgrown. I was in my little car in my suit. I had just come from the courtroom and was not prepared to go on a trek through the jungle. I could see the potential in the house even from a distance. That is when I decided to clean it up and either use it as an investment property or sell it. But, Carly, about that…" He starts but is interrupted by a beeping. My phone alarm starts going off.

"Shit, I set an alarm for picking up the girls," I had set the alarm in the car so that I did not lose track of time, which apparently was an excellent idea. It was now to the point where I had only 5 minutes before I had to get in the car and even that was pushing it, due to the rain. I return my attention back to Henry, "Thank you so much for sharing all that with me. I could tell it was not easy, but I appreciate you opening up. Can we put a to-be-continued on this conversation? I really like learning more about you and where you come from."

"Absolutely, if you have to run, go ahead, I will finish up here," he offers. I think I look a little frantic.

"I have about 3 more minutes, can I pay for dinner tonight, please?"

"No way, it is my treat, though that feels odd after a story including male chauvinism about gender roles," he says, making light of the heavy story he shared.

"Well, thank you. Honestly, it is nice being taken out and cared about a little bit. And trust me, you do not give off any chauvinism traits," I assure him, because it is true. His entire personality is so comforting but also motivating. When we are talking about my work, he builds me up. He does not scoff at my ideas or goals.

"I'm glad to hear that. Can I see you again soon?" Henry stands up and offers me a hand to help me up. He takes my now-dry coat off the hook and holds it open for me to slip on. Once I do, he quickly spins me around and plants his lips on mine for a kiss that starts innocently enough but escalates into borderline inappropriate for a public forum.

Our waitress walks by us and says, "I'll be right over with your check, lovies."

I did not know how red my face could be until this moment. Kissing Henry genuinely felt like everything around us disappeared. Damn, I have to leave right now, or I am going to be extremely late for the girls and have to hear a Jake-lecture about how irresponsible I am.

Henry must see the panic on my face because he says, "Go on! I will finish up here. I will text you tomorrow to figure out when we are free next."

I let out a grateful sigh for his understanding and give him another peck on the lips, careful not to let it get heated again. I ran out the door to my car and am heading towards Jake's house seconds later, I cannot stop smiling and thinking about how easy the connection I feel with Henry has been.

Chapter 27

⚜

The morning after our diner date, I had an appointment with Dr. Rose. We worked on trying to pinpoint my insecurities and when they make my emotions go into a downward spiral. It was a tough, but good, appointment. I head over to Amber's afterward for some baby snuggles, because who can feel anything but calm while in the presence of the new baby smell?

As I pull into her driveway, I see a little white Toyota Camry also in the driveway, which means Patti is also here. Amber's mom is the best and I hardly ever see her anymore now that we are all grown up with families of our own. Remi and Millie absolutely adore her too, they will be excited to hear that I saw Grandma Patti, as they call her. Seeing her car there helps wash away more of the stress that is residual from my therapy session.

I let myself into the front door quietly in case PJ is sleeping, but as soon as I walk in, I hear the wailing noise that only newborns can produce. My first thought is that I do not miss hearing that in the middle of the night. Then almost at the same time, I feel an unfamiliar pang of missing the baby stage and wishing I would have had another baby. I shake my head at myself. I am beyond blessed to have my girls, but I could not imagine having had another kid with Jake. He was so selfish and absolutely no help with taking care of the kids. I had to take care of Millie completely alone while recovering from giving birth to Remi, plus did everything for Stevie when he was with us every other weekend.

I hear stories about this generation of dads being different from our dads. They want to be involved and take on half the work where they can, but while cherishing their partners as strong women. It is hard for me to picture what that could look like because I had the complete opposite experience. I shudder at the memory of being told that I was fat and lazy for trying to take a nap when Remi was only about a week or two old.

I walk down the hallway off the foyer towards the crying. Amber and Paul's house has an open floor plan for the kitchen and living room. The staircase to the second floor is on one side and leads to the overlook area at the top landing. The openness of the room makes PJ's crying echo through the space.

Coming around the corner into the area, I halt at the view. In the living room is Amber bouncing a red-faced, crying PJ trying to offer him a pacifier and Patti standing next to her making soothing noises trying to help keep them both calm. The kitchen is where the real shocking sight is. Paul is standing there in a pink floral apron, using one hand to mix a bottle, one foot to close fridge door, another hand is pouring water that he must've been using to heat the bottle in the sink, all while he is yelling over to Amber and Patti asking if either of them needs a refill on their waters.

"Hey, Carly!" Paul sees me first. He is calm and does not seem overwhelmed at all by the million things he is doing. He gives me a quick hug on his way over to Amber. He turns his attention to her and asks, "Do you want me to feed him so that you can visit?"

My mouth is agape with the contradiction to all the memories I had walking in here. Paul is one of my best friends, of course I knew that he would be a great dad, but I was not ready for this level of hands-on parenting.

Amber looks up at me, as Paul takes PJ out of her arms and gives him the bottle. He quiets right down and Amber sighs out a relieved breath. She runs over and grabs me into a hug, "Yay, you're here!"

"I'm here, everything okay?"

"Oh yeah! We switched over to formula feeding this past weekend, breastfeeding was just not right for us. We are still getting in the routine of making bottles *and* warming them up before PJ loses his fucking mind," Amber as she leads me into the living room with her.

"Language!" Paul says, pretending to cover the baby's ears.

"Like he didn't hear you cursing at the Patriots losing? I think there is something about throwing and glass houses that I am way too tired to remember the exact saying, but it fits in here," They banter back and forth, but it is clear they are just messing around. Paul walks over to where we stand to give Amber a kiss over their baby boy.

"That's fair, but he should probably learn early how to be disappointed by them." He laughs to himself but is distracted by a beeping in the kitchen. Paul, still in his pink apron with the baby resting on his arm with his hand reaching around to hold the bottle, walks back into the kitchen. He grabs an oven mitt and twists his body so that the baby is a safe distance away from the oven before he opens it. He pulls out a dish to set on the stovetop to cool and closes the oven door. He looks closely at his creation and nods approvingly. "Brownies are done cooking. Give them a bit to cool and then I'll dish you ladies up some treats. I grabbed vanilla ice cream to go with it."

He takes the empty bottle away from the baby before hoisting him up to pat his back for a huge burp in record time with a bonus splash of spit up right down Paul's back. He shrugs and sets PJ down in his baby swing. He is wearing a button up shirt, so he takes the apron and the top layer off to reveal a basic t-shirt from our alma mater, then goes back into the kitchen to start making us brownies.

As he walks over with a plate for Amber and me, he says, "What's wrong with you? Why are you being so quiet?"

I snap back to reality and pinch his arm hard.

"Ow! What the fuck was that for?"

"Just making sure I'm not in some weird dream, you were wearing a pink apron when I walked in the door and baking brownies. I mean brownies without weed in them!" I quickly look over at Patti with a guilty look and she just shrugs her shoulders like whatever.

"You are supposed to pinch yourself to check for a dream, asshole," Paul says, rubbing his arm.

"But that looked like it hurt, why would I want to do that?" I retort and Amber breaks out into a giggle.

"Don't worry, babe, I like the pink apron. Once the doc clears me, maybe I'll have you wear the apron with nothing—" Amber is interrupted by her mom loudly clearing her throat to save us all from having to continue that conversation, "Alright fine, come on. Let's go sit."

Amber and I walk into the living room where Patti is and the three of us make our way towards the sectional couch to eat our brownies. As I get settled, I feel my phone vibrate in my sweatshirt pocket. I sneak it out to check it quickly.

Henry: Hey, hot stuff.

I can't help but smile.

Me: Hi... hot stuff? Is that what we are going with for pet names? Okay, hunk.

Henry: Hunk?? I do not think I have ever been called that. In fact, I do not think I have even heard someone use the word in decades!

Me: Well now I feel old.

Henry: You are distracting me from my mission.

Me: Mission?

Henry: Yes. My mission of figuring out when I can see you again, you have the girls this weekend right?

Me: I do... the next time they are at their dad's is next Wednesday.

Henry: And I would love to have dinner again then... but I can't wait to be able to kiss you without giving a restaurant full of people a show.

Me: Not an exhibitionist, huh?

Henry: Not usually, but with you I am not sure how capable I am of behaving myself.

I cannot help but smile and laugh under my breath at my phone. I get a wave of the feeling that I am being watched and as I look up, I realize that I am. Amber and Patti have stopped talking and are both staring at me. I have no clue how long this has been going on.

"What?" I ask them.

"Don't what us! Who are you texting and smiling about?" Amber prods, "Is it the hot neighbor?"

"Who is this neighbor? I haven't seen you like this in a very long time, sweetie." Patti was and still is the cool mom. She always knew about our crushes and bought plenty of ice cream for our broken teenage hearts, back in the day.

"Henry, he owns the old farmhouse next door. He is fixing it up currently, so he's not really my neighbor since he does not live there, but I guess technically he is—"

"Stop rambling and get to the good stuff," Amber says. Patti shoots her a look telling her to be nice.

"Well, we connected when we both ended up at the same wedding coincidentally and through a wild series of events, we have now gone out on a couple dates," I say with a huge smile which transitions into a bit of a scowl, "But of course my time is limited, since I have the girls all but four overnights a month, pretty much. I mean the girls have met him but as the guy next door. And we are not officially anything at this point, so I can't include him in with the girls and I when we are doing something or hanging out."

"That is great that you met someone, but it sounds like you want more time with him, am I right?" Patti asks.

"Yes, I have considered hiring a babysitter for tomorrow night, but they are charging an arm and a leg these days, especially for two kids," I explain.

"Why are you hiring a babysitter? I can take them! It's about time that I get a full night to give them way too much sugar and let them stay up late," Patti offered. When I was getting ready to leave Jake and shortly after, Patti was such a help. She took the girls the afternoon my furniture was delivered so I could focus on setting up the house. She watched them on the day the divorce finalized so Amber could take me out for dinner.

Patti and Amber have been my family for so long. My mom moved out of the state the same day I moved into my dorm in freshman year of college, and she has only been back about a dozen times. I do not resent her distance though, since she put her life on hold for so long to raise me all alone. Usually, the kids and I go to visit her, which I did not mind before since it was a break away from Jake with just girls. But now, my mom has not been to New England even once since the separation and divorce. We talk often and she is supportive, but she is just not here to lean on. She got married a few years ago and seems to be genuinely happy, but she feels even more distant than ever. I think she feels bad telling me how happy she is while I have been going through a divorce.

Pretty much all my holidays in my twenties were spent at Patti's house, even now the girls and I will be spending Thanksgiving at her house. Amber's dad passed away when we were sophomores in high school and Patti has been so determined to keep Amber's world somewhat normal.

I never knew my dad and my mom has never given me any information to try to find out more. The only thing I know is that 40-something years ago, he was living on the West Coast. I even tried to do one of those ancestry DNA tests, but nothing came back for me. Not even distant cousins other than ones I knew of on my mom's side. My mom did her best and she was always there for me growing up. Every track meet, she was in the stands. Every academic award, she was cheering for me in the audience. However, she was never my confidant or the type of mom I could talk to about dating or high school drama with. That is where Patti filled in.

Millie and Remi have never spent the night with Patti, but they love their time with her, and she is easily one of their favorite people. They would love that, and I would feel less guilty not spending time with them on my weekend. The mom-guilt is real. Even though I have them about 70% of the time, I have a hard time feeling okay about taking a night for myself on the weekends that they are with me.

"Are you sure?" I ask timidly, waiting for the offer to self-destruct.
"Absolutely!"

"I can bring PJ over to see them for a little bit too!" Amber said. They
will freak out with excitement if they hear that they are spending the
night with Grandma Patti, plus get to see Aunt Amber and baby PJ.

"Thank you so much! Let me see if he is free tomorrow night, but
it would be nice to see him before next week. I feel like a teenager
again."

*Me: The girls have a sleepover at grandma's house (my best friend
Amber's mom) tomorrow night, are you free?*

Almost immediately my phone pinged with a response.

Henry: Yes!

Henry: So... does that mean I get you all night?

*Me: If you want, but whatever will we do for a whole entire
night?*

Henry: Obviously play scrabble.

Me: Obviously. {devil emoji}

"He's free," I say as a smile takes over my face and I start to feel giddy.

Chapter 28

Henry has invited me to his house to cook dinner and watch a movie together. Low key and comfy. I am happy to throw on a pair of black joggers and a plain pink T-shirt.

I am not sure how tonight will escalate. I know how much I would like it to, but I do not want to be presumptuous about spending the night. I grab my big purse so that I can easily sneak my toothbrush, hairbrush, and extra underwear in without being too obvious. I have so little recent experience and no clue what protocol is anymore for sleeping over, especially since we are not officially dating.

Henry lives in another area outside of the city than I do. It takes me about 25 minutes to get to his house. I pull into the driveway and see the truck with the trailer next to it. He has not been bringing the trailer to the house much lately now that the weather is looking more like winter and there is no need to mow or anything. There has not been another snowfall that has stuck enough to need plowing. His appearances at the farmhouse are becoming far and few in between. On Wednesday, he had mentioned that there was an issue that required a plumber to come out, but was not deemed emergent, so they were not rushing to come fix it. Other than that, I really do not know what the status of the house really is.

I head up to the door which is cracked open a little bit with a screen door over the entrance. I knock on the screen door.

"Come on in!" I hear from somewhere inside. Inside the entryway, I toe off my shoes and make my way back towards where I heard Henry's voice... I think. The house is nothing like I imagined. It is very nice, but Henry and the house just do not match. There is not a lot of warmth in here, while Henry is an intuitively warm person.

The first turn I make is a wrong turn. It brings me into what I would guess would be called a parlor or formal living room. The furniture looks staged, uncomfortable, and unused. There are gorgeous built-in bookshelves on the wall filled with encyclopedia looking collections or special edition leather hardcovers of classic works of art. I read smutty books with morally grey book boyfriends. I have not read anything labeled as classic reading since a painful English class in college that was a requirement.

I back track out of that room and try again turning into another room. Success. I walk into a massive kitchen with all state-of-the-art appliances. There is even a screen on the refrigerator door. Henry stands next to a stove that looks like it is off the set of Chopped, stirring a pot. He looks so sexy with a pair of tight dark jeans, not like the ones he wears to work around the house, and a crisp, form-fitting black T-shirt, plus a white kitchen towel draped over his shoulder. I cannot stop staring at his butt in those jeans, but finally am brought back by the amazing aroma filling the room.

"What in the world are you making? It smells absolutely incredible," I ask. I feel like a cartoon floating in the air towards the food. Henry puts down the wooden spoon and as I near him, his arm wraps around my waist and pulls me close. His lips take mine in an unapologetically intense kiss with his tongue coaxing my mouth open to take me even deeper. At least a minute must go by before he releases me, and my breathing is trying to regulate back to normal.

"The other night you were saying that you never get seafood because the girls do not like it. So, mademoiselle, I am making you seafood alfredo with cheesy garlic bread and a fresh salad," He says the last part in a bad French, maybe Italian- I really do not know, it was a real bad- but cute- accent, "Can I get you started with a glass of wine?"

He made a dish based around my preferences, even more so, he listened when I said I never get to eat seafood. I love it when he shows that he is paying attention when I talk. He makes me feel so seen.

"Wine sounds great and dinner sounds tasty. Thank you."

As he finishes cooking, I sit at the stools at the kitchen island. We are chatting about our days and about how he likes to cook, and I like to bake. Even though he is busy with making all the components of the meal, he never lets my wine get empty. He announces dinner is ready, so I start to head towards the little 4-seat table in the kitchen.

"I have the table in the dining room all set for us," he gestures towards the archway off the kitchen. I walk through it and there is an ample size dining room on the other side. I had to stop for a moment and count how many chairs were around the table. Four on each side. One at each end. Ten people can easily fit at the dark wood table that looks like it weighs more than a car. The dining room is decorated in a deep burgundy red and gold with a chandelier with gold accents hanging from the ceiling. Just like the parlor, it is lovely and well staged, but there lacks warmth. A tablecloth covers the entire table, but thankfully, Henry has set up our two-plate setting and one end, sitting across from one another. I might have died if I had to keep a straight face if we sat at the heads of the table trying to talk across the span of it. In between our plates, he has set up a pair of candlesticks and a pretty floral centerpiece. Even in a room this stodgy, Henry's true nature of being incredibly caring bleeds through. I can tell he put a lot of thought into tonight and genuinely wants to make it a special night. This is not just a night about coming over to get it on. No, this is about him bringing me into his world, even though it seems a little mismatched, the thought is there.

Dinner is just as delicious as it smells. Henry can cook. I mean like really cook. The alfredo sauce was homemade and perfect. He said he went to the fancy grocery store to get fresh seafood. He even made his own salad dressing. I feel spoiled and I do not hate it at all. I cannot remember ever having a man cook for me, especially not to this caliber. We eat and drink some more wine, while chatting some more. We do not cover anything deep. Our conversations, both in person and over text/phone, have become less about our life stories and more about just keeping each updated on our day-to-day... or occasionally a disagreement about the important things, like the best Adam Sandler movie. Just Go With It, obviously. Typical guy, he is going with Happy Gilmore.

As we finish, it is seamless and natural to clear the plates together and place them in the dishwasher. He blows out the candles before turning the lights off in the dining room. I put the last fork in the basket and close the dishwasher door, just as his arms wrap around me from behind. I let out an audible sigh as I lean back into his hold. His length is pressed up against my back and as I lean my head back a little, exposing my neck, I can feel it twinge against me. Knowing that I have this effect on him and that he wants me sends heat between my thighs. He has seen all of me and I have not seen barely any of him. My insides start getting a little wild with the desire that I want to have him fill me.

Henry puts his mouth on my neck, and he sucks while flicking his tongue on the skin. I moan and grind back against him, which he responds to with a moan of his own. He is even harder against me now and it feels like he is going to burst out of his jeans. That does me in. I am delirious with how badly I want him.

It is my turn to have control. I know he likes to be more of the domineering partner, he has told me just that, and he can have control back later, but right now I am in charge. Maybe it is the wine giving me courage or just the fire this man builds inside of me, but I am on a mission as I turn around towards him and kiss him harshly, entwining our tongues together. I must put more force into the movements than I thought because he falters back a little until he is leaning up against the kitchen counter.

He has the kitchen towel over his shoulder again from us cleaning up. I grab it off him, as I break the kiss, and toss it on the hard vinyl floor in front of him. He gives me a perplexed look like he has no idea why I would do that. It is only as I drop my knees onto the towel that he realizes and there is a hitch in his breath. I am sure my fingers are giving away some of my nerves as I go to unbuckle his jeans. It takes me a couple tries, but I get it and carefully guide the zipper down. I look up at him to find him intently watching what I am about to do like he is in disbelief of where this could be going. I return my focus to what my hands are doing. I gently guide his jeans down his legs, and he steps out of them one leg at a time, as I help him. He is still covered but I can see the outline through his boxer briefs of just how large he is. I think I should be scared for multiple reasons, like he is huge and might break me apart, or that I do not just get on my knees in front of a partner like this unless I feel obligated.

That is the thing with Henry, I do not feel like I have to do anything, but I actually feel an overwhelming pull and desire to do everything with him. My body reacts to just the thought of him, even when he is not with me. Now here with him in front of me, my brain has completely short-circuited, and I am officially only thinking that I want, no need this gorgeous man's cock in my damn mouth. I want to see how I can make him come undone. I want to taste all of him.

I press my lips against his inner leg just below where his underwear is, sneaking a look up at him as I do. His pupils have taken over his eyes and he looks completely feral as he watches my every move. I move my lips to his other leg and this time I give a little nip at his skin. He groans and instinctively rolls his hips towards me.

I push him back against the counter again. "Mmm patience, Henry."

He wriggles against my hands a little as I say his name, raspy in between heavy, wanting breaths. I continue my path along the hem of his boxer briefs with more kisses and nips, as he rolls his head back and groans. My hands are still on his hips, and I take a finger on each side to hook into the elastic waistband. Slowly I start to slide them down, carefully pulling them over the tent they've become. Finally, he is sprung free, and he is uncovered in front of me, ready for my mouth to take him. I force myself to finish what I have started by taking his underwear down the rest of the way until he has stepped out of them too. My hands glide upwards along the back of his legs until they are on the ass I have been dreaming about touching all night. His cheeks are firm as I squeeze them a little before bringing my right hand around to the front. I palm his whole length as he lets out a sharp exhale. I have never thought of a dick being attractive, but this one is.

I place my tongue in a swirl around the tip, licking up his precum. Then I lick one long stripe from his balls to the tip before pumping him again with my hand.

"Carly," he says my name into the quiet space of the kitchen. It comes out more of a hiss than anything. In response, I take him in my mouth part of the way and pull back off. He groans at the loss of my warm mouth around him. I return him to my mouth but this time I breathe carefully through my nose and take him all the way to the back of my throat. Immediately he reacts and rolls into me pushing farther until tears sting my eyes, but to see him like this is worth it.

"Oh my god, your mouth feels amazing." In response, I suck a little harder and as deep as I can. "Oh baby, I am not going to last long if you do that."

I take that as an invitation and reach my hands back around to each grab a butt cheek. Grabbing onto the tight flesh I push him into me, forcing his body to fuck my mouth. The noises coming from him are just that, noises, no words are forming. I keep feeding off his reactions to learn what he likes. The noises he makes are turning me on and I let out a throaty moan around his cock. His entire body responds to it.

"I'm so close, oh my god." With that I dig my nails into his ass and harden the force that I am pushing him into me with. That is it for him, with a strained yell, he explodes against the back of my throat. I back off him just enough to let the forceful spurts go down my throat as I swallow every last drop out of him. Only after his body starts to go limp, do I start to take him out of my mouth, but I do give a flick of my tongue to his still sensitive cock and the sensation causes his whole body to jerk involuntarily.

I sit back onto my feet to stare up at him. His eyes are still closed, and he is breathing heavily. Slowly his eyes open and I smile up at him.

"Fuck that was incredible. You are amazing. I have only one complaint." My brows scrunch and I get nervous that I did something wrong. It has been a long time since I have done this. But then he finishes, "My complaint is that you are wearing way too many clothes!"

I let out a giggle and shyly look down at my fully clothed body. He offers me his hand to help me stand up. My knees give out a little bit when I put weight on them, but Henry is there to support me. I guess I am not in my twenty-year-old body anymore, my knees will suffer if I am on them too long at this age. I am distracted from the woes of my aging body by Henry's mouth finding mine. His tongue plunges into mine tasting himself as he buries a hand in my hair to push our heads closer. The hand untangles from my hair and both hands reach down to the hem of my shirt. He breaks the connection as he pulls it up and off.

"Jesus, I am almost ready to go again. What do you do to me? I am not used to relinquishing control, but that was something else to watch you take what you want from me," Henry says and I look down to see him half-hard again.

"So, you're not mad that I took charge of you?"

"Oh no, you are definitely getting a spanking for that. But first I am going to make you so desperate to come until I am ready to fuck you so hard you are screaming my name so loud the neighbors can hear." Henry picks me up and hoists me over his shoulder. He gives my still clothed ass a hard smack as he carries me down the hallway. My head is just above his naked butt, and I think I am completely obsessed with this man's ass. Before we reach our destination, and I lose the opportunity, I reach to grab a handful of his cheek and squeeze. He jumps.

"Sorry. You just have the nicest ass ever and I just want to keep it as mine," I say, laughing.

"Baby, you can have it all. My ass, my dick, my mouth, my heart, my all, it is yours for the taking. You can have whatever you want because I'm lost in you, Carly. I am yours."

I freeze at this. I think I want it all and I am not sure what that really looks like yet, but all sounds right.

"All," I say softly into his back as we turn into what I assume is his bedroom.

At first, I think he did not hear me. He plops me down on the bed and slides over me. He brings his lips to my ear and whispers, "Then all of me is yours."

Chapter 29

I am laying on the bed stunned by the possibility that he could want me as much as I want him. Before I can overthink it, his lips kiss the sensitive spot by my ear. He stands up at the end of the bed and peels my joggers off, leaving me in just my bra and panties.

"You are so beautiful," he says as he places a kiss on my stomach. He kisses up to my lace bra and grabs my nipple through the fabric. My body reacts with a jerk. "Oh, it seems that you like that. Let's try it without the barrier."

I moan with anticipation and buck myself up so he can reach behind to unhook the bra before sliding it off me. I lay back down flat, just as his mouth takes in my bare breast. He flicks his tongue against the peaked nipple before lightly nipping it, sending a surge through my entire body. He continues to enjoy sucking there, while his hand moves down my center. Henry teases my senses by stroking over the lace panties a few times before bringing his hand back to my stomach. I would normally feel so self-conscious being so exposed, especially having someone touch my stomach, but Henry makes me feel desired just the way I am.

His hand slips under the front of the lace and he pulls them down my legs before throwing them aside. With one finger first, he parts my slit then he adds a second. The fingers slide back and forth with ease from how wet I am. He moves so slow that it is almost painful how much I need more, and he knows it. He looks up at me from his spot at my chest with a sly smile before sucking my nipple into his mouth again. I nearly come apart, but I need him to give me more friction or I will be stuck on the edge indefinitely.

"Please, Henry, harder. Please, I need more." I beg.

"I know, baby, but not yet. You're not coming until I can feel it on my dick." His words add to the need and edging. "You got your turn to play, now it's my turn."

With that, his teeth grab onto my nipple and pull hard. I nearly jump off the bed, as I am so close to climaxing without actually hitting it. Henry's hand leaves my soft center and I arch my back to try to chase it. He takes the opening and slips the hand underneath me to flip me over onto my stomach on the bed. He pulls on my hips to bring me up on my knees in front of him and I can feel his cock against my backside, fully ready to go again.

I rock back against him to press against his length and his grip on my hips tightens as he moans. He puts a hand around himself to slide it along my center.

"Please," I say through my breath. I am so close to exploding if he does not make me come soon.

"Shit, hold on. I need a condom," he starts to back off and away from me, but I twist my feet around his legs. He could have easily broken through the hold, but the surprise of it kept him in place.

"No, I need you now. I am on birth control and got a clean bill of health a couple weeks ago at my annual, as long as you are clean, I need you to fuck me right now." I have no clue who I am at this moment. I have never suggested that so early on. He must like the idea because I feel him get even harder against my ass.

"I got tested last month and haven't been with anyone since. I'm clean. But to be clear, you are giving me the go-ahead to ride you bare tonight?"

"Only if you stop fucking talking and do it," I say with desperation, "Or I will do it myself."

I receive a hard smack on my butt cheek for that, but the pain quickly melts into pleasure with all the need built up inside me. He reaches a hand around me and puts a couple fingers back on my clit. I jerk back into him as he gently rubs, again not hard enough to take me over the edge.

"I'm the only one who is touching this spot, got it?" He whispers behind my ear.

"Yes, yes, okay. Please, more," I beg.

And with that his hand leaves my center again but the disappointment only lasts a moment as he pushes me down against the soft bed to drive into me from behind. The sensation of him filling me is almost enough to make me come instantly, but I manage to stay on the edge as he thrusts up against me. I meet his rhythm and our bodies work in tandem.

"Oh my god, you feel so good." He says as he rocks his hips to drive even deeper.

I am starting to see stars as he hits my spot inside with every hard thrust, which brings me closer and closer. He finally releases me from the edge as his hand reaches around.. This time he is not teasing and gentle, but rather gives my clit all the friction I need to make my body shake and clench around his dick. I am not expecting how explosive it is and just as he asked, I am screaming his name along with some other gibberish mixed with curse words. He slows his pace as I ride through the orgasm.

Once my body stops shaking, Henry picks up his pace again. I can feel that he is close after I came around him.

"I'm so close, baby. Oh my god you are so beautiful. Yes, baby, yes, yes," And he grunts and spills inside of me. He does not pull out immediately but rather lays his head against my back wrapping his arms around my waist. The gesture is so sweet and intimate.

He kisses my back and says, "You okay? That was... well, that was just wow."

"I'm amazing, my entire body feels so relaxed and satisfied right now," I respond.

"Are you telling me that I am so good in bed that I can satisfy your pinky toe?" Henry laughs as he carefully pulls out. We both flip over onto our backs on the bed, his arm underneath my neck. He brings me in close to him to rest my head in the crook of his arm. We lay in peaceful silence for a moment before we start a comfortable conversation about everything, anything, and nothing.

We spend the rest of the night in bed, talking mostly. Our hands are either intertwined or touching somewhere on each other. Eventually, his fingers start making circles around my nipples and that instigates our hands to find all the sensitive parts until he is on top driving inside of me until I scream his name again. After that, our conversation lulls as we both begin to fall asleep.

In the morning I am woken to sweet kisses along my shoulder, followed by a sweet, sensual love making before we head to the kitchen where he makes me a coffee with a splash of oat milk creamer.

I get home around nine in the morning. I do not have to pick up the girls until noon from Patti's, but I want to take a shower and get ready before heading over there.

After the shower, I throw on some baggy jeans with a slouchy sweater. I do not have anything planned for the girls today, figuring they are going to be overtired anyway. I probably should try to pump them with some broccoli and carrots to offset the sugar they undoubtedly consumed with Grandma Patti. As I walk into the kitchen while towel drying my hair, I am making a mental menu in my head of what to make for dinner. I smile to myself thinking about the amazing meal Henry made the night before, and then remembering after the meal. It is hard to explain how confident I feel with him. I want to make him feel good because he makes me feel safe, important, and seen. I have been looking for that for a long time and he seems to be it.

As I am lost in my thoughts, I am brought back to reality by the sound of knocking on my front door.

Chapter 30

K nock, knock, knock.

    I swing my hair up into a towel on top of my head as I walk towards the door. It is probably just Barb stopping by. I do not generally get unexpected visitors.

Opening the door preparing to see my neighbor, I am shocked to be face-to-face with a well-dressed woman around my age. She looks vaguely familiar, but I struggle to place her. She is dressed in a pencil skirt and royal blue silk blouse with high heels that seem impractical for the snow that is forecasted. Her shoes perfectly match her calf length trench coat in a plaid pattern.

My visitor's makeup appears to be airbrushed on and camera-ready. Her impeccably styled blonde hair contrasts with my towel wig. I think she walked off a magazine cover to stand on my front stoop.

Why is this woman on my front stoop? She's probably trying to sell something. I really do not want to hear the spiel about her makeup company and the amazing opportunities if I sign up.

"Hello, may I help you?"

"Hi, there, Ms. Kennedy?"

Okay, she knows my name. That is some extreme solicitation research for a sales pitch.

"Yes, but I'm sorry— I have a busy morning and I am not interested in buying anything."

"Oh gosh, I'm not selling anything," she starts looking taken aback, then her face scrunches and she continues, "well I guess I am selling something—"

"And like I said, I am not interested, have a great day." I start to shut the door. I am proud of myself for not letting her sell me something just because I cannot say no.

Except, as the door is closing, she quickly says through the opening, "Please, that's not what I meant. I am working with Mr. Reid and need to talk to you briefly."

Henry? Why is she mentioning the man whose house I slept at the previous night? I open the door back up. She has my attention now.

"Oh, thank you! I am sorry. I should be clearer here. My name is Sadie St. Clair, I am a real estate agent." She explains. Now I know where I have seen her!

"I knew you looked familiar! I have seen your benches all over town. How can I help you Ms. St. Clair?"

"Call me Sadie, please," she smiles at being recognized, "I am working with Henry Reid on selling the property. While we haven't listed it just yet, I am in the process of preparing the details since I have already had some informal interest."

Selling? I knew Henry was probably not keeping the house, but I guess I did not realize he was at this point of having a real estate agent involved. It all starts to come together in my brain now. She is probably looking for some information about the neighborhood. Henry does not live around here, so he would not be able to give her the specifics about the area. The only weird part is that he did not mention hiring Sadie to sell the house.

"I see, and how can I help? Do you need some information about the neighborhood, the school district, I don't know, the mailman?" I am deflecting the awkwardness with humor now. Besides, our mailman is a sweet gentleman who is planning to retire in a couple of years and the whole street adores him.

"Not exactly, but I would love to hear the feedback about the area that you may have at some point!" She claps her hands excitedly, "No, I was hoping to be able to set up a time to take pictures of the whole property. I have several developers that may be interested, and they need to see all the structures to decide what they would opt to keep, in order to decide the direction they would take with the land."

"Developers? I am not following."

"Yes, 50 acres of natural land is a hot commodity!" Sadie says much too enthusiastically, "Henry said he would take care of the photos of the houses for the listing, but I thought I would give him a hand and see if I couldn't grab some photos during the week."

"I still do not see how I can help here—wait, did you just say houses, like plural?"

"Yes, I will need interior photos of both the houses. Both the main house and the guest house." As she says it, I am suddenly figuring out the conversation she is having with me and my heart flops into my stomach. She must see it on my face. "I'm sorry, but Henry said he was going to speak to you about it and apparently, I have put my foot in my mouth."

"I am just very confused. I do not rent from Henry. My landlord is a guy named Doug."

She looks down at her padfolio in her arms and uses her finger to scan the page.

"Ah, yes! Doug Tenny with Tenny Property Management, LLC., correct?"

I just nod my confirmation.

"Yes, that is the company that Mrs. Reid— Henry's mother— has used for years to rent out this smaller house to basically cover taxes and property maintenance."

"Are you saying that once Henry sells the property, which I was not even aware that I was a part of, then I will be evicted?"

"I'm sorry, but yes that is a possibility. That is just how the real estate world works." She says it kindly, but it is abundantly clear that this woman has never worried about there being a roof over her head, much less her children's heads. The rest of the conversation is a blur. I look down at my watch and realize I need to go pick up the girls from Patti's house. I also need to process everything I just was told and the fact that it came from a perfect stranger, not the guy that had made me coffee this morning.

"Sadie, I do not mean to be rude, but I have somewhere I need to be. If you want to leave a card, I can reach out or something." I will myself to not start crying. I honestly think the shock is still lodged so far in my heart and gut, that I am not ready to react.

She reaches into her pocket and retrieves a business card. Sadie begins to say something else, but I just take the card and turn around, shutting the door in the process. I run around finishing getting dressed before slipping on my Kohl's boots and Target jacket. For some reason despite the spinning feeling I am somehow thinking about how average I look next to people like Sadie St. Clair. That is probably the usual type of woman Henry goes for. I must be delusional thinking there was something serious brewing between us. How could he not tell me this if he cares about me at all?

I get behind the wheel of my car and just stare in at the dashboard for a moment. Robotically, I press the button to start the engine and the clock lights up. Crap.

Before putting the car in drive, I pick up my phone to send a quick message to Patti to let her know I am running late. I hit send and immediately my phone is ringing through the car. Startled and jumpy, I look to find Lana calling. I take a deep breath before answering.

"Hello?"

"Hey, girl! Do you have the kids in the car yet or can I be NSFW? Well NSFK, not safe for kids, not work in our case."

"I am in my driveway just leaving now." I answer with zero emotion in my voice. I do not laugh at her jokes or match her upbeat demeanor. I am so lifeless inside right now.

"I was going to say that I wanted to see how your date went, but your tone is making me worried it did not go well. Everything okay?"

"The date was amazing. Phenomenal. I have never felt so good with someone and comfortable. He doesn't even snore! But then I got home, and it went to shit." Backing out of the driveway, heading to Patti's.

"Oh no, what happened? Did Jake pull something?"

"Jake?" I did not even realize that when I get like this it is usually because of something Jake has said or done. It is the hollowed-out center feeling that I walked through life with for a decade. Lana understands that because she has gone through that with her ex-husband as well. "Oh no, not Jake. Henry is going to kick me out of my house, and I found out from the bus stop bench lady that teenagers always graffiti dicks going into her mouth around town."

"Um, what? What about bus stop dicks?"

I let out a single, hard laugh that has no humor behind it.

The lack of emotion must be clear because she says, "Okay, Carly, start at the beginning."

"I can't fully unpack it yet. I am driving to pick up the girls from Amber's mom's house and I cannot untether. But the cliff notes version is this," I take a deep breath and pause to gather my thoughts. "You know the house next door that Henry has been fixing up?"

"Mmhmm"

"Well apparently that house is on a 50-acre lot. All that land behind us is part of it," I swallow harshly trying to force the next words out, "Plus my house. My rental house is part of the larger property which Henry is selling to a developer. Or at least that is what I was told by Sadie St. Clair—"

"Oh! The bus stop bench real estate lady! Sorry, continue."

"Yes, her. Well, apparently Henry hired her to sell the house and she knocked on my door this morning to take photos of quote-unquote my part of the property. Apparently, Henry's mother hired a property management company to rent out my cottage to pay for the taxes and upkeep of the property, so she did not have to. My lease is through that company, not Henry's family, or so I was under the impression." I'll stop there.

Those are the facts; I cannot venture into the emotional side at this point. I am not ready to break through the shield I have up right now. I want to punish myself with this broken, empty feeling for falling for someone again that did not care about me in the same way I cared about them. I am forty years old, and I have never felt the compelling love that I do know exists—just not for me, apparently. I started to imagine Henry in my life already in the short amount of time since we met and I do not deserve to feel the feelings right now, because I brought this on myself by letting down the guard around my heart. I can't be emotional right now, because I already let my emotions take over and this is where I have ended up. I just want to curl up and begin to accept that I am forever going to be alone.

"Wow. I mean—wow." Lana stutters out, "That is heavy. Where are you right now?"

"In the car, about 5 minutes from getting to the girls. Then I will probably do some rental shopping until the girls fall asleep, then break down."

"Okay, no, this is what you are going to do," Lana's tone has zero messing around in it and I listen because, honestly, I do not have the brain capacity to think. "Pick up the girls and come over to my house. My kids are home, so the girls can play with them. My daughters would love to play with little kids, they want to start babysitting so badly but I think they are just a little too young. I think we need—you know what, never mind, I got this, and you don't have a choice. We will rally and sort this out."

"I don't know…"

Lana gives me a quiet-down type noise and says, "Straight here with the girls or I will come to you. No negotiations are allowed."

"Fine."

We hang up as I pull into Patti's driveway. I am sitting staring at the house building up my mask to go in there acting normal. With a deep breath and a fake smile, I head up to the house and manage to mask the internal destruction I am feeling.

Chapter 31

We pull into Lana's driveway about 45 minutes later. I managed to be chipper enough to make it through picking the girls up and small talk with Patti. The girls had so much fun, and Patti was gushing about their time together.

"Huh..." I say out loud.

"What, mommy?" Millie asks. The girls are excited to meet Lana and her kids. They are in the stage where they idolize older girls.

"There are more cars than I expected. Hey, wait, I know that red Mini." More to myself than answering Millie. Marti's bright red Mini Cooper is parked next to Lana's SUV. "Ugh, what is going on?"

Millie, Remi, and I walk up to the front door of Lana's large house.

"Mommy, this is bigger than Aunt Amber and Uncle Paul's house!" Remi looks up at the house with wide eyes.

I knock and before I even take my hand away from the door, it swings open. A girl that I am assuming is Lana's daughter opens it up with a big smile.

"Hi! Are you Millie and Remi?" she asks as she opens the door wider for us to walk in out of the cold. "I'm Lindsey."

Lana walks out from another room behind her.

"You're here! Hi, girls, I'm your mom's friend, Lana. Would you guys like to check out the playroom with Lindsey? My other daughter, Trinity, is up there too."

"Yes, please!" Both girls look at me to make sure it is okay. I give them a little smile and a nod, then they are off. They disappear up the stairs holding Lindsey's hands.

"Don't worry, we won't see them until they get hungry. Those kids have way too much shit up there that I keep meaning to donate a bunch of it, but who really has time to do that." She is walking down the hall towards an open area that has a family room and a kitchen with a dining area. My suspicions are confirmed as we walk in. Marti is at the counter slicing limes and tossing them into a large pitcher. Jayna is also there, pouring tequila into it.

"Carly!" Jayna and Marti speak at the same time. Their faces show that they know to tread carefully around me because I am fragile, damaged goods.

"Hey, girls. So, what's everyone doing here?"

"Well, since you couldn't be at the cafe this morning, I decided to bring it to you. From what you told me, this whole situation is complicated and multi-layered, so you need your community to back you up. You may be the new kid around here, but you're already a part of our little found family."

"Do you all hang out regularly outside of Saturday mornings? And, Jay, don't you have your son this weekend?" I ask, wondering if I totally missed something, suddenly feeling a pang of being left out.

"Yup, Wyatt's upstairs with the older kids. We do not hang out too often, but we totally should," Jayna says with a shrug, "During the summer, Lana does a themed barbeque which we all come to, and we all usually end up being the last to leave. Last year, most of us were too drunk to drive and the kids were with us, so the girls had a sleepover in the playroom, the boys slept in Max's room and we all slept scattered around the house. Please don't judge us."

This actually got a laugh out of me. I try picturing it in the space around me.

"Oh, also when Dylan's ex-wife left for good," Marti adds, then for my benefit she says, "Kayla had been come and go for years, then about a year ago she announced that she was officially moving to England with her new boyfriend to open a pub because she felt that she mastered the perfect fish and chips recipe. I think Dylan and his girls had always hoped she would come home and stay put, so they were a mess when this happened. We rallied and got his house back in order, pitched in to help with taking the kids where they needed to go, etcetera. As far as I know, they have not even heard from her since."

Jayna scoffs under her breath and says angrily, "She's an idiot to not see how lucky she is to have a hard-working, handsome guy who is a good dad. He's a rare gem and she just tossed him away."

Lana, Marti, and I all just freeze and look at her. It takes her a moment to realize we are staring.

"What?"

"Nothing, just never knew you felt so passionate about the situation and Dylan."

Like saying his name summoned him, he rounds the corner holding a casserole dish. Jayna's face turns beet red. There is no telling what he just heard, but I definitely notice that she becomes a little stiff and nervous around him. I do not think anything is going on between them. Jayna is in her twenties and Dylan is around my age. That is a significant age gap. Plus, as Dylan comes in, he does not look in her direction other than to scan the room. He looks at us all the same, with a quizzical look.

"What about Dylan?" He asks. It seems that he only heard his name, not the rest.

"We were just telling Carly that the last time we gathered like this was when—where are the girls?" Lana says, looking behind him.

"Annie had a sleepover tonight, so I dropped her off on my way. Sarah went upstairs to find the rest of the kids."

"Got it. Last time we gathered like this was when bitch-face left." Lana finishes, referring to Dylan's ex-wife.

"It's true. Both the bitch part and the you all gathering to help me out part." He just shrugs his shoulders and sets down the casserole dish. "I made a layered taco dip while I was waiting for the girls to get ready."

I am standing next to Jayna now, close enough to nudge her and quietly say, "hmm, add makes homemade appetizers for reasons he's a catch."

Her head whips to look at me and when she sees me laugh a little, she does too, but stiffly. I do not push anymore and just leave it alone.

"Okay, I brought my DD, please tell me Marti made her famous margaritas!" Miles comes walking into the room with a baby sitting on one hip and bags hanging from the opposite hand. A slightly taller man walks in behind him with another baby strapped to his chest, two folded highchairs in each hand and a full backpack with a stuffed giraffe peeking out over his shoulder. Lana and Marti run over, and each take a baby from them, while Dylan grabs the highchairs and Miles sets the bags on the countertop.

"Thanks!" the other man said and then he saw me, "Hi, you must be Carly, we haven't met yet. I'm Cal, Miles' husband."

I shake his hand. "So nice to meet you!"

"And those are the twins, Rosie and George," Miles says while trying to grab the pitcher Jayna is still working on putting ingredients into. She slaps away his hand and he pouts. Cal is setting up the highchairs side by side and begins to pull things out of bags to set the kids up.

"They are not fully walking yet but they are pulling up on everything and can crawl faster than their dada runs to a sale at Bloomingdales." Cal gives his husband a subtle wink. And we all laugh.

Over the next couple minutes, Gwen, Paula, and Talah all filtered in as well until the ten of us all had beverages in hand. Most of us have one of Marti's margaritas but Cal did not want to drink, so he grabbed sparkling water. Talah and Paula say they overindulged last time on the margs, so they stick to wine. Everyone has brought something to add to the gathering. It had only been about an hour and a half since I first talked to Lana and now, we are all sitting around the huge table with the babies in their highchairs munching on snacks that look more like communion wafers than food. I was in such awe of all this that I almost forgot they were here for me, and it was now time to talk about it.

Time to rip off the band aid and lean on this group that has only known me for a couple months, but they have welcomed me with open arms. I go through the entire play-by-play, with certain details left vague from last night, and into this morning. I recap the exact conversation, as I can best remember it, with Sadie when I got home.

"So basically, my luck with my love life has *not* turned around and I will be homeless soon." I end my story and look around the table. I give a smile with just one side of my mouth and sigh loudly.

"Holy shit." "What the fuck." "I know a guy." Came from various places at the table, talking at the same time.

Marti puts her fingers to her mouth and lets out a loud whistle. The whole table falls silent except for the babies giggling at the noise.

"Again." Rosie babbles clapping her hands. George joins her and they both are saying "again" and clapping. This makes us all chuckle.

"Okay let's unpack this one piece at a time." Marti says diplomatically. "So, the property is not officially on the market yet, correct?"

"No, she was just getting a head start on gathering photos."

"How long is the lease that you signed?" Talah asks.

"One year, which is coming up in late winter."

"Have you talked to him at all? Maybe it is a misunderstanding." Dylan adds and he receives nine glares for that.

"Typical straight guy answer." Miles rolls his eyes.

Dylan holds his hands up defensively. "Hey now. I am not saying he is not totally wrong in what is going down, no matter what, but you need to confirm if and when the sale is planned for. It will give you an idea of how much time you have to find a new place."

"Okay, you make a good point," Miles concedes.

"I just don't understand why he wouldn't tell me from the beginning that my house is part of his property. It's one thing when he was the grumpy neighbor but now, he has seen me naked, and he did not bother to mention it." I am mad. I am devastated. But right now, I am mostly just confused. Dylan is right, I need to ask for some answers.

"Well, I have a small apartment above my garage that you are welcome to use, if it does come down to you having to move out. It may not be the best long-term option for the three of you, but you can stay there as long as you need rent-free. My kids have all lived there at some point or another, it was never meant to be income gaining, just a spot for them to get a little privacy." Paula says down the table to me. I feel tears forming in my eyes with the generosity of the offer. My circle of trust has always been small. My supporters have pretty much been Amber, Paul, and Patti for my entire adult life. I know all three of them would each offer us a place to stay too, but this group has known me for just weeks and they have circled around me to help lift me out of a hard time.

The tears start flowing heavily now. I am full-blown sobbing as I try to say, "Thank you," to Paula. It comes out like gibberish.

"Oh, Carly, I didn't mean to upset you. I am sure you will find something more permanent, but I just want you to know that you have options."

I shake my head and attempt to explain that I am touched by the offer. A box of tissues magically appeared in front of me at some point during my sob-fest. I take a moment to gather myself. This is so embarrassing. I am sitting at this table with a group of people I just met, one of them I legitimately just met today, losing it. I can feel my face turning bright red. I start babbling apologies.

"Nope, do not do that. We may be new friends, but that is the thing about our little group, when someone is meant to join our fold, they find their way to us. And it is usually obvious very quickly. People talk about finding their soulmates, but sometimes that means a found family rather than a love interest. In my opinion, that's even rarer and more special, so we are all the lucky ones to have this table full of people. You are not the first person here to be brought into our group swiftly, and I would be pretty confident in saying that you will not be the last person. I guess I will just have to buy a bigger table." Lana says, looking at me directly in the eyes to make sure I hear every word she is saying. Then she shrugs her shoulders and finishes with, "It's Marti's doing, she started the group. I am convinced that she is really a witch or fairy godmother or something."

"For the millionth time, Lana, I am not doing anything crazy or casting any spells to make you all be friends with me and each other!" Marti says with a huff. Lana gives her a side eye look and a small grin. Her face spells out that she does not believe Marti. I think I am questioning her powers a little bit too.

Chapter 32

⎯⎯⎯ ❧❧❧ ⎯⎯⎯

I finally pulled myself together. We talk a little more about housing options and it turns out that Gwen works as a mortgage broker. She mentions she could meet with me to help me plan what I would need to buy a house in the same general area. I will have to find another rental in the meantime, but maybe it is time to get something that I own. When she asks what kind of house I would like, I find myself subconsciously describing the farmhouse next door, though I know I cannot afford to buy it. Even without the amount of land associated with it, the house is historic and large. I never had a chance to see inside but there has to be at least five bedrooms and Henry has mentioned that the kitchen was a massive country kitchen. Gwen does not pop my dream bubble; she just says that we will schedule something and see what my price range would look like.

The items everyone had brought are the makings of an impromptu barbeque. The weather is relatively calm and not too frigid today though, for late Fall. Dylan and Cal take plates full of hotdogs and hamburgers to Lana's outdoor kitchen while the rest of us busy ourselves setting out sides and desserts.

We call the kids down and it is the first time I am seeing all the kids together. A few of them have ventured downstairs for this or that, but now I am amazed that they all get along great, and my girls seem to be having a great time. The older kids are helping the little kids, and they all find seats around the folding table that we set up for them. The weight of feeling so lost earlier has been diluted by this gathering.

I am standing against the counter looking at the kids all chatting away when Lana slides up next to me. She puts an arm around my shoulders and says, "On a scale of 1-5, 5 being a lot, how badly did you want to kill me when you realized I gathered everyone?"

I chuckle lightly and answer, "A solid six."

"And now?"

I roll my eyes and say, "Zero."

"Okay, good. There is something about this crew that is good for the soul. Everyone brings a piece of the puzzle that puts something broken back together." Lana says. It is very true when I think about it. Her face becomes more serious. "So, what are you going to do about Henry? You still haven't spoken to him, right?"

"No, but he did text me while we were making dinner just asking how my day was going and that he loved waking up next to me this morning." I huff out a breath. "He says it like his actions are not derailing my entire life today. Like he did not lie to me, or withhold the truth, whatever you want to call it."

"I call it douche-baggery." She says defiantly.

"I'm just not ready to respond. Even if I was, how do I begin?"

"Maybe just let him know the realtor stopped by and let him shit his pants trying to figure out what you know. Let him be blindsided like you were."

"Hmm, I don't know. I think I am too drained by all this to be calculated. I think I need to just call him and talk it out, but I do not want to do that with the girls around."

"The girls are welcome to stay here tonight. They can have a sleepover in the playroom with my girls."

"Thanks for offering, but they just spent the night at their grandma's last night and I kind of want some time with them this weekend. With a look at them it always grounds me and pushes me to make things happen. The way my world revolves around them is probably a little unhealthy, but I don't have any biological family nearby other than them, and I have to protect them at all costs."

"I completely understand. How about they hang out here for a little bit so you can have a conversation in private and then when you give me the thumbs up, we will drop them off at home. If you need longer, the sleepover option is still open. Just leave me their car seats."

I nod in agreement to this suggestion. I do need to take care of this today, so that I know how long I have until I need to find new housing. "You are too good to me. You all are. Thank you for today"

She squeezes me in a side hug and rubs my arm. "You're one of us. You would do the same for any one of these people in this room."

* * *

I am driving home from Lana's when my phone rings. Henry shows up on the Caller ID. I had planned to get home to call, but I guess we will do this now.

"Hello?" I say, indifferently.

"Hey!" Henry sounds so upbeat, and it reminds me of how this day started, "I am going to be by the house tomorrow to work on a few things and was wondering if I could grab some lunch for us to have a living room picnic with Millie and Remi. What do you think?"

To my right is the middle school, I cautiously pull into the empty parking lot. I do not want to be driving as I have this conversation. My heart aches by how much I want to just ignore everything I know and just say yes. I would be lying if I said that I had not pictured our relationship growing into exactly what he is proposing. But I cannot ignore reality.

"We can't," I say flatly, trying to work up the courage to say the rest.

"That's okay, do you girls have something fun planned tomorrow?"

"Fun? No, my plan tomorrow is to distract the girls with their tablets while I scour the internet to find any rentals that are in my budget and in the same school district." I press my lips together trying to not cry... yet.

"R-rentals?" Henry is stammering and I am not sure if it clicked that I know, or he is genuinely confused.

"Ah, yes, rentals. After my little chat with Sadie St. Clair this morning about needing photos for my house for the sale of the property, and I quote, for Mr. Reid— and while you have not issued an eviction notice to me yet, I figured I would get a head start." I pause to see if he has anything to say, but the sounds coming from his side are not actual words. He is shocked. Good, he can feel blindsided like I did this morning after all.

"Carly, I'm sorry. I asked her not to go over to your house." He stammers out. I physically jolt backwards.

"You mean *your* house, Henry," I say sharply, "And someone had to fucking tell me and obviously you were not volunteering to do it."

"I tried telling you so many times, but we were always interrupted. And nothing has been finalized, I am in the early stages of selling," His tone is very defensive and is only making me angrier.

"Always interrupted?" I ask, "Maybe you could've taken your face out from between my legs long enough to say hey before I make you scream my name and give you false hopes of a future together, I should probably tell you that I am going to make you and your children homeless."

"You want a future together?" he says quietly, "Carly, please listen to me. That is what I want too! Maybe you and the girls can come live with me, or if you are not comfortable with that, I can pay for an apartment for you."

"I don't want, nor do I need your charity. But a little common courtesy and respect would've been nice. And no, we will not be moving in with you. I do not want you anywhere near me or my children. I do not want to leave my house!" My anger is starting to break, and the tears are threatening to start flowing.

"I'm sorry," His voice is more solemn than defensive now, "I really cannot keep the house. I couldn't do that to my mother. She has so many horrible memories of that place that I barely even mention it to her. I need to sell it away from our family. I couldn't imagine telling her that I would consider keeping it and trust me, I love that house. I would love to live somewhere like that and let you keep your house, but I just can't."

"I get that, I really do. It's not the selling part that I am mad about. It is not telling me that my house was a part of that sale that has me upset! Henry, I had not the slightest clue that you owned my house. I pay rent to Doug Tenny's business with no information about your family owning it." I explain so that he knows where the wrong turn here was.

"Carly, I promise you will have ample notice when the property sells. And I will help you search for a new place. And the buyers may even keep it as a rental, who knows. Please just let me help you with all of this." His voice is full of begging.

"Thank you, but the only way you can help me right now is by hearing me when I say that I do not want to speak to you again. If you are next door, do not even wave hello to me. Do not talk to my girls or me. I—am—done." I pause in between each of the last three words to emphasize how serious I am. As much as I am dying inside right now, I cannot change my mind.

"Please, don't do this. You just said you wanted to be with me. Can you honestly tell me that you can't feel that there is something special between us? I have never felt so connected to someone before the way that you and I meld." He is full-on begging now.

"Yes, dammit. I do feel it, that is why this lie— or omission of truth, whatever you want to call it—has torn me to pieces. But I need to be strong because this is not only my heart that I am making decisions for. My girls are about to have their home rocked again for the second time in the past year." I shake my head realizing that maybe it had been too soon to start dating again. I never meant to have the girls involved in my dating decisions at this point, but I failed them. I let them know Henry, even if they did not know we were romantically involved. I let them feel like we were in a solid house for a few years until we bought a permanent house. But that was all wrong and I failed them. Now the tears come freely.

"Carly, don't cry, please don't cry. I promise we can work through this. I want to plan our lives together. This cannot be over before I can even tell you that I love you, because I do. I know it's early, but I know I do love—-"

"STOP!" I cut him off. "Do not say that to me again. That is not fair. If you loved me, you would have protected me and been honest with me. You did neither. So, while I really had hoped to move forward together, that is just not possible. I am done. I am going to hang up now. I do not want to hear anymore. Goodbye, Henry."

"Carly! Wait—" That is all I hear as I disconnect the call and block his number.

Chapter 33

꧁ꕥ꧂

The next day Henry does not show up at the house.

On Monday, there are two vans and a truck parked in the driveway of the farmhouse. The vans have business names for the electrician and the plumber on the side, while the truck has a construction company logo on it. No sign of Henry.

Tuesday brings a van for the roofers and the truck for the construction company again. Still no Henry.

Wednesday morning, there is the truck, plus now a big box truck for the construction company with several guys going in and out of the house with supplies. Additionally, Sadie St. Clair is out front in what look like winter boots but have at least a four-inch heel on them. She is parked along the street getting something out of her trunk. I pause in my car long enough that I am able to watch her pull a "For Sale" sign out of the back with a large rubber mallet. I feel a stab in my heart that it is actually happening.

My attention is fixed on Sadie as I question how she plans on getting that sign into the cold ground. Much to my surprise, she impressively lines the sign up sideways, so that each side is facing cars coming from either direction, and she brings the hammer down with incredible force. It takes her only four hits to have the sign secured in the ground. She goes back to her car and pulls out two smaller signs. She inserts them into slots on the top of the sign with her face on it. She is standing in front of them, so I can only read them once she moves away. My breath hitches as she does.

"50+ Acre Property"

"Two Houses on Property"

I knew my house was a part of the sale of the farmhouse but seeing it in writing in front of me makes it extra real. I am losing my home and there is nothing I can do about it.

* * *

"Wow."

"I feel like as my therapist you should not be speechless right now."

"I'm just processing everything you just told me on top of everything I already know about you." Dr. Rose then bites her lip, deep in thought, "You've really had one hell of a couple months here, haven't you?"

"Again, aren't you supposed to make me feel optimistic and find the silver lining positives in it all?"

"Carly, I'm not a TV therapist. Our sessions are not scripted," she says with a small laugh, "I am here to help you not bottle all this up. I am here to validate that you are indeed going through some crazy shit right now."

I cannot help but laugh at Dr. Rose swearing. It's like a little kid hearing mom swear.

"I just don't know what to do. I have been ignoring dealing with it. I mean I am looking at rental listings, though nothing worthwhile and in the right school district, is popping up. But the emotions are just packed deep down and I really just want to keep them there." I admit.

"Okay, I can understand why you would feel like that, but can you honestly say that is the healthiest thing for you?" She asks me.

"I know it is not, but I feel like once I pull on that string, I will fully unravel."

"That is fair. Okay let's talk about it this way. What part of it weighs you down the most? What consumes your thoughts?"

"That I failed."

"Failed? How so, Carly?"

"I promised my girls I would protect them, and I promised myself I would not let them be negatively impacted by me dating again. I was not blind to the fact that dating would have its ups and downs, but I had no intention of it all trickling down to my kids' world, especially not like this. They like Henry a lot and they like our home a lot, now both are gone or going."

"That makes sense, but you have not failed them. You are showing them that we can persevere through difficult times. That is what they will remember. Can we call it a hurdle rather than a failure?" Dr. Rose asks me. I think about it and nod, though I am not sure I am there yet.

"Okay the kids aside, what about you and Henry? What is weighing most on you there?"

"Hmm-" I stall while I am thinking that question through. I decide to be completely honest and tell her about our phone conversation. In the retelling earlier in our session, I said there was a phone call, not word for word. "He said he loved me."

"Okay, that's huge. Do you believe him?"

"Yes."

"What makes you believe him?"

"Because I was falling in love with him too. I knew it was very quick and I said I would not jump into being serious again after Jake, but this was a different emotion than the love bombing that Jake pushed on me in the beginning. My connection with Henry is, well was, from the core, not just surface level. It was the type of love that you struggle to tell your friends about because words do not exist for it— not the love that you show off on Facebook because it just looks good."

"That's rare, indeed. And there is no chance of reconciling?"

"How can there be? Love *is* rare and when it breaks, it shatters."

"Do you want to trade chairs? You are doing really well at unpacking this and explaining it."

"Thanks," I say with a half-smile, "I guess I wish we could get past this, but this did not just break my heart, it broke my everything."

"I know you are capable of taking a seemingly impossible situation and turning it into the best. Look at how far you have come since you left Jake. Would you have ever stood up against him like you did with Henry?"

"No, definitely not. But I did not feel safe with Jake like I do with Henr—y…" I trail off realizing what I am saying.

"So, even during a disagreement that ultimately ended your relationship with Henry, you still felt safe? Am I hearing that correctly?"

"Yes." My voice is almost a whisper.

"Interesting. I guess my professional advice is," She makes finger quotes around professional, "Be open to all options. I am not saying run back to Henry because what he is putting you through is not great, but also don't force yourself to stay closed off, if you feel yourself fighting against your own barriers."

"I will try, but honestly, I think I am putting dating on the back burner for a while. It was good to get back out there. I felt wanted and truly sexy, but I need some time before I venture down that path again."

"That is fair. There is nothing wrong with taking time to focus on you and the girls."

We ended the session talking about the housing market and what I am looking for in a rental. She mentions that she knows a few people with duplexes, and she would reach out to them to see if any are available. I am walking out feeling a little lighter and a little more ready to take care of business. Dammit, she got me to unpack what I said I was going to keep buried. She really is good.

* * *

The rest of the week goes by in a similar fashion. The construction company is next door each day, along with miscellaneous other professional companies, but no Henry. I do not hear from him, though I do still have his number blocked, but there are no attempts any other way. It appears that he is respecting my wishes.

We are at a new coffee house this week called The Bean Counter Cafe for the Early Bird Cafe Club. As an accountant, I appreciate the current coffee shop that Marti picked, since "bean counter" is slang for accountants.

We all get our coffees and snacks before we sit down at a large table in a far corner of the dining room. The whole crew is here.

"Guys, I just want to thank you for last weekend. I know you are all so busy and it means a lot that you came over to Lana's for me." I try to express how grateful I am to them for their support.

"You are welcome, but that is what we do. No matter what each of our actual families looks like, we have our own found family together." Marti says and pats my hand.

Our conversation shifts to talking about the kids and how much fun they all had playing together at Lana's house. For a group of kids with a wide age range, they did great together. The older kids were amazing with the little ones, and I know that my girls have not stopped talking about how cool the big girls are. We decided that we would try to have another family night for Christmas.

As we walk out to our cars, I speed up to get next to Lana. I bump her hip with mine and say, "Hey, you were unusually quiet today?"

"Unusually quiet? What do you mean?"

"It means that you are normally loud and opinionated, which we of course love you for." I say with a laugh, but I give her a genuine look to let her know I am serious.

"I'm just feeling done with online dating. It is so stressful and everyone is either boring or absolutely insane. I am starting to feel like I will never meet someone to last long enough that I don't have to watch Wheel of Fortune alone every night for the rest of my life."

"Wheel of Fortune, eh? I love that show, I will watch it anytime with you." I offer up.

"Thanks, but you know what I mean."

"I do. I really do, but you have so much to offer, I refuse to believe that the right person is not out there somewhere for you." I wrap my arm around her waist and squeeze.

"Thanks, I am really glad you ended up being a keeper around here." Lana smiles over at me.

"Thank my therapist, she made me do it," I laugh as I remember exactly how I ended up here.

* * *

When I get home, I try everything to keep myself busy. I know I would have been with Henry today in an alternate series of events. I miss him even though I know I should not. With the girls at Jake's and my social calendar empty, the quietness is deafening in the house. I put on Taylor Swift's The Tortured Poets Department album as loud as I can as I do household chores and some extra cleaning. I sing along to her heartbreaks like they were written for me. I am belting out to *I*

Do It with a Broken Heart when I hear a knock on the door. I swear if this is Sadie St. Clair again, I am not promising my ability to be nice.

It's not Sadie that I find, but rather three different delivery vans with three different drivers lined up at my door. First in line, a very large bouquet of Autumn flowers.

"Delivery for Carly Kennedy."

"That's me."

"Great, here you are," he said, handing me the flowers before continuing, "The card is attached to a ribbon around the vase, but there is an additional message with them. Mr. Henry wants you to know he is incredibly sorry and begs you to please forgive him. Thank you, ma'am."

I reach for my purse to tip him, but he waves his hand in front of him.

"It is greatly appreciated, Ms. Kennedy, but Mr. Henry has been very generous and already given me a tip. Likely the same for them too," the florist delivery driver hooks his thumb behind him at the line. Three heads poke out around their items to nod in agreement. Three?! When the hell did a fourth delivery driver get here?

The line continues in a similar fashion. They each handed me a gift with a message that there is a note attached and that Henry was sorry and asking for forgiveness. I finally close the door and stare at the pile I have collected. There are flowers, along with an Edible Arrangement and gourmet soft-baked cookies from the local bakeshop. The last delivery driver had my go-to complicated cafe drink—Mucho Latte with Oatmilk and 1 pump white chocolate and 2 pumps peppermint with cocoa powder sprinkled on top—I am slightly impressed Henry remembered that. The driver removed it from some contraption it was held in to keep it warm, which worked well since it was still too hot to drink.

I survey my loot for the day and my surprise morphs into anger.

The card on top of the cookies catches my eye and I remember them all emphasizing that there was a note with it. I look closer and see on the cookie the envelope has written on it "Open this one 3rd." As I examine the writing, I am shocked because I am pretty sure it is actually Henry's handwriting. The first two gifts have the same message on the envelope, with a different number, and the same handwriting. The coffee came with the verbal message but no note, unless...

I pull down the sleeve that is wrapped around my latte. Under it I find written on the white cup, in the same handwriting:

Please read the other notes. I mean everything. You can wait until you are ready to, but please read them. I am not going anywhere. <3 H.

Chapter 34

I have not read the notes, at least not yet.

I am not ready to forgive him. I cannot imagine a world where we can get past this. This situation was life-altering and I deserve to be mad at him, at everything. I am not only mad at Henry, though he does own most of it, but I am also mad that I am in this predicament because I married someone who did not give me real love. I am mad because I feel like I may never know what that is like. I am mad because I started to be able to imagine it happening to me but then the rug was pulled out from underneath me. I am mad because I am not giving my girls the best that they deserve right now. They deserve a home to grow up in with their mom, not getting bounced around house to house. So, no, I am not ready to read the notes yet.

* * *

I had calmed down enough to let Sadie come take photos, she was just doing her job and I was not going to hinder her because I was mad at Henry. She came in, took a handful of photos and left without giving any information about prospective buyers or anything about the sale.

The whole interaction lasted about five minutes.

I just went through the motions. A few times I have seen Sadie over there walking people around and they would stop in my front yard. She would point to the house, but they never invaded my space.

There are more deliveries with quick notes saying that he was sorry and asking for forgiveness. Tuesday night, a full course meal showed up from Pacino's, which did not go unnoticed since the restaurant is usually closed on Monday and Tuesday every week. So, he called in a favor to his friend.

There were lots of coffees and baked goods. A box that exploded paper butterflies in the air when you open it and there was a piece of cake in the middle. The cake was red velvet. This just made me more upset that we were not able to have the favorite flavor talk yet before all this happened. I hate red velvet—I find it weird that it looks like it will taste like berries but then bam— it's weak chocolate. He was not giving up, that is for sure, and he was trying to be intentional.

I am not ready to face it still, but somehow it feels safe. By safe, I mean that at no point through these gifts, or even when we fought, did I feel like I must forgive him or that my feelings of being hurt were not justified. He has validated that he did wrong and that it is up to me whether I want to speak to him ever again. If there were Google reviews for dating, I would mention that in his currently 2-star review.

* * *

I am battling with placing yet another flower bouquet that I had at my door when I came back from dropping the girls off to school. I am trying to consolidate the past three flower deliveries by putting the flowers that were still alive and thriving all in the largest of the vases. I was running out of counter space.

The white roses are hard to decide whether to keep or not. They started out so vibrant but have dulled. Not brown or dead, just dull. I get it, roses, I get it. As I decide to keep them and try stuffing them into the already too full vase, there is a knock at the door.

Ugh, what delivery is it now? I am half expecting to open the door to find a live cow so that I can milk it to make the freshest of ice cream. Or a singing telegram professing his apology for the whole street to hear.

But when I open the door, I am surprised to see an older woman. She is dressed nicely in slacks, a long puffer coat, and sensible winter boots, even if they were Moncler and probably cost more than my monthly car payment. She must be lost, maybe she was supposed to meet Sadie.

"Hi, there. If you are here to meet Miss. St. Clair, I normally see her with clients over in the other yard."

The woman shakes her head at this, "No, no. I am not a client of hers, per se. I was looking for Carly Kennedy, but just looking at you, I am sure you are her. You are just as pretty as he said, but your eyes have the same sadness as his."

"Okay, this may be the strangest delivery that Henry has sent so far."

"I'm not delivering anything, my dear. In fact, Henry has not the slightest clue I am here."

I study her for a moment. Her face looks so familiar, but it takes me a minute to place it. The shape of her eyes and nose gives it away finally.

"You're Henry's mother, aren't you?"

"Yes, I am Stella Reid, and I needed to see firsthand who has my son all twisted up in knots." My heart starts racing at this, trying to figure out how much she knows. He said that he did not talk to his mom about this property, and I assumed that included me, "Though from the sounds of it, he deserves it."

I must look like a fish out of water gulping in the open air. I regain composure, somewhat, and say, "Is that right? You're not here to sell his case? Or to talk him up?"

"Not particularly, I came here to meet you and talk to you. I have not seen him like this since—well, actually I have never seen him like this. He wouldn't tell me what was going on, but then I gave him way too much wine at our family dinner last week and he told me everything. Drunk as a skunk and crying, but he gave me the details." Her look of deceit as she talks about how she got the information washes away into a grimace.

"Okay… sorry I am a little thrown off balance here. Um—would you like to come in?" I gestured to invite the woman who owns the house into it.

"I was actually hoping that you would be willing to go for a little walk with me," she nodded towards the farmhouse. "It's chilly but the wind is calm, so it should be pleasant enough to do so."

I nodded my head and started to pull on a jacket, hat, and boots. She has my attention without a doubt right now. Mrs. Reid has a commanding presence. I can tell she usually gets what she asks for.

We start down the walkway in silence, she stares at the house. I wonder when was the last time she was here.

As if she was reading my thoughts, she says, "I have not stepped foot here since the 1970's. I tried to visit a few times to see my mother, but my father forbade it. He said that I would fill her head with my wild woman ways and ideas. Henry said he told you a little bit about my history here, correct?"

It's my turn to speak. I paused long enough for it to now be awkward.

"Not much, but he mentioned that you and your father did not agree about your schooling. He said you went on to achieve a lot and become a mentor. It sounded like you did not have fond memories here."

We have crossed over the yards and are standing in front of the big house now. She stops and looks up at the tall peaks.

"Not all my memories are horrible. I love this house and the land behind it. My brother had built me a treehouse far back in those woods over there. It had a secret compartment in the floor where I could hide my books. I would go back there and read for hours. My brother was a simple man, but a good man, nothing like our father." She looks deep in the direction that she pointed. It is just a patch of trees. I cannot even see a path or anything. It would be so amazing to explore this place when the weather gets nice again. The thought is like a sucker punch to the stomach as I realize that we are not going to be living here much longer.

"Your brother sounds like a nice person. I know Barb and Bud across the street said nice things about him."

"Oh, my word. I remember them! They were the first to buy some land. Such kind people, I doubt they would even remember me."

"No, I know Barb remembers you. She is the one that told me Henry owned the property. Funny story, I thought he was a random hired landscaper at first." I laugh slightly. That seems like a lifetime ago, not a couple months, "It does not sound like you have as much of a distaste for this house as Henry made it seem. He made it sound like you would be incredibly triggered by even hearing about it, much less visiting it. I was under the impression that was why he wanted to sell so badly."

She turns to look at me and her face twists in what I think is concern and/or confusion.

"Hmm—" She murmurs as she frames her chin with a delicate hand and strokes her cheek. "Is that right? I suppose I should have seen that. My Henry has always been protective of those he loves and sometimes he pushes that protection so far that he misses the part of asking what a person really needs."

I am not sure how to respond, but she continues before I have to.

"I knew something was bothering him. A mother always knows

when something is not right. Henry mentioned that you have two daughters, right?" I nod my head to confirm, and she keeps going. "He talked about how he failed to tell you about the sale of the house and that as a result he destroyed something real between you two. He's obviously had past relationships, but I have never seen him so vulnerable. Henry is quick to put a wall up and I did not see that when he told me about you, even after the bond was damaged. I may be overstepping but I felt compelled to meet you."

We keep walking around to the back of the house. The ground is solid with barely a dusting of snow, making it easy to walk in the yard. She is surprisingly easy to talk to and looks bright as she tells me more about the property. Apparently, they had an old red barn in the back that was destroyed by a massive blizzard in the 1960's and she talked about a whole big group of people coming out to help her dad and brother build a new one. They had animals back in those days and crops as far as the eye could see. As much as I enjoy talking to her, it is killing me from the inside out. She is making me fall even more in love with this place all while looking at me with the same eyes as the man I love.

As we come back around to the front, she slows down in front of the house. "I now wish I had told Henry I was coming. I would have gotten the key to look around inside too. I would like to see it all once more before he sells it. He just seems to be rushing it now and is ready to have this off his plate. I know he wanted to do a lot of the work himself, but it sat vacant for years, I can only imagine it was too much for him."

I cringe, "Or it may be because I told him I did not want to ever see him again. I was probably a little harsh."

"Not at all. You like living over in my brother's old cottage, is that right?"

"Very much so. When I was getting ready to leave my ex-husband,

I had imagined that I would end up in a boxy apartment in an even boxier building until I was sorted out and settled enough to buy a home. But then I saw the posting for this place and felt a weight off my shoulders knowing that even though I was not in a spot to own a home yet, I was able to give my girls a real home until that point. Now, I feel like I am going to be moving them around from place to place too much."

"I can understand that, and it is valid. I am sorry that you are going through this, but I promise you that in what Henry has mentioned and from now meeting you, I have no doubt that you will come out of the other side of this in an even better spot. There is nothing quite like being a parent; the smallest of humans give you the largest amount of determination." She takes my hands in her gloved ones and gives them a little squeeze. Then, much to my surprise, she pulls me into a hug. "I wish Henry was not such an idiot, I really think I would have liked having you around."

"I think I would have liked that too." I say, whole-heartedly.

We break apart and head back to my area of the property. She gives me another hug as we say goodbye. Watching her drive away feels like another pull at the loss I feel at almost having a life with Henry. For a split second I mourn that Stella would have made a fantastic mother-in-law. I shake my head at the ridiculousness of that, since Henry and I did not even make it far enough to think about the little things, much less the marriage sized things.

Chapter 35

ꮯꭹꮻꮻꭹꮯ

CLANG!

Lana jumps next to me, "What the hell was that?"

"Oh, just the music school downstairs," the Property Manager with really white teeth says. She keeps smiling like she is reminding herself to smile in her head. I know she said her name on the phone and again when we came in here, but I do not have the slightest guess what it might be.

"A music school?" I do not know how I missed that while walking into this apartment. Maybe it was due to the massive flight of stairs I had to walk up because there is no elevator.

"Yes, isn't it lovely? You would have the joy of the next generation of musical arts right in the same building!"

"Mhm…" I say simply because anything else I say will not come out as nice. I am tired, I am hungry, and I have little hope. Lana and I have looked at three apartments before this one and they have all been awful. The first one was a studio listed as a three bedroom, the second one had a smell that there would be no hopes of cleaning out, and the third one came with a cat in the lease. Yes, a cat. The tenant was required to care for the cat that lived there. Well, said cat hissed and attacked Lana's feet so we quickly decided that two small children would not be the right humans for him.

Now, number four comes with a symphony of misfits downstairs.

As we walk out onto the sidewalk, Lana looks at me, "We have a couple more on our list, should we keep going?"

"I can't, Lana," I am defeated. Nothing will compare to my cottage. Well, Henry's cottage. I sigh and gesture towards the car. It's Wednesday, so I do not have to pick up the girls for a bit. I just want to go home and sulk some more.

An hour later I am sitting at my desk by a window that overlooks the front of the house. I am trying to do some work for a client that is conducting an internal audit next month, but, in reality, I have not even moved off the first page of the report I am studying.

Movement catches my eye at the street. Sadie St. Clair is there in another long trench jacket and a different pair of heeled boots. This woman's closet must be insane. I am picturing her wearing an outfit once then throwing it into the garbage when real-life her catches my attention. She is using an apparatus to pull the For Sale sign out of the ground. Once it is pried free of the cold ground, she throws it into her trunk and drives away.

Well, I guess that is that. The property has been sold. Time to decide which move is next.

We have multiple offers from the people around us to stay with them. Patti has two extra bedrooms in her house, Paula reminded me again about her offer for the garage apartment, and both Lana and Amber offered for us to stay with them. I feel grateful that we have such a support system around us, especially after I felt so lonely during and coming out of my marriage.

Breaking away from my desk, I start putting away the clothes I folded earlier today. As I open the top drawer to put away my underwear – a bunch of comfy, not sexy, pairs that I have been wearing in solidarity of not admitting to myself how much I miss Henry—I stop short. The pile absently drops out of my weak grip as I see the notes from the first delivery sitting there, unopened. I knew they were there but I had stuffed them so far back in my mind so I would not fixate on them. I had put them under a pile of socks in that drawer and I must've quickly grabbed the last pair covering the notes this morning. It is just proof of how long I have put off doing laundry. Sue me, mom-police, but laundry sucks.

I grab the three envelopes and sit on my bed with them. I shuffle them around in my hands trying to decide if I am ready yet or not. My talk with Stella made me miss him on a new level and I was curious if there was information that I did not already know in them. And, honestly, I just want to feel connected to him. I pick the envelope with #1 on it and set the other two down next to me. As I break the seal, I can feel my pulse on the paper through my fingers. It's not a long note, but at the bottom I see written in his scratch writing, "Continue with #2." I take a deep breath and read:

> *Carly,*
>   *I knew you were not going to read these the day they were sent, as much as I had hoped you would, but I know you and you probably needed time to work up to it.*

I shake my head at the accuracy.

> *I am sorry. That is the number one thing I need you to know. I never intentionally hurt you. In my own, completely wrong, way, I was trying to prevent hurting you. I failed in that, and I failed at being a safe spot for you. If you give me another chance, I will spend every single day trying to make it up to you, Millie, and*

Remi. I want to be there to support you three, not make your life more difficult.

CONTINUE TO #2...

I grab at the second envelope greedily. His words are the closest I have felt to him in so long and now I am addicted.

Thank you for continuing to read. I know you could have just tossed these in the garbage and really closed the door on me. Any who... part two:

I meant what I said on the phone. I have fallen in love with you. I know it is quick and we have a lot of long-term talks that we never got to, but the way I feel so much like myself around you is undeniable. More than that, the way it feels like you are a part of myself creates a vulnerability I only have around you because I am talking to a similar heart. I am sorry I broke your heart by not being strong enough to tell you what was going on.

The house has been in my family for generations and I think I could not say it aloud to you, because once I did, it would become real. I would be making it real that I was selling away the only material connection I had left to the side of the family I did not know. I do not feel that I can ask my mom, she has so many horrible memories in the house and with my grandfather. I do not want to force her to talk about something that brings her pain.

CONTINUE TO #3...

I pick up number three and spin it in my hands, not opening it. I think back to walking around the property with Stella and how much she enjoyed telling me stories. Henry is making all these assumptions for his mother without being honest with her about his own feelings.

This is the last note... I promise... for today.

As I was saying, I had every expectation to just come in to clean up the house and sell it fast. I kept creating more projects for myself so that I could drag it out longer. I did this not only because of the hot neighbor, though that was certainly a bonus—

I roll my eyes at his letter.

...but also because of the family history I was learning. I found old photo albums of people I never knew and would not be able to identify without my mom's help, if she even knew. In the barn is a woodworking project my uncle must have been working on when he died, because it looks very much "in progress" with the tools still spread around. He was an artist, did I ever tell you that? He created brilliant art in his woodworking, but also there are tons of sketch books around the house. He would draw my grandmother a lot. Of her sitting in her rocking chair while knitting. Her kneading bread dough in the kitchen. Her tending to her roses. I learned more about her than I could have ever imagined and my uncle too, through his drawings. I wanted to keep finding more and learning more.

The pain of knowing that I hurt you makes it not as magical coming there. I did not tell you what was going on because I was so wrapped up in my own head and emotions. It was not fair. I should have told you about selling, and I should've leaned on you with the inner turmoil I was experiencing. Please do not worry, I am not selling to anyone that will not include a clause in the contract that they must give you at least six months' notice to move. I hope that will give you plenty of time to prepare. Maybe they will like the side income and keep it available to you. Either way I am sorry this disrupted your and the girls' lives. I care about you all very much. You are such an amazing mom and role model to them. I have so much respect for how you stood up for yourself and them when you confronted me with finding out. You are an incredible woman and I love you so very much. I am going to stop rambling on now, but just know that I will forever hold a spot open in my heart for you and if you forgive me, I will make sure you never regret it.

All my love,

Henry

The tears are rolling out of my eyes now. Thank goodness I do not have any client meetings scheduled today.

I believe every word of his notes. I know he is sorry, plus his added clause explains why no one has been banging on the door to kick us out. Sorry as he is, I still feel damaged by this. However, reading these notes may have added a little glue to the broken parts. I want to forgive him, I want to move forward with him, but I need a moment to gather my thoughts. I can't make a knee jerk decision over some well-written notes.

The first step is taking his number off 'blocked' in my phone. I am sure he has long figured out that I had him blocked, but maybe I will get the courage up to start the conversation. I will think about that tomorrow. I can only take so much at a time.

The girls are at their dad's house overnight. Normally they just stay for dinner, but they have only a half day tomorrow and Jake asked to switch the custody around a little with Thanksgiving next week. I have nothing to distract me from thinking about the notes and Henry. I cannot help but hyper fixate on what our life could have looked like together. One vision is us in a house of our own, another vision is us living in his house, or us living in the farmhouse. The last one is my favorite, but also the one that hurts the most since the truth of the farmhouse is what got us into this mess.

I pour myself a large glass of wine and settle onto the couch with a blanket to catch up on the Hallmark Christmas movies. I am scrolling through the DVR list when my phone pings with a text. It is probably Lana cancelling lunch tomorrow or something.

My breath hitches when I look at the screen to see "Henry" as the sender. I am fumbling with my phone, and I cannot seem to remember my password to unlock it. All the blood feels like it is rushing to my head. Finally, I manage to get it open and click on the message.

> *Henry: Hi, again. I know I shouldn't but I can't help myself from sending this message every night. I hope you had a good day, beautiful. I love you and I miss you. Okay, until tomorrow's message, goodnight.*

Gasp! He has been sending me a message daily since who knows when. He has not given up on us, maybe it's time that I fight for us too. In time though, I need to ease into it. I do not respond to his message, but I read it about a hundred times before bed.

The next night a similar message came in. It was slightly different and at a different time, so it is something he is actively doing. He is not giving up and I don't think I want him to.

Chapter 36

❧

"Sweetie, I think you are just prolonging the inevitable here. You know you are going to forgive this boy, right?" Gwen asks. The girls are at Jake's still, which lets me sneak over to the Early Bird Cafe Club today.

"I know," I say so quietly that I am not sure anyone heard me, and I cannot tell because I am avoiding eye contact with the whole table.

I only know they heard me when Miles yells from down the table to me, "Girl, make him sweat it out for just a little bit longer—because he deserves it—and then lock that shit down."

This makes my head pop up and look in his direction. I let out a little laugh. I notice that several of the other people at the table are nodding.

"I can honestly say I have never even considered sending multiple deliveries to a girl's house at one time with a three-part handwritten note." Dylan adds. He makes a good point.

"The part that I am struggling with the most is questioning my own judgement. I stayed with Jake for too long." Pausing to take a deep breath. "I constantly made excuses about why he hurt me—not physically, but emotionally and mentally. I questioned if he was even really doing what I thought he was. I lost all sense of whether it was real or not. I am scared I am setting up to let things go with Henry when they may actually be red flags. I can't let myself get stuck into that level of controlling behavior by a partner again. I will not survive it again."

"Oh, honey," Marti pats my hand soothingly, "Just because Jake did not value your kindness and ability to forgive, does not mean you should never allow yourself to forgive again. People mess up. Good people mess up sometimes. The biggest difference here is that when Jake made you forgive him, he made *you* feel guilty. With Henry, he is *asking* but not demanding that you forgive him because *he* feels guilty. Trust me, if we were concerned about you going back with him, we would be grabbing our pitchforks and torches to go after the monster, but truly he sounds like a good and solid man who just wants to be there for you and your kids."

"I see what you are saying. And you are right, but I think I still need a moment to process it." I shrug my shoulders and let them slump slightly after.

"Take your time. This is a holiday week. Let yourself enjoy Thanksgiving and worry about it in December or something. You do not have to decide this second." Marti says.

* * *

Over the week, the construction trucks increased at the farmhouse. At one point I saw a delivery truck from a local furniture store. Even though Henry's letter said that I would not be forced out quickly, I did expect to at least hear something regarding my new landlords, unless they decided to use the same management group that Stella had set the cottage up with before. It just confused me that I have not been told anything about the sale.

I make a mental note to reach out to Doug after the holiday weekend to find out what is going on. I should have thought to do so already, but there is not an instruction manual regarding this situation.

Jake and Riley are apparently going on vacation to Aruba for the long weekend, which is why he needed to switch days around. How nice for her that he suddenly wants to take vacations. I may be a little bitter, but I get a little extra time with the girls, so that is a positive.

Thanksgiving dinner at Patti's house with Amber, Paul, PJ, and some of their extended family. I have been coming to this dinner for over twenty years, so the aunts and uncles see me as their niece almost as much as Amber is.

"Hey, penny for your thoughts?" Amber says sliding up next to me as I stare out the backdoor of Patti's house. She has a beautiful yard. It is fully wooded, and she does incredible landscaping. Even in the colder months, she manages to make the outdoors look like a magazine. Right now, she has her Fall decor up and I know that she will work tirelessly all weekend to switch it over to her Christmas wonderland. The girls look forward to it every year, and I would be lying if I said I do not, as well. It really is magical.

"Oh nothing, just zoning out looking at the yard."

"Nope. Talk."

"What are you talking about?"

"I know you and this is not your daydreaming stare. You were thinking about something not in this room or out that window." Amber is too good at calling me out on my bullshit, "Thinking about Henry stuff?"

"It's stupid."

She gives me a probing look.

"Fine. Now that I have met his mother, I can't help but wonder how nice his family gatherings must be. I was picturing what it would be like to split our time between here and his parent's house. We could run all over the place and complain about it in the moment but end the day looking back at how grateful we are. Don't get me wrong, I am so grateful for all that we have this year too, but that is just where my mind floated off to."

Amber nods along as I talk.

She wraps her arm around me and says, "It's okay to let yourself be happy with him. And you know I would never say that if I did not think you probably should. Remember, I have a sixth sense for these kinds of things. I hated Jake before I ever met him. There was an instant change and defensiveness in the way you spoke from the get-go with Jake. This is not the same."

I know both Amber and the EBCC crew were all right. There was no rule set in stone that says I can never go back to him. I am going to be present to enjoy this time with my friends and family, then I will resume obsessing about what I will do next when Monday comes.

After an incredible dinner at Patti's, we leave with our arms full of leftovers, to head to Lana's parents' house for dessert. I stopped by Lana's house a week or so ago to drop off something and her mom was there. They were planning their family's Thanksgiving, when Betty asked me if I hosted, or we visited family for the holiday. I mentioned that my mom never comes into town for the holidays, but my childhood best friend's mom has us over every year. Betty insisted that, if possible, in our schedule, we must stop by in the evening for desserts and drinks. It was impossible to say no, nor did I want to when she mentioned that she has all her desserts made by the woman who owns Sliced, the bakery downtown that has the longest waiting list for personal orders. Betty told me that she has been going to her long before the wait list and has standing orders for all the holidays. The Sliced Pumpkin Pie is rumored to have the ability to make all other Pumpkin Pies subpar for the rest of your life. She opened a store front about two years ago and I have yet to go. When Betty saw how I fangirled about the Sliced order, she promised to call her up and add an extra Pumpkin Pie for me to take home. I think I almost fainted with excitement.

The girls know Lana and her kids, but they were not prepared for what we just walked into. The Harrington Family Estate, because seriously calling it just a house feels so underwhelming, is massive. The front door is so tall, and the girls are practically clinging to my dress now. I am ready for some Addams Family shit to happen and the door to swing open, while creaking, all by itself. Instead, the door flings open with Betty smiling at us.

"You came! Come on in, girls, let's get those coats off and warm you all up with some hot apple cider." She shuffles us inside the grand foyer. I feel like I am in the mansion in Clueless with the staircase that has a fork in it to go either left or right the rest of the way up. We follow her back to an open room with various seating arrangements spread around. There is a buffet table full of baked goods and another beverage station with everything one could imagine to drink.

The girls are still clinging to me. I have not seen Lana anywhere yet. I haven't even seen her siblings that I met at her cousin's wedding. The only person I recognize is her uncle's wife that got mad at Lana's dancing.

"So, holidays around here are a bit of a free-for-all. It may look fancy, but everything is help-yourself-buffet style. I give the entire staff the long weekend off to enjoy with their families. If they do not have anywhere to go or just would like to come, then they are guests here for the day." Betty points to a slender, older woman with dark gray hair, "That is Nakita, my house manager. Her and her husband and two children, who are now grown but still come, have been living on the property since it was my husband's parents living here, though she was on the kitchen staff back then. And over there is our property maintenance manager, Raul, and his husband, Leo. Their families disowned them both when they came out and decided to marry. They were going to just elope when I found out and they had their wedding right here at the estate. It was so posh! Anyway, my point is that no one here is working, so if you need anything help yourself or find one of the Harrington's tonight."

"That is so sweet!" I really do love this family, they constantly surprise me. Betty hands both the girls a mug of hot cider after pouring a little cold apple cider in it to temper it for them to drink. She hands me a larger mug filled with smells that float through my soul, but it is not cider. I lift it to my nose to investigate.

"Mulled wine, my grandmother's recipe," Betty helps.

"Millie! Remi!" Both girls look in the direction of their names being called to find Trinity coming towards them, "Come on, all the kids are in the arcade room! Gigi, did you give them their tokens yet?"

The girls and I all look to Betty to figure out what Trinity is talking about.

Betty laughs, "Chill out, Trin. They just got here. I was trying to be a good host and getting them drinks and dessert first."

"Gigi! The big prize is still in play," Trinity is talking a mile a minute and I am struggling to keep up.

"Okay, okay. Girls, all the kids that come to the house for the holidays get a token for the claw machine we have in the game room. Each token gives you one turn to get a prize egg, but it is play-until-you-win." Betty has obviously given these instructions a bunch of times because she is very animated as she tells them, "There is something in every egg, but they vary in prize levels. Some just have candy. Some have small toys. Some have gift cards. But there is one egg every year that when you open it there is a second, slightly smaller, gold egg inside it. The big prize changes every year. The kids who are here Thanksgiving and Christmas Eve all get one try on each of those days to play. And all the eggs that are not found by the kids by the end of the Christmas Eve party are then in play for the adults only at the New Year's Eve party."

"Wow, that's elaborate!" I cannot believe how well Stella thought out this evening.

"Yeah, it's pretty cool," Lana showed up out of nowhere next to me, "And for the adults only party, she'll throw a bunch of airplane liquor bottles in there! Then everyone gets heated about bartering over 3-ounce bottles of liquor to get your favorites."

Betty shrugs with a smile, "It's true, I'm a shit-stirrer. I throw some Banana Pucker in there, just to really get people going. No one wants that crap."

"Not wrong. I've never had that, and I would like to keep that streak going," I grimace.

"Here you go, girls. A token for you each," Betty says to Millie and Remi as she pulls shiny copper coins out of her pocket.

"Thank you, Mrs. Gigi," Remi says, getting a laugh out of us all.

Betty thinks it over for a second and responds, "I kind of like it."

"Okay, thank you, Mrs. Gigi," Millie says too as Trinity starts pulling them away through the crowd. I try to squash the uneasiness of them going off somewhere that I am not familiar with. Lana must pick up on my concern, and Betty is getting pulled away by some relatives.

"Come on, I'll show you where they will probably be all night." Lana links arms with me and leads me through the crowd to a room in the back of the house that overlooks the outdoor pool. The pool is closed, and all the patio furniture is absent, but I imagine it being a fun site during the summer.

The girls are in line at a claw machine straight out of my childhood arcade memories. A boy probably around 9 goes first. It takes him three tries but he gets a bright blue egg. He opens it up to find Fortnite bucks, which he seems very pleased with. A little girl, who I am assuming is his sister, goes next. She keeps missing until the Fortnite bucks kid helps her a little. She gets a purple egg and opens it to find a bunch of Hershey Kisses. She, like her brother, seems very happy with her haul.

Millie goes next and it takes her a few tries before she catches a green egg. She opens it with a big smile and holds up a $20 gift card to the big bookstore. That is perfect for her.

Remi is up next. I lean down over her and whisper, "Remember any surprise is great and we are grateful for whatever is in your egg, right?"

"I know, mom. But I am totally winning this game," she says defiantly.

"It's not a game, honey, it's just a surprise egg."

"Got it, mom. Now, I'm going in for the gold."

I step back because there is no reasoning with my stubborn wild child. Hopefully she got something that she is excited enough about that she is distracted that it is not the golden egg. She loves candy more than anyone I know, so it shouldn't be too hard.

First try, she grabs a pink egg. I know it is the one she was aiming for because everything is pink for her. She has her back turned to me and I hear the pop of the egg opening. She flips around and looks me dead in the eyes, "Nailed it."

That kid is standing there with the golden egg in her hands. My mouth drops open. The kids in the room all start screaming, and Betty comes running in. It is pure chaos but in the most joyful way. Millie is poking her, telling her to open it. Remi pops the smaller gold egg open and inside is a rolled-up piece of paper. She unrolls it with her sister over her shoulder. It is Millie that reads it aloud, because obviously my 4-year-old golden horseshoe cannot even read yet.

"Good for you and 9 of your family and friends to spend three hours of private time at Zoomies." Millie and Trinity are jumping all around Remi who is jumping up and down in her spot. Zoomies is an indoor go-karting place and apparently Remi just won a private party there. Their excitement is contagious, and I feel so warmed by how my found-family in the Early Bird Cafe Club has trickled down to my children, because their circle of family has grown too.

They spend the rest of the evening playing all the arcade games with the other kids at the party. And I ate the Pumpkin Pie that lived up to its reputation. It has been so nice to be chatting with adults and drinking cider – I switched to non-alcoholic after the dangerously delicious, mulled wine.

The girls are half asleep before they even buckle their car seat and I drive home with the full Sliced Pumpkin Pie that Betty had hidden away just for me, riding shotgun. Between Patti's earlier and the Harrington's tonight, this has been an internal refresher that I needed to be ready to move forward and make the next move with Henry. I know that no matter what, I will be okay because I have a village around us now. I am not alone in this.

Chapter 37

***

"How about this one?"

"Too green."

"Millie, how can a Christmas tree be *too green*?

"Um, like that, mom." Millie points at the tree I am standing next to with more sass than I care to deal with in this busy lot. It seems everyone in the city had the same idea to get their tree today.

It is our first, and probably last, Christmas in the cottage, as just the three of us. I left Jake shortly after the New Year. It seems unreal that it was such a short amount of time ago, when it feels like a lifetime ago.

"This one!" Remi is jumping up and down pointing at a tree. Millie stops in front of it and looks it up then down. She is rubbing her chin with her thumb and forefinger, ticking off some list in her head. Remi stops jumping and we both stare intently at Millie for the verdict.

"It has a good structure. Perfectly round. The green is a nice deep shade," She leans in and takes a huge sniff of the tree, "Smells very piney. This tree is approved."

Remi goes back to jumping up and down. I give Millie an incredulous look. I cannot explain the way her mind works, but it is fascinating.

Thirty minutes later and the tree is loaded on top of my SUV by the teenage kid at the tree lot. I have never done the Christmas tree thing alone. The girls are in the backseat excitedly planning the decorations. I am just praying that this is not a Christmas Vacation situation with a squirrel jumping out after it is in the house.

As we pull into the driveway, I have myself freaking out that there is a spider nest living in this tree and a million baby spiders are going to invade my house. I wonder if I have the physical strength enough to shake the tree of all its possible critters before bringing it inside.

Luckily, I had enough foresight to remember to grab the scissors to cut the ropes holding the tree to the roof. It's not that big of a tree, I will be fine. I picked it up at the lot just to make sure I did not need help carrying it, though grabbing it down from above my height seems challenging.

I cut the ropes on the passenger side, so far so good. I walk around to the driver's side and tug it a little, only to realize that there is a rope tangled in the branches and netting they put around it. That's when a big white truck catches my eye in the driveway to the farmhouse. There is a man that I do not remember seeing around the property before unloading a box down the metal ramp from the box of the truck. The new owners must be there now.

I grab the stuck rope, tugging through my frustration, and it is just not giving. I let go of the rope to grab the scissors from the ground next to me and as I turn around, I see a puff of green hauling at me. I let out a scream as the tree rolls off the roof onto me, throwing me backwards.

Everything goes fuzzy around me. I do not lose consciousness, because I can hear the girls yelling in the background. I know I need to get up. I do not want to scare them any more than I already did, but I cannot seem to gather my bearings. I see a person running towards me from next door but then it all goes darker.

"Carly!"

I must be hallucinating now. The new neighbor sounds like Henry. I am trying to sit up, the tree rolled to the side, so there is not anything weighing me down. I feel a warm arm stretch behind my back stabilizing me.

"Mommy! Mommy, are you okay?" I can hear the girls asking in the background. It sounds like they are crying. I shake my head to try to sort myself out. I need to get to my kids and let them know I am okay.

I push my hand on the ground and start to stand up, getting my left foot grounded but when my right foot digs into the ground the searing pain from that ankle drives through my entire body.

"Ahh!" I yell and start to fall over again. As two strong arms wrap around me, I remember that there else is someone here. I look over and am met by the frightened eyes of Henry. My Henry. It was not a dream that I heard him. He is here holding me up.

"Henry?" I ask weakly and confused.

"Yeah, I'm here. Come on, let's get you on solid ground." I am about to ask what he is talking about when I feel his arm scoop under my knees, and he is carrying me. "Millie, can you grab the front door?"

"On it!" I hear her switch into task mode.

"Remi, can you please put the pillows together on the couch for your mom?"

"Ye-ye-yeah," Remi says softly through her tears.

"Oh, honey, don't cry. Your mom is going to be okay," Henry says to Remi in a soothing voice. He sets me down on the couch and grabs her into a big hug to assure her.

I need to pull myself together and figure out what is happening.

"Henry? How are you here?" I say shakily.

"I was next door and heard you scream. When I looked over, I saw a tree rolling off you and you on the ground." Henry explains.

"Next door? I thought it sold? I saw the sign come down and there was a truck and a guy there today," I hope that I am making some sense because my head hurts and I do not want to think any harder to clarify.

"That guy over there? That is my brother, Grayson. And the truck is our rental that he is helping me unload. And the sign? Sadie took it down here and put it back up at my house." Henry has a matter-of-fact tone.

"It's at your house—next door or across town?"

"Across town. But I guess that is not really my house anymore since most of my belongings were unloaded into the house next door today before I had to help a damsel in distress." Henry smiles sheepishly.

"So, you're our neighbor for reals now?" Millie inputs and I startle. I did not realize that the girls were still standing right there.

"For reals," Henry says to her, but his eyes are still on mine.

His gaze makes me feel unprepared to face the reality of this moment. I swing my legs over to the side and stand up. As soon as my weight hits my right side, I let out a yelp. I fall back onto the couch.

"Okay, goddess warrior," My breath catches a little at hearing him call me a goddess again, "You need to sit still and elevate that ankle. You really need to head to urgent care to have it looked at."

"No, no, it's just sore. It will be fine."

"Carly, it is blowing up like a balloon." He says and I can feel it as confirmation without even looking.

"I do not need a doctor, I swear," I insist.

"Hold on, I'm getting a professional opinion of whether or not you need to go to urgent care." Henry grabs his phone out of his pocket and quickly spits off a text.

"What does that mean?"

"If you won't go to the doctor, I am bringing the doctor to you."

"Huh—" There is a knock on the door.

"Come in!" Henry yells in that direction.

The man I saw unloading the van walks in the door with a small duffle bag. I can now see the resemblance of this man to Henry. He also looks like Stella but not as much as Henry does.

"Hey, so what is going on here?" Grayson asked while removing his shoes.

"She hurt her ankle when she was attacked by her Christmas tree and refuses to go to the doctor," Henry gives me a smile like he won. "Carly, meet my brother, Dr. Grayson Reid. One of the top orthopedic surgeons in New England, if not the country. And he is going to be the deciding factor of whether you need to go in or not."

"Jesus, bro, I thought someone had a nasty splinter or something. I didn't know I was coming into the full throttle showdown here."

"Doctor? And you are a lawyer," I say point at Henry, my mouth is a little a gape. "So, what, is your sister a rocket scientist or something?"

Grayson smiles knowingly as Henry laughs and replies, "No rockets. Cancer research scientist rather."

My mouth drops open completely now.

"Okay, let's see what we have going on here." Grayson crouches down at the end of the couch next to my foot. "Ooo you did a number on it."

He feels around and asks me in several spots about tenderness. He gently moves it in one direction and then another.

"I think it will be fine. There is not a fracture or break on the foot, you probably sprained it or bruised the bone. I am going to wrap it for you, and I want you to ice it for at least 20 minutes several times a day. And keep it elevated. You can take ibuprofen for pain and swelling. If the swelling does not go down by tomorrow night, I want you to call my office and I will get you in for some X-rays. Deal?" Grayson offers, his voice is so soothing and assuring. I can see how he would be considered a top in his field, at least based on bedside manner.

"Deal. And thank you," I say to him.

"No problem. Wish it was under better circumstances, but it is nice to finally meet you." Grayson smirks, he looks over at the girls, remembering their prying eyes and ears. He does not say any more about mine and Henry's involvement. "Hey there, girls, can you help me in the kitchen to find stuff to help make your mom an ice pack?"

They both nod enthusiastically, happy that they are getting asked to do something.

As they walk away, I say, "Your brother is so nice and great with kids. Does he have any of his own?"

"He has never settled down; his career has taken so much of his ability to have a social life. So, no kids for him. Fallon, our sister, is the only one married with kids. She has a boy and a girl around the same ages as your girls. They live in Minnesota; she works for the Mayo Clinic." He says this in his sweet quiet tone. I soak it in because I have missed hearing him.

Grayson and the girls walk out of the kitchen with a plastic baggie full of ice and a towel. He quickly wraps my ankle in a tan bandage and gently sets the ice pack on top, using the towel to cover anywhere the ice might hit that is not protected already.

"Alright, you should be all set. If you need to move around the house at all try to lean on furniture or the wall to keep weight off it." Grayson turns to Henry and continues, "Hey, man, what do you want to do about the rental van? I could take it back and have someone come pick me up, but your truck is still there."

"Damn, I was not even thinking that we had to get that thing back."

"Henry, I appreciate your help, but I am fine. Go ahead and finish up what you were in the middle of— I don't want to completely derail your day nor leave you stranded without your truck." I try to sound convincing that I do not want him to stay, when really my body is aching to keep him close.

It must work because he replies in a hesitant voice, "Alright, yeah. I don't want to push you. But if you need anything, you know my number. Promise you'll call before you overdo it."

"I promise I will take it easy. And don't worry, the girls will be good helpers and we are going to just have a chill night." I say with the most pleasant smile I can muster.

Chapter 38

﹏჻⟡჻﹏

With a couple more tips from Grayson and another round of thank yous, they leave to walk back. From my vantage point on the couch, I can see the big truck pull away. The girls have settled in to quietly watch their tablets. As I am staring at them on their devices, I realize that I have no clue where my phone is, plus I have to pee badly. This was not going to be as easy as I thought.

I sit up and pull myself to stand with all the weight on my left foot, using the couch to balance myself. Millie notices me and rushes over. She helps me hobble to the bathroom, acting as a crutch when no furniture is available. It takes 15 minutes for a simple trip to the bathroom. Maybe I should call for some help. Jake is still on vacation, so I cannot even ask him to grab the girls this weekend. Maybe Lana will come over and help. I am avoiding the offer of help I just received before Henry left. It does not matter though if I cannot find my phone.

"Mom, I'm kind of hungry, are we going to eat dinner tonight?" Remi asks. Mom-guilt hits me like a ton of bricks because I had not remotely thought about food. There is no way I am going to be able to stand in the kitchen to make something. I could order something, but I have no idea where my phone is still. Using Millie's tablet, I manage to locate my phone—either in my car or on the ground in the snow next to my car. I wish I could remember if I took it out when I started taking the tree down.

It is almost dark outside now and it is starting to snow. I know the girls would be scared to go outside alone right now.

"Okay girls I got this." I do not 'got this' but I am going to have to power through. Just shy of adding the food delivery app to Millie's tablet, which would do no good since my purse is also in the car, I needed to run out to the car. The hobble to the front door is rough looking. My ankle is swollen, and I am not sure how to fit it in my boot.

"Mommy, someone just pulled in," Remi is at the front window, but shields her eyes and walks away. "Bright headlights."

Before I have a chance to question it and to stuff my foot in my boot, there is a single knock on the door before it is pushed open.

"Carly?" Henry's voice feeds around the door before his face follows. "Carly! What do you think you are doing? You need to be on the couch!"

I abandon the feeble attempt of trying to get this damn boot on to look at him, still halfway in the door. I am exasperated. "Well, Henry. I am a one-mom show around here for two great, but small, kids. They can help me only so much. I would call for help but my entire purse and phone are in the car. It is dark, so there is no way I could ask the girls to go get it. So here I am trying to be injured but still having to mom. And for god's sake, what is that smell??"

He pushes the rest of his body through the door revealing a pizza in his hidden hand. I think I might be drooling.

"I figured that you would not want to cook, so I grabbed this on my way home to drop it off for you. Let me put this in the kitchen and then I will run out to grab your stuff in the car. Get you situated back on the couch. And then I will leave. I just couldn't sleep tonight knowing that you are right next door, hurt. So, feeding you was my excuse to check on you." Henry is already walking to the kitchen with comfort around us. I make it back to the couch before he can try to help me. I might crumble at feeling his touch again.

"So, you are really moving in next door? Like you're sleeping there tonight?"

"And every night after, my old house is an empty shell. Move-in-ready for its next owner. I'll be back with your stuff, then I'll head out." He swiftly heads back out the front door towards my car.

"Mommy, ask Henry to stay for dinner with us." Millie scolds me, her brow furrowed.

"What are you talki—" I am interrupted by Henry walking back in with my purse, phone, and car keys.

"Okay girls, I think you have everything you need for the night. I also propped that murderous Christmas tree of yours up against the porch for tonight."

"Thank you, we really do appreciate your help." I say to Henry as he starts to open the door.

Millie dramatically fake clears her throat with a mouth full of pizza. She gives me a look that honestly has me scared of getting grounded. Through clenched teeth she says, "Mom."

"Uh, Henry—" I start quietly, slightly stuttering. I know he heard though because he stops at the door, turning his head just so his ear is facing me. "I was thinking—I mean we were hoping—but if you are busy don't feel obligated—maybe you would like to have some pizza with us."

His body turns slowly to face me. "Are you sure? Don't feel like you have to ask me to stay."

"I would like you to stay. I would really like that a lot."

A smile consumes his entire face. He toes off his boots and heads towards the kitchen. "Alright girls, let's make your mom a plate and find you two a movie to settle in with."

He jumps right into it with the girls, and they eat up every fiber of attention. The way he just fits into our family seems natural. In this moment, watching him make them laugh while plating food, I feel the last of my wrath towards him release. I am done fighting the feelings that are so consuming. He belongs with me. He belongs with us— though there are a few things we need to talk about.

We all sit around eating pizza for a bit, chatting a little bit here and there, nothing deep. Henry grabs the plates to take to the kitchen and I tell the girls to go put their pajamas on.

"Mom, can we work more on our friendship bracelets before bed?" Millie asks as they come back out in matching Barbie PJ sets.

"Sure, at the kitchen table and please pick up any runaway beads." They run to get their little kits that they have been obsessed with lately. Hey, it gets them off the screens a little more so I will encourage it.

Henry comes back out of the kitchen as the girls fly by him. He is wearing his emotions on his face right now. His eyes dart between the couch I am on, the chair, and the door. So, I decided to put him out of his misery.

"Come sit on the couch with me so we can talk without them hearing," I gesture towards the girls in the kitchen.

He looks relieved as he gently lifts my feet and slips underneath them. A calmness floods my body at his touch.

"Carly, I am so sorry for everything. I just want you to kn—" He is begging.

"Stop." I say firmly. "That is not what I want to talk about. I know that you are sorry, and I am sorry that I did not tell you that earlier. I needed time to get there. I have some questions and stuff first."

"Ask away, I am here to be a hundred percent open with you, which I should have been from the start."

"True, but okay let's start with explaining why you are moving in after being so adamant that you would not be doing that." I pause to let him answer.

"My mom told me she came to visit you and the property. It opened the door to a conversation about her childhood and my assumptions that she associated those years directly to the house. She admitted that she would have loved to see her family home turned into a place with great memories. When I tell you that I was shocked, that doesn't even begin to cut it." Henry explains.

"I can imagine, because I was taken aback by the joy in her voice as she walked me around here. She made the place sound magical." I smile at the thought of Stella's visit. "Your mom really is a wonderful woman."

"She really is." Henry smiles a little. "In that conversation, I was able to talk to her about how the hard work I have put into the house has forged an attachment to the house. Not only have I put my mark on the house, but I learned so much about my ancestors. I never felt that kind of connection with the house I was living in. It was nice and met my needs, but it never felt inviting to me. There is a warmth in that farmhouse that encircles me when I am inside."

"It's beautiful on the outside, so I am sure it is fantastic inside too."

"Once you are up and moving again, I will give you the tour."

"I would like that very much. Do you feel good about the move and settled with your decision?" I am excited to see inside that house. The architecture on the outside is original and Henry mentioned before that the inside has a lot of original features.

"Almost, but it is missing something still." Henry is acting slightly shy, which is out of character for his normal confident self.

"Do you need more furniture or something? What is it missing?"

"A family."

Gasp! My eyes connect with his, which have a sparkle in them.

"A family?"

"Not just any family. Our family. You, me, and the girls."

"Henry, I don't know about that. We haven't even figured ou—" I say but he holds up a defensive palm to stop me.

"I don't mean right away. But, Carly, I love you and I really have grown fond of Millie and Remi. I want nothing more than for us to ease into becoming a family." He explains. "We can be neighbors for however long makes you feel comfortable. You can live in the cottage, and you can all spend time in the farmhouse getting used to it. Then when the time is right, you three can move into the big house with me."

"Can we get a dog too?!" Remi's voice jolts my attention away. The girls are standing at the doorway listening to everything. I never saw them walk up.

"Mom, are you and Henry dating?" Millie asks inquisitively, but there is no concern in her voice.

"What?!" Remi says catching up to what her sister already figured out, "Are you boyfriend and girlfriend?"

Henry looks at me and I give him a slight nod with a smile. He grabs my hand in his and we both turn to the girls.

"Yes. Yes, we are."

Epilogue

We made it to March 2nd and Henry's birthday. I have been planning and plotting for about two months to throw him a surprise party. The girls did not even know about this party because I did not want them to slip up. Millie probably could have been trusted, but Remi would have undoubtedly told everyone on the street and Henry. Our lives have been magical since that fateful Thanksgiving weekend.

Henry and I wasted no time combining our lives. We had family dinners at his parent's house. I have FaceTimed so much with his sister, Fallon, that it's hard to believe that I have not seen her in real life yet. I tried to talk her into coming out for this, but she had a work convention that she was already traveling for. We go on double dates with Amber and Paul. Lana shows up unannounced and we commandeer the huge wrap-around porch on the farmhouse for wine nights.

We have started to move into the big house over the past month. We are sleeping there full time but have had a lot of projects to tackle to get ready to do so. The girls each picked out a bedroom, thrilled not to have to share a room anymore. Henry's parents and brother come over almost every weekend to help us, especially now that we are heading into Spring. Millie and Stella have grown incredibly close almost from the moment they met. Millie even picked Stella's childhood bedroom with the built-in bookcases and the same white oak desk that Stella used as a girl in it. Remi and Henry's dad, Ted, are buddies now too. He is teaching her how to play poker and she is becoming quite a little hustler. They are only playing for Skittles right now, but I can see that escalating.

Amber and Paul are coming tonight, so they were able to bring the girls for me for the dinner part at Pacino's, then Patti is going to come by and pick them up for the night with PJ, so the grown-ups can have a night on the town.

Dom helped me arrange the whole dinner, closing the restaurant for the entire evening. He even sold the story to Henry by saying there was a private party of investment bankers from Hong Kong coming in, but he has the side dining room not being used so that we can come in for a birthday dinner just the two of us.

It was not going to be a large party. Just our families, some friends, and Dom invited some of their friends from college to join us. Maybe a dozen people total. Dom and I worked out how we would get everyone in and the signal to turn the lights on. I got us a party limo bus for after dinner, so no one had to drive. We told him that the private party was coming in on that and then all our guests parked in the overflow lot behind the building, so he would not recognize any of the cars.

I think I have covered all the bases. We are parking and he does not seem to be questioning anything. I sigh in relief.

"What was that sigh for?" Henry asks amused.

I try to not look too nervous, but I am sweating profusely in my sweater dress.

"I'm just glad we are here. I barely ate today—" Not a lie, well not completely a lie. "So I'm looking forward to a good meal."

He gets out of the car and comes around to open my door, offering me his hand as I stand up. I will never get over how handsome he is. I could get lost in those eyes every night for the rest of my life.

"I wonder how rowdy the private party is, that is one impressive looking limo." Henry gestures to the limo bus sitting in the parking lot.

We get up to the door and my stomach is flip-flopping with nerves. The door opens and the entire restaurant is dark, as we planned. It is my turn to say the code phrase to trigger them jumping out.

"Hmmm... It is really dark in here." I say loudly and slowly. I must sound strange, but it does the trick.

"SURPRISE!" Everyone yells as the lights are turned up. I look out in the crowd with complete confusion.

I look out to see far more than a dozen people and I try to process everyone who is standing there. Henry's family is there, including Fallon and her whole family. Next to them is my mom and stepdad. And next to them is the entire Early Bird Cafe Club and their families. Then stands Amber, Paul with PJ on his hip, Patti, and my girls standing in front of them looking wildly excited. I can even see the Harrington's in the crowd. Plus, a whole bunch more friends of Henry's than I thought were coming.

"What is going on?" I turn to Henry to see his reaction and gasp.

Henry is still next to me but has lowered to one knee with a small blue box in his hands. He grabs my hand into his free hand.

"Carly, I have loved you since the day you came barreling at me in red hot anger and made me destroy the bushes," There is a light rumble of laughter in the crowd, "I have grown to love you more every day and that love has extended to include an indescribable love for Millicent and Remi."

He pauses to look over at them and gestures with his head for them to come over with us. They are running up to flank me on both sides.

"I promise to love all three of you for the rest of my days, if you will have me. Carly, will you marry me?"

Tears stream down my shocked face as I start vigorously shaking it,

"Yes. Yes. A million times, yes."

Everyone bursts into cheers and the staff is already passing out champagne or cider for everyone.

Dom lifts his glass, and everyone follows suit. "To the happy couple and happy family. Oh yeah and happy birthday, buddy! I think this is going to be a great year for you."

"Sure is," Henry says, taking a sip from the flute before pulling me into him and kissing me as the rest of our lives begins—together.

CHECK WWW.ELVIECANN.COM FOR A BONUS EPILOGUE OF THIS EVENING FROM HENRY'S POINT OF VIEW!

About the Author

Elvie Cann (she/her) writes books about characters falling in love while punching their ticket on the hot mess express. Elvie lives with her two daughters and their cats in the Western New York area. When not writing, she can be found reading smut, trying a new short-lived hobby, or impulsively traveling.

You can connect with me on:

🌐 https://www.elviecann.com